Decoherent rocks! Recommended. A fine debut novel.

John Shirley,
author of *Stormland*

*   *   *

Steve Holley's *Decoherent* is forged like a Masamune katana, layers of steel folded one into another until, deliberate and with utmost purpose, the final, fatal form is revealed.

The work is a laminate of disparate literary steels—martial arts meditation; quantum physics pontification; hard-boiled sci-fi detective case—welded together and honed to an eerie sharpness. Every layer is described in perfect clarity, explained with a professorial surety that manages to impart to even the most ignorant reader a sense of familiarity with everything from the practiced specificity of *Goju Ryu* karate to the wanton tedium of internal police politics.

Propelled by Holley's masterful interweaving of genres, the weather-beaten Florida cop story is transformed into something that transcends time and place; like a samurai side-stepping through the multiverse, the novel seethes with a focused energy that translates into an immutable, respectfully understated but still weapons-grade power.

Paul d. Miller,
author of *Albrecht Drue, ghostpuncher.*

*   *   *

Steve Holley's first novel, *Decoherent,* is a winner. This is a police procedural that nails the cop-shop dead-on, has martial arts out the wazoo, interesting characters, and a quantum quirk that adds just enough pepper to heat it nicely. Well-written, and a page-turner, and there is even a dog. Go for it.

Steve Perry,
New York Times Selling Author of
The Man Who Never Missed

*   *   *

Decoherent has everything—police action and procedure, martial arts, and so many twists and turns you'll want to see how each one turns out.

First-time novelist Steve Holley is a life-long student of the martial arts and a 36-year veteran of police work, and his experience shows in the story's realism. In this unique police thriller, he combines his mastery of martial arts and the years of patrolling the mean streets to bring the reader a gritty sense of realism other writers can only hope for. This one is as true as it gets and will keep you turning the pages long after your bedtime and reading into the wee hours of the night. Steve Holley is a writer to watch.

Loren W. Christensen,
best-selling author of 60 books.

DECOHERENT

A NOVEL

J.S. HOLLEY

A Montag Press Book
www.montagpress.com
Montag Press
777 Morton Street, Unit B
San Francisco CA 94129 USA

Montag Press, the burning book with the hatchet cover, the skewed word mark and the portrayal of the long-suffering fireman mascot are trademarks of Montag Press.

Printed & Digitally Originated in the United States of America
10 9 8 7 6 5 4 3 2 1

DEDICATION

To Debbie, who was certain that this book would get published, even when I wasn't. Love you, babe

ACKNOWLEDGMENTS

To Charlie Franco, Editor Extraordinaire, without whose relentless beatings, this book would not have been nearly as good

To Loren Christensen, fellow writer, retired cop, and life-long martial artist, who read the entire first draft and gave me advice along the way. I've spoken to an Ophthalmologist, and he says your eyes should stop bleeding any day now.

To John Shirley, for your encouragement and advice but, most of all, your friendship

To Peter Watts, who has taken the time to correspond with me on many subjects, an astonishing percentage of which has involved either cephalopods or raccoons, and has been a sounding board I've relied on. And thanks for your input on the last chapter.

To Eric Cline, who has always been available when I've needed some help. Eric, you're a mensch.

To Steven Barnes, whose writing, and writings about writing, have influenced the way I think about the craft. You never know who you will influence along the way.

To Steve Perry, who kindly read my novel, offered some sage advice, and gave me a dynamite blurb. Thanks for that and for Emile Khadaji.

DECOHERENT

The afternoon sun hammered Detective Second Grade Alex Dorn through the windshield of his unmarked, slate-gray cruiser, making him squint and wish for the umpteenth time that he hadn't forgotten his sunglasses at the department. He was fighting a headache building behind his eyes, the result of a three-hour deposition on a traffic homicide case. The sun wasn't helping. He sighed, shifting his weight to give the Glock on his right hip a little extra room against the center-console radio-mount. He could feel a bruise there. His hip had been tender for three days now, ever since he'd taken a spill when jumping a fence in a foot pursuit

"I hate it when they run," he muttered under his breath.

The air conditioner did its best to keep up with the heat, struggling with the Florida sun. He adjusted the vent to cool the inside of the cruiser. Sweat beaded his face and stained the armpits of his white dress shirt. The car was four years old, but vehicle wear on a police car is like dog-years compared to human-years. He threw his jacket in the back seat, loosened his tie, and rolled the sleeves of his shirt up his arms to just below the elbow. None of it helped.

Alex had spent the afternoon in a defense deposition on a traffic homicide case, a holdover from his work in patrol. The defense attorney, Johnny Ramirez, had raked him over the coals for three hours on minuscule, technical points of the crash, most of them irrelevant. The cops called Johnny "Sleazy John," and it was rumored that you couldn't use a phone to contact him. Instead, you drew a pentagram on the ground and summoned him up from the depths of the abyss. Alex didn't mind any defense attorney doing his job, but Ramirez delighted in embarrassing and ridiculing cops on the stand in open court.

Alex looked at the three-inch-thick case file lying in the open briefcase on the passenger's seat. It was thorough and complete, containing diagrams, calculations, lab results, photographs, and supplementary documentation concerning the crash he'd been deposed on. The suspect was an eighteen-year-old kid driving a Ford Mustang GT with a five-liter engine, a machine with a top speed of 264 miles per hour, according to its factory specs. He and two friends had bought beer that night with a fake I.D. that they'd gotten at the flea market. It was crappy I.D. but the bored clerk hadn't given a shit and sold them the beer anyway. Between drinking, playing grab-ass with each other, driving fast, and yelling, the driver had failed to negotiate a curve. He had been traveling well above the curve's critical speed, the yaw marks on the road testifying that he'd realized his mistake at the last second. The super-elevation of the roadway had caused the car to vault, spin, and smash into a pine tree fourteen feet off the ground. The vagaries of physics and the certainties of modern engineering had conspired to save the driver's life but not that of his friends.

Alex had been out on patrol checking the back of a closed building a quarter of a mile away when he heard the crash. He radioed that he'd heard something suspicious in the area and started searching in that direction, coming upon the scene within minutes. The vaulted vehicle had made contact with a pine tree on the passenger's side of the grill, activating the airbag and pinning the driver to his seat. The front-seat passenger had been ejected through the windshield, catching his neck on a jagged piece of metal as he exited, slicing through his carotid artery.

Alex found him later, bled out in a thicket seventy-three feet from the point of impact. The rear seat passenger had remained in the car. Unsecured he had rammed face-first and dead-center into the dashboard, shattering his skull and all of his cervical vertebrae.

Fire/Rescue got to the scene soon after Alex, stabilizing the vehicle and cutting its roof off with the Hurst Tool — aka, the Jaws of Life and its 5,000 PSI of metal-chewing power. With the roof removed, it had only taken moments for the first paramedic to check the passenger and pronounce him DRT, Dead Right There. They found the driver unconscious and unresponsive but alive. They then extricated and back-boarded him, strapping him to a rigid piece of fiberglass and immobilizing his head and limbs. Then they shoved him, gurney and all, into the back of the Fire-Rescue vehicle. Alex, squatting in the cramped back of the squad with the paramedic, smelled beer on the kid from three feet away. The paramedic had looked at Alex and said, "ETOH", Alcohol. Hearing this he'd un-assed the squad and gotten the blood draw kit out of his trunk. Upon his return, the kid had started to regain consciousness and seemed lucid enough for Alex to explain the Implied Consent law; that, by accepting his driver's license, he agreed to be tested for sobriety. He refused, telling Alex to go fuck himself. The paramedic had the vial in his hand for the blood draw and looked at Alex, the question written in his expression. Alex had smiled, nodded to the paramedic, and held the cursing, squirming kid's arm steady while the paramedic stuck him. The blood had come back from the lab three weeks later at a .16 BAC, twice the legal limit.

With all that, Alex had taken his case to the State Attorney's Office and the kid was charged with two counts of manslaughter. But as luck would have it, the driver had parents with money. This brings us to now. Enter Sleazy John.

Jesus. Three hours of deposition. Torquemada was surely kinder and gentler. Alex massaged his temple with his right hand, his left hooked over the steering wheel at the wrist as he meandered through the afternoon traffic.

Alex considered going back to the PD and closing out some paperwork on another case he was working but that took him in the opposite direction from his home and, frankly, he was too keyed up and exhausted from the deposition to sit at a desk right now. Besides, his partner, Deni 'Don't call me Denise' Johnson, had also been at the criminal courts complex, so there was no one at the station that needed to see him. They'd had lunch together and planned their strategy for investigating a series of burglaries/rapes in the southwest section of town. Patrol had done a field interview card on someone at 0300 in the area that had a rap sheet as long as his arm. Pretty much every criminal charge but air piracy. Deni had wanted to scoop him up and sweat him, but Alex argued they should plant a GPS tracker on his car and see if they could get something incriminating on him before hauling him in. Deni had grumbled between sandwich bites but said she'd go with him on this one. Alex had smiled. With Deni, he lost as many as he won but there were few people he'd rather have as back-up when things went pear-shaped.

So he decided to play hooky, cruising instead in the direction of home. He considered stopping by a small used bookstore on the east-side of town and killing time by going through the semi-organized stacks of books, looking for an unexpected treasure that might lurk in the musty ranks of print and smelling of the peculiar perfume only old books possessed. Just thinking about it made him relax until the radio broke squelch, crackling to life, "All units, 10-33 on Channel 2. Units out on a Domestic Call at 4215 S Main Street. Shots fired. Officer down."

"Shit," Alex said. "Shit, shit, shit," smashing his palm on the steering wheel with each exclamation, bending the wheel back with each blow. He cursed himself for not having monitored the radio traffic, losing precious seconds punching up the call that should have already been on his in-car computer. He spun the steering wheel, making a sharp and illegal U-turn and cutting across two lanes of traffic. Three vehicles locked up their brakes, sliding to a stop, horns blaring. Alex spared them a dark glance, activating his emergency lights and siren as he completed the turn. He stomped on the accelerator as he came out of the turn, fishtailing and leaving rubber on the road, accelerating away from the angry drivers. He reached for the mike to the in-car radio, prying it out of the mount on the dashboard.

"Delta Two Eight, responding to the Domestic. Two minutes out, going to Two."

"Delta Two Eight copied, responding, going to two," the dispatcher answered. Alex smiled tightly. The dispatcher was Karen, one of the best in communications. She was probably champing at the bit to get to Channel Two. She regarded every officer working as one of her "boys" and God help the rookie who pissed her off.

Alex listened to the radio traffic on Channel Two as he drove in. The radio chatter was a typical Charlie Foxtrot with patrol units setting up a perimeter and the on-scene supervisor calling for SWAT. He read the call notes between dodging traffic, weaving back and forth between cars. They said there was a domestic disturbance involving a man, a woman, and two children. The man was reported to be behaving erratically, possibly high or intoxicated, and was seen to be verbally abusive toward the woman and kids. There was no evidence of physical violence before the arrival of the first responding unit. The officer had gone in without backup and, according to the last person out the door, had taken a round and was still inside.

Tires shrieked and Alex jerked his head up to see the vehicle in front of him lock up its brakes and go into a four-wheel skid, rubber peeling off the tires, smoke billowing from under the Buick's chassis. He yanked his wheel to the right and hit the accelerator. As his front end cleared the right rear corner of the car, Alex pulled the wheel back to the left hard, causing the rear of his vehicle to fishtail to the right, clearing the skidding, smoking hulk, and slamming his tender right side against the radio console. He grunted with the pain and said a silent prayer of thanks to the Police Gods that he was driving one of the Crown Vics with its rear-wheel drive and not the underpowered 6-cylinder unmarked cars the administration had bought to "save money." He glanced at the driver as he sped past. She looked to be about eighty years old, clutching the wheel like grim death. Her face was frozen in a rictus of terror, staring at the road between the top of the steering wheel and the dash. Alex shook his head. *Needless driving.*

Thirty seconds later, Alex rolled up to the scene at the Family Discount Food Mart, positioning his unmarked car behind the Sergeant's vehicle. Both cars were parked sideways to the market to afford the officers cover. The setting sun baked the entire scene, heat rising off the asphalt and turning it soft and sticky. The storefronts faced west, the plate glass windows blazing the setting sun back into the eyes of the police cordon, killing their ability to see inside the store and ratcheting the heat up several notches. As usual, the commotion had drawn the curious and the stupid, forcing officers to use manpower already stretched thin to herd them back and away from danger. Two rookie cops were stringing yellow crime scene tape as fast as they could run.

Before he got out of the vehicle, he took a moment to settle himself, cultivating the *feeling* of turning a corner, of making a choice. It felt like he was making a ninety-degree turn in his head as he felt the familiar sensation of something *twisting* between his shoulder blades. It took only a second and then, satisfied, he stepped out of the car and kept low as he ran to the back of the sergeant's cruiser. Alex recognized the on-scene supervisor. Bobby Hull was a small man, distinguished by the gold chevrons on his dark blue sleeves. He was turned away from Alex, crouched on the side of his cruiser, giving orders to a much larger patrol officer with an AR-15 slung behind his shoulder. Bobby was issuing orders at a break-neck pace, trying to get the units organized into some kind of jury-rigged perimeter while SWAT geared up at the station and prepared to respond.

"Look, Pazlowski, I need you and the other two patrol units with rifles to set up anywhere you think you might get a clean shot at the suspect. Make sure the other two know there's no green light unless or until I say so, got it? Good. Go!" Bobby told the officer in front of him, sending him off with a slap on the shoulder. Alex was glad it was someone as stable and street-smart as Bobby in charge. He'd been in Vice before his promotion and had once bet he could go up to a house wearing a Goofy cap, carrying a gallon of milk and a box of Oreos, and buy drugs. Alex had lost twenty dollars on that bet.

"Hey, Sarge, you all by your lonesome out here? Where's the El Tee?", Alex asked.

Sergeant Hull pivoted around, still in a crouch, to face Alex, sweat streaming down his face and glistening on the crown of his bald head, clearly annoyed.

"Gee, I dunno, Dorn. It's 4:30 on a Friday afternoon. My guess is he's at home enjoying his first cocktail or blowing the captain. Maybe both".

"Maybe I can help. What have you got?" Alex asked.

Hull grimaced, wiping the sweat from his forehead with the back of his forearm. "Ah, it's a cluster fuck, Alex. All we know is the suspect is a white male in his late-thirties/early-forties, short brown hair, bad teeth, probably strung out on something. From the description the cashier gave, I'd guess he's a tweaker. Victims are a woman and two children. And now, Carstairs," he said.

"Carstairs is the cop?" Alex asked, struggling to place him without success. Bobby nodded.

"You wouldn't know him. He's a rookie, just out of field training. Apparently, he decided not to wait for backup and charged in to save the day. He took a round and went down, at least according to the last cashier to get out of the place. We don't know his status."

Alex scowled. It was a rookie mistake they'd all made at one time or another, but most people didn't suffer this kind of consequence.

"OK, Sarge, I'll get the number of the store and try to make contact with the suspect. See if I can get any more info," Alex said. Hull nodded in reply, already turning away and talking on the radio, trying to coordinate the crime scene. SOP called for establishing an inner and outer perimeter as well as a command post. As usual, there weren't enough officers on scene to get things done, so the result was a hodgepodge effort that tried to accomplish the mission with what was available; so it was pretty much a soup-sandwich.

Alex got out his department-issued phone and called Dispatch, using the direct number.

"Bay City Police Department, this line is recorded, how may I help you?", the call-taker asked, stress and tension in his voice.

"This is Dorn, Delta Two Eight. You got a phone number for the store yet?"

"Yeah. Hold on. I'll pull it up. It's...352-258-3080."

"Got it. Thanks," Alex said.

"Hey, you on-scene? You didn't call out."

"Oops. Yeah, I'm here. Sorry, it's a little hectic."

"No problem. We have you on-scene. Be safe," the call-taker said, cutting the connection.

Alex took a minute to think about his first contact with the suspect. He had to establish his identity and authority but, beyond that, remain a blank slate. *Tabula rasa.* Let the subject project onto Alex whatever he needed Alex to be, whatever it took to resolve the crisis. It was like walking a tightrope, feeling your way along during the negotiation, letting the hostage-taker feed you information. Alex heard the report of handgun rounds being fired and froze. The sound was subdued, dull and indistinct, unmistakably coming from inside the store.

One...Two...Three...a pause...Four... a longer pause...Five. For a long second, everyone froze.

Alex went numb. He heard Sgt. Hull advise units closest to the store to take the door. They had prepared and were set up to breach. Three officers, stacked belly-to-butt, moved as one unit to the door. The first officer yanked it open and crouched, waiting as the second and third entered dynamically, clearing the "fatal funnel" and fanning out to opposite sides. Secondary units began to close the gap to the store to provide fire support if needed. Alex watched it as if it was an exercise, distant, uninvolved. *Textbook entry.* Alex could see them in his mind. *The officers responding direct-to-threat to neutralize the shooter, moving efficiently toward the back of the store, covering the angles as they advanced, each man knowing which sectors he was responsible for. They functioned like parts of a well-oiled machine, using the exaggerated heel/toe "Groucho Walk," clearing the store as they moved.* Within a minute, the lead officer called an "all clear". The building was secure.

Alex walked beside Hull as they moved toward the grocery store. Hull's face was set into a mask, blank, stoic, expecting the worst.

"What's the status on Carstairs?" Hull asked over the radio.

There was a pause and then, "Signal seven."

"Fuck," he said, then keyed the mike again. "And the other subjects?"

"Signal Seven, Sarge," came the response. "They're all signal seven. Including the suspect."

Hull faltered and stopped, looking down at the ground He took a deep breath, his eyes unfocused. Alex stepped up to his side and said, "I'll take the investigations side of things from here, Sarge. I'm already involved and on-scene."

Hull shook himself, straightening his back, turning to look at Alex, "Damn right you will, Dorn. Figure out where this shit went sideways. And do it before the brass shows up." Alex nodded.

As they walked to the front of the store, Hull got pulled to one side by a patrol unit. Alex went on, taking in the exterior scene. The grocery store was located in a short strip mall, a ubiquitous architectural fixture in South Florida that said "Shop here. We're cheap". This particular strip mall had seen better days and was generally run down, housing at most a dozen retail storefronts, several of them unoccupied units that stood out against the decorations of the struggling stores like decayed teeth. The neighborhood was lower middle class, the working poor, and the local grocery store, tiny as it was, saved the residents from having to go uptown by bus or friend's car. As he approached the doors, he considered a course of action. Alex grabbed the patrol unit closest to the door.

"Hey, Officer!" he shouted. The patrolman jumped as if struck. The adrenaline still edging his nerves like acid. He turned toward Alex, a cautious look on his face.

"Congratulations. You just became keeper of the crime scene log. No one goes in or out without you logging them. And no one goes in at all without my permission." The patrolman's face looked like Alex had forced him to eat a live toad.

"What about the brass?"

"That goes double for brass," he said.

"Yes, sir," he said, looking equal parts pleased and worried.

Nothing makes a patrol officer feel better than screwing with the brass.

Alex passed through the door as the cool air, scented with a dozen ethnic spices, washed over him. He took in the front area of the small store. There were three check-out lines at the front of the shop with old-fashioned electronic registers, no laser scanners. The floors were gummy and had not been waxed in a while. The front windows were all plate glass, but half of them were taken up with advertisements, current and past, some yellowing and curling from the sun while others looked fresh. The entrance and exit doors were on opposite sides of the front of the store, with the entry on the south side. There were no pressure plates, so the doors did not open automatically and an old, tired fan system struggled to create an air curtain to keep the cool air in and the bugs out.

The meat department was against the north wall, to Alex's left as he entered, the meat cases at waist height with the aisles running parallel to the cases. As Alex approached the shooting scene, he could see the suspect had tried to barricade himself and his family behind the meat case, piling boxes of canned hams at one end. Both kids lay face down with the mother lying halfway across the meat case, a twelve-inch butcher knife still clutched in her right hand. Her position made it clear she'd been trying to stab the suspect when he shot her. Most of her face was gone. Three cops were standing around Carstairs while a fourth knelt beside him. They stared down at him, looking lost and angry. In contrast, his face was peaceful. He'd been shot through the side of the head, bits of brain and skull splattered against a display of canned peas. Brain matter extruded from the exit wound. His body lay face up, twisted slightly to the left.

The other cops on the scene inside were milling about aimlessly. Seeing one of their own lying lifeless on the floor deflated them and made them feel helpless. It was easy to slide into a state of shock. *You had to clamp down on your emotions. Control them or they controlled you.* The only real antidote is to give the officers direction, to give them a purpose, and to stop their brains from thinking.

There was a flurry of activity as Fire/Rescue and paramedics moved into the store from where they'd been staged. There were four of them and they moved to Carstairs and the children first. Alex thought about limiting their access to one paramedic in order to get an official pronouncement of death but decided a pissing match with FD would be counter-productive. *The juice just isn't worth the squeeze. It won't matter in the end, anyway.*

Alex ordered one of the younger-looking officers to get some of the yellow evidence tape and seal off the actual shooting scene, and anyone not actually doing something to vacate the scene. Left to their own devices, cops will trample all over the evidence at a crime scene. Especially a scene as charged with emotion like this, with one of their own lying dead. It's like they never learned Locard's principle in the academy: everyone who enters a crime scene brings something with them when they enter, which they then leave behind, and takes something away when they leave. *And Brass is the worst. It was like they do it to prove how important they are.*

At last, Alex got to the suspect. The man lay on his back with the revolver by his left hand and Carstair's Glock jammed into his waistband. He had held the gun to the side of his head when he pulled the trigger; the bullet taking a turn in his skull and exiting through the top of his balding head. Alex looked up to see the blood spray had painted the ceiling above him. He stepped gingerly to one side, avoiding the fallout area. The suspect was stretched out across a case of canned hams with his head tilted back, his mouth wide open. He had an advanced case of "Meth Mouth". Most of his teeth had jumped ship some time back and the few remaining hung on gamely, looking like little brown pegs set haphazardly in his gaping maw.

Tweaker for sure. Alex spent some time getting the exact location of the suspect and the geometry of the store layout, looking for angles of fire from various places in the shop to the suspect's location, trying to estimate how long reaching any position of advantage might take from the moment of entry into the store. Satisfied he'd covered as many of the bases as he could, Alex took one last look at the scene in front of him then reached *back,* mentally, to the space between his shoulder blades. *Back* to where it felt like there was a knot - twisted, torqued, and under tension. He reached *back* and felt himself *pull* on that knot. He set himself and, just for a moment, the tension increased and then *released.*

*   *   *

With the feeling of a sudden jarring stop, Alex found himself back in the cruiser as he had arrived at the scene. Just before he'd gotten out of the car. Exactly where he'd set the waypoint. He took a moment to orient himself. No matter how many times he jumped, it was always a little unsettling.

Alex opened the door, standing up outside the cruiser. *I don't have much time. Better get to work.*

Chapter 2

"You stupid motherfucker!" Cheryl screamed. "You shot the cop! I ain't gonna die 'cause o' you and I ain't for shit-sure gettin' my kids killed!" She confronted her live-in boyfriend with her arms spread wide, keeping her children behind her, partially shielded. The kids alternated between cowering behind her and sneaking a peek around her side to see what was going on They looked out from beneath her arm where the worn and frayed red-and-blue flannel shirt she wore open over her stained white wife-beater made a half curtain that seemed to offer protection.

Rafe's head felt like it was going to explode if she screamed one more time. Every screech was another nail in the side of his throbbing melon. He squinted at the frizzy-blonde bitch-demon he lived with, trying to remember what he'd seen in her in the first place. *Christ! Wasn't it enough he hadn't had any decent crank since Billy's lab blew up?* Billy had fled the state since the lab had taken most of the farmhouse and his grandparents with it. Shit, he hadn't even smoked weed today. *Weed, for chrissakes!*

"Shut the fuck up, Cheryl," he yelled. "I gotta think."

"Well, you shoulda started thinkin' before you pulled that goddamned trigger!" she snarled.

"It ain't my fault! He shouldn't a' tried to hassle me. I'm...I'm a free man, traveling upon the land," Rafe smiled, nodding at her with satisfaction. *Take THAT, bitch!* He met with his boys every other Wednesday. They called themselves the 'Swampboy Militia' and, while they were supposed to practice military operations, they usually just drank beer and talked about how the government and the immigrants were screwing them over. Sometimes they watched programs that talked about how they were the last hope of the free white men in the world, the last hope against the mud people. Sometimes they watched porn. Rafe liked porn nights the best.

"Oh, that's just one of the stupid sayings you learned when you go meet with your *idjit* friends on Wednesday night. Then you come home half-drunk and wantin' some pussy. That don't mean shit."

"It ain't stupid. We are sovereign citizens and we don't need no gub'mint tellin' us what to do!" As Rafe said this, he was dimly aware he was on welfare and food stamps and the kids got nutritional assistance and free lunches at school. *Hell, that don't mean nothin' to me. I'm a Free Man, dammit! And I'm a member of the White race that built this country and made it great before the niggers and spics and kikes screwed it up. They owe me, dammit. OWE me!*

Hank Carstairs watched this exchange with a mixture of disgust and self-loathing. *How could I have gotten taken out by THIS shit-for-brains?* He grunted, shifting position to take pressure off his right arm. He'd responded to a simple domestic call and thought he could clear it in time to meet his girlfriend for coffee after she got off work. *But no, dumbass had to go in without backup*. He'd located the couple right away…well, Hell, it wasn't difficult with all the yelling and cursing…and approached them with his best 'Hi-I'm-Officer-Friendly-and-I'm-Here-to-Help-You' smile when he noticed the male part of the domestic had a gun in his hand. He'd yelled "freeze!" as he went for his service weapon but the perp had fired first, the bullet going through his lower arm, breaking the radius (which now stuck out of his arm at a jaunty angle) before impacting his bullet-proof vest, knocking him down. His gun had fallen from his lifeless hand, skittering away down the aisle. The perp seemed as surprised he'd shot Hank as Hank was that he'd been shot and so it took him a moment to gather what wits he had and run down the aisle to retrieve Hank's Glock. He'd picked it up from the floor and jammed it into the front of his greasy jeans.

"You…you stay right there," the suspect had said, pointing his revolver at Hank, who was still doubled over on the floor with the breath knocked out of him. Hank could see the muzzle of the gun as clear as day, even though it was bouncing around like a pinball in the suspect's shaking hand.

"I'm not going anywhere," Hank had managed to grunt as he attempted to sit up, pushing up with his right arm. "Fuck!" he'd exclaimed as he grabbed his right arm with his other hand and face-planted onto the floor. He'd curled into a fetal position, cradling his injured arm. The pain subsided after a moment, at least to a bearable level, and Hank pushed himself back up to a seated position using only his left hand.

"That's right! That's right! You ain't doin' nothin' but what I tell you." The remaining bullets in the cylinders of the cheap handgun made a tapping noise as Rafe's hand continued to shake.

It was then that Cheryl, who'd been huddled over her children, started in on him. The kids were watching everything with extreme concentration; their bodies coiled like springs. They had learned to read the signs through countless episodes of domestic violence and, when it came time to run, hesitation only meant a beating. Rafe and Cheryl settled into a pattern of argument and abuse that was like a choreographed dance, a *pas-de-deux,* a play, with their roles clearly defined, their rejoinders well-rehearsed. And, as the children and Hank watched, the drama began building to its inevitable and violent climax.

Chapter 3

Alex got out of his cruiser, walking quickly behind it and toward the front of the store. Perimeter patrol units lifted the crime scene tape for him, not questioning him. The gold shield on his belt guaranteed their cooperation. Sgt. Hull was crouched, his back to Alex, talking to Pazlowski. Sgt. Hull was giving Pazlowski his orders when he saw him look past his shoulder, his eyebrows raising.

"Uhhh...Sarge? You might want to turn around," Pazlowski said, pointing at something behind Hull.

Hull pivoted in place to see Alex making a bee-line for the front of the store. "What. The. Fuck." he said, for a moment having trouble actually believing his eyes.

"Dorn! DORN! Oh, I am going to have your ASS for this!" Hull pivoted back to Pazlowski. "Ok...change of plans. I have no idea what Dorn's doing - and he better have a damn good reason for doing it — but I want you and the other rifle-qualified officers to form up and move into position to back his play."

"You think that's smart, sarge?"

The expression on Hull's face looked like an elementary school teacher being forced to explain something for the fifth time to an especially slow second grader. Hull stared at him for a full five seconds before he blinked and answered in a low, threatening voice."I don't think I have much of a fucking choice, Pazlowski. Now move!"

Hull turned again so that he could see Alex approaching the entrance to the grocery store.

"I don't know why you're doing this, Alex," he murmured. "But you'd better be right."

Alex was halfway to the front of the store when he heard Sgt. Hull calling his name. He smiled grimly, his mouth drawn into a tight line, knowing full well what Bobby was saying about him. *Ok, I got no time here. No time*, Alex thought as he eased the door open just far enough to squeeze through, holding it as it slowly shut, then moving in a semi-crouch down the first aisle. His Glock 40 was drawn, held tight against his rib cage, barrel leveled and trigger finger indexed along the side of the gun. *Muzzle first to danger.* He could hear the arguing to his left as he moved down the aisle. He walked deliberately, heel-to-toe, being careful not to allow his feet to slide or scuff as he made his way between the dishwasher detergent on one side and rolls of toilet tissue on the other. He approached the end of the aisle which featured an end-cap of canned baked beans arranged artfully into a tower.

"You gonna help me move these goddamn canned hams or whut?" Rafe bellowed as he shifted another box into position, panting and red-faced. He was sweating profusely now despite the air conditioning, partly from the exertion but mostly from withdrawal and adrenaline. His faded yellow T-shirt proclaimed him to be, in fact, the World's Greatest Lover and was completely soaked through.

"What the Hell do you think that's gonna stop, you fuckin' retard?" she snorted.

"Don't call me that! Don't you EVER call me that!" Rafe turned on her and shouted, his fists balled in rage

"What? Retard? Like your brother? Re-Tard! Re-Tard!" Cheryl taunted in a sing-song voice, a wide, malicious smile splitting her thin face.

"Shut the fuck up, you whore! Your daughter's gonna be JUST like you! A whore! A dirty, filthy, fucking WHORE!" he screamed, veins bulging in his thin neck, his Adam's apple bobbing up and down furiously.

Alex cleared the end of the aisle, going to one knee. He could see the male suspect clearly. He was turned away from him, oriented toward the sound of the female voice. Leaning a little further out, Alex could just barely see the woman. An adolescent girl moved out from behind her mother to the right of the male subject. Her face was screwed into a mask of hatred, her teeth bared in a snarl.

"I ain't no whore and you ain't my daddy!" she screamed.

Rafe reacted immediately, stepping forward and backhanding her viciously across the face. Her mouth snapped shut with a hard *clack,* one of her teeth flying through the air, banking off the side of the cooler and skipping across the floor. Cheryl reached across the meat case and seized a twelve-inch steak knife, pivoting back toward her boyfriend with the knife in an icepick grip, blade protruding from the bottom of her fist. Her daughter dodged back behind her. She lunged for Rafe, eyes wide, screaming, beyond caring about the gun in his hand, just as Alex yelled, "Freeze, police!", his weapon up and covering Rafe.

Rafe's gun had started to come up to shoot his girlfriend but his head snapped to the left at the sound of Alex's voice. He saw the detective in a two-handed shooting position, kneeling at the end of the aisle with a dead bead on him. He tried to turn the gun toward his left and Alex fired two quick shots in response, catching Rafe in the chest, under the armpit. Rafe's knees buckled slightly as his reflexes kicked in and he fired a round that went wide, hitting a can of baked beans that exploded, showering the left side of Alex's face with sticky, molasses-smelling goo. At the same instant, Cheryl hit Rafe high in the chest with her knife plunging downward into the hollow behind his collarbone, slicing through the subclavian artery and lodging in the heart. Rafe fired another round as his fist clenched from being stabbed, the bullet hitting the overhead fluorescents above Alex, showering him with glass and dust. Reflexively, Alex squeezed off another round, hitting the woman in the side of the neck as her body crashed into Rafe's. They both went down in a heap. Dimly, Alex heard the kids screaming.

Alex moved as rapidly as caution would allow toward the couple, keeping his weapon trained on them. The woman lay quietly on top of the man. Not moving, not twitching, not breathing. He saw the entry wound on her neck. *Probably severed her spine.* Alex obeyed the dictates of training, treating the incident with clinical detachment. The man lay with his eyes open and staring, seeing nothing, as his body twitched and jerked spasmodically, his heels drumming against the floor. Alex kept them both covered, working his way around the man's head to his side, stepping on his gun hand to secure the weapon.

"You killed my momma! You fucking pig! You killed her!" the young girl was screaming at Alex as she emerged from behind the meat case, spittle and blood flying from her lips, while the younger boy stood stock still, in shock, watching the entire scene. his eyes were vacant, unblinking. Alex stood helplessly, caught in amber between guilt and training, locked into position. Time stopped. She came around the stack of canned hams, gathering herself to charge Alex when the first patrol rifle unit showed up, coming between the two of them. Within seconds, there were a dozen cops in the store. Alex stepped back, the frozen moment now past. Time flowed again. Peripheral vision and normal hearing returned. He took a deep breath. Alex stood stock still for a few moments, steadying himself. He concentrated on his breathing, lowering his heart rate until he heard the familiar voice of Sgt. Hull behind him.

"Well, that was some Rambo shit, Alex. I sure as Hell hope you got a good explanation for it 'cause I.A. is gonna wanna hear it."

"I didn't think we had the time," Alex near-whispered.

"Time for what, Alex? To wait for SWAT?" Hull asked, concern plain on his face as he walked around to face him, trying to gauge Alex's mental state.

"Yeah."

"And just how the Hell would you know that?"

"I don't know," Alex said, looking away. "I just did."

Chapter 4

Alex stood to one side, watching the chaos of the post-shooting scene evolve. In textbooks, the crime scene gets roped off with surgical precision. Forensics descends on the scene like angels from on-high, working diligently to preserve every scrap of evidence. The reality is not so pretty. Paramedics swarmed the crime scene, attending to the injured and contaminating everything they touched. Their mission was different from and, frankly, more important than forensics. Cops in general and detectives in particular still referred to them as EEUs – Evidence Elimination Units. They worked on Carstairs first, getting him stabilized for transport. He was going to need surgery. One paramedic was talking to the kids as another examined the girl's mouth. The boy was uninjured physically but seemed to still be in shock, standing in one spot and swaying back and forth, staring straight ahead. Another paramedic looked over the shooter and his girlfriend.

Alex saw the paramedic about to turn the woman over when a patrol officer stopped him, having been stationed there and assigned by Sergeant Hull to preserve the scene. The paramedic was becoming visibly upset at having been interrupted, gesturing and raising his voice. Both of them were getting louder as they went back and forth. The tension of a shooting scene, adrenaline, and testosterone were escalating their behavior. *This kind of pissing contest doesn't do anyone any good.* Alex usually sided with the paramedics in this see-saw battle between crime scene sanctity and medical assistance but, in this case, the woman was clearly dead and the paramedic was being unnecessarily territorial. Alex had seen dramas like this before, one party staking out a position and then defending it to the death, even if they're wrong. Especially if they're wrong. Since they had forgotten him in the general chaos and had nothing better to do, he decided to intervene.

"Look, you have to let me do my job," the paramedic said, his voice raising several octaves as he became exasperated

"Your 'job'," Alex could hear the air quotes in the cop's voice, "is to attend to the injured. She's dead."

"Well, I haven't determined that yet, have I?" the paramedic asked, sarcasm dripped from his words as he leaned in and looked closer at the officer's name tag. "Officer Hughes."

"Hey, guys," Alex said, and they both turned to him, completely astonished that someone else would insert themselves into their dispute. Alex looked directly at the paramedic, "Why don't you just check her neck for a pulse? I think the bullet transected her spine."

"And who might you be?" the paramedic asked, crossing his arms across his chest and staring at Alex.

Alex leveled his gaze, "I'm the one who shot her".

Both the cop and the paramedic were startled. The paramedic blinked, saying nothing for a few seconds, then realized this intrusion gave him a face-saving interruption. He squatted, pointedly ignoring Officer Hughes as he used the first two fingers of his right hand to feel for a carotid pulse. Finding none, he stood up and entered the information into his pad.

"Aren't you going to check the guy, too?" the officer asked, smiling, enjoying his small victory.

"His pupils are fixed and dilated, but sure, if it'll make you happy," the paramedic shrugged and squatted again, performing the same procedure on the male.

As the paramedic entered the information into his pad, Alex stepped closer to him and put his hand on his bicep. He looked up. Alex nodded and smiled.

"Thank you," he said," I mean that."

The paramedic nodded back, mumbled something, and moved off. Alex rounded on the police officer. His first few words wiped the smirk off the officer's face.

"That was entirely unnecessary, Officer Hughes. He was just trying to do his job. Like you're trying to do yours. Everyone here is tense and nervous. People are not going to be at their best. But we're all on the same side. There's no percentage in being a dick to this guy. Especially since, if you get shot like Carstairs over there, he may be the person working his ass off to save your life."

Hughes opened and closed his mouth a few times, like a fish out of water. He looked down, his face coloring. "Yes, sir. Sorry," he muttered to the floor

Alex sighed, then remembered he'd forgotten an important post-shooting detail. Very important. Probably the most important. He turned away from Hughes and was going straight for the front door. He walked past Carstairs as paramedics were placing him on the gurney, his injured arm in an inflatable cast. He paused to give them room and turned, checking for the kids, but they had been moved outside to be away from the scene of the trauma. As he started to walk forward again, a hand caught his left forearm. He looked down and saw it was Carstairs, lying on the gurney and using his left hand to seize Alex's wrist.

"Thanks," he said, looking up at Alex.

"You'll be fine," Alex said, smiling down at him on the gurney. "The paramedics are going to take good care of you. I hear there's free morphine in the ambulance."

Carstairs groaned, "God, I hope so." Alex motioned for the paramedics to get him moving. They needed very little encouragement.

As Carstairs left the store, Alex turned, surveying the scene, his hands on his hips. Things seemed to be calming down. He turned and followed the gurney out the door, catching a puzzled look from the officer with the crime scene log. It was the same officer Alex had tapped for the job before he reset his waypoint and changed the outcome of the hostage situation. He almost laughed out loud at the absurdity of it. *Some things are destiny. The universe just wants it that way.* Alex squinted as he got out his phone and shaded the screen with his left hand, searching for and finding Rick Norton's number. Rick was his PBA Rep and Alex figured he was going to need a lawyer. This was one of the reasons he paid his dues. He hit send and Rick's voice came over the speaker.

"I'm on my way, about ten minutes out," Rick said tersely.

Alex took his phone from his ear and held it in front of him, looking at it like it was something alien. He put it back up to his ear, "How did you...?"

Rick cut him off. "Deni. She called me as soon as she heard. She's on her way, too. Do me a favor; keep your mouth shut until I get there."

Ah, mystery solved. He heard a noise and turned around to see Sgt. Hull standing in the doorway with his hands on his hips; his head cocked to one side. He did not look pleased.

"Uh, sure thing, Rick. I gotta go. See you when you get here," Alex said, hanging up. Hull didn't say a word; he pointed inside the store. More of a stabbing motion with his finger, really. Alex held his hands out, palms up, in an expression of supplication. Bobby re-emphasized his unspoken order by jabbing his finger at the door again. As Alex walked the few steps back to the store, he noticed the camera crews from the local news setting up.

Hull looked at him with an expression of resigned dismay as he passed, asking, "You want to be plastered all over the evening news? What were you thinking?"

Alex had been too busy with his phone to notice the growing crowd of vans outside emblazoned with the insignia of media outlets. Reporters were setting up cameras, looking for the best backdrop for their shot. "I don't think I was, sarge, thinking that is. Thanks," Alex said. "I just phoned Rick Norton."

"Smartest thing you've done all day. There should be a shooting team here soon, along with forensics and, God help us, command staff. You need to be ready," Bobby said. He studied Alex's face, concerned.

"Thanks, Sarge. I'll be inside, out of everyone's way."

Alex went inside and stayed away from the actual shooting scene. He found a place on the far side of the store where there was a raised office area that gave him a commanding view of the entire area. It was about three feet above floor level with a waist-high wall around it on three sides, the fourth side being the Store's south wall. It was festooned with papers scotch-taped to its chipped and fading green paint. On the side opposite the wall was a two-foot-wide, laminated press-board shelf, jutting from the half-wall about a foot down from the top. It held an ancient computer and printer on it as well as an old-fashioned adding machine and some paperwork. Inside the enclosure were two black faux leather chairs on rollers that had electrical tape in places where the material had cracked. A banged-up, beige filing cabinet completed the ensemble.

He noticed that Bobby had set up an inner perimeter using crime scene tape inside the store, using the store itself for his outside perimeter. *Smart.* Control was getting established over crime scene access now that the wounded and civilians had been evacuated. He thought about his conduct in the shooting and decided he was within departmental guidelines and state law. He regretted he'd not established a waypoint before entering the building. He couldn't think of any good reason why he hadn't. Stress, adrenaline, tunnel vision...they were all factors but, in the final analysis, he just didn't do it. He turned it over and over in his mind, parsing all the possible outcomes.

If he had set a waypoint, he might have been able to correct the incidental shot that killed the woman. He'd have been tempted, but there was no guarantee it would have gone any better. Alex might have missed the bad guy, or not disabled him with the first shot. The wild shot he got off might have gone into Alex, one of the kids, or Carstairs. Getting a second chance didn't ensure things were going to work out perfectly, or even to one's liking. In the end, he decided he'd saved three lives - four counting his own - and would live with that outcome. *Otherwise, you could "What If" yourself to death over every decision you make.*

Alex inventoried his own emotional and physical state. He felt confident in the outcome of any investigation but that didn't mean he was morally or ethically justified. *I could beat that to death, too.* He had already put the experience into a box, compartmentalizing it, keeping his mind clear so he could focus on the present. He'd long been aware of this ability to control his emotions and deal with things objectively even when those around him were freaking out. It had saved him from injury or death on multiple occasions. In his more reflective moments, he was sometimes concerned he had sociopathic tendencies. He was comforted by the fact that he could form strong attachments to those closest to him. *Maybe I'm a higher-level sociopath. A kinder, gentler sociopath, with a conscience. Yeah. That's it.*

Alex noticed they had monitors on the shelf in the office that were linked to cameras focused on various places in the store. He sat in one of the dilapidated chairs and examined them closely. They showed the register area, the front door, the office, and a back room used for storage. Nothing was centered on the area in front of the meat case, where the shooting had occurred. *So, even if they are hooked up to a working recording system, and that's a toss-up, they wouldn't be of any value to the investigation.*

From his vantage point, Alex saw Rick arguing with the rookie at the front door. He was taking his duties very, very seriously. He got up and headed for the door. He was halfway down the stairs when Sgt. Hull beat him to it and let Rick in. Alex waved to him until Rick waved back and started toward him. Rick looked disheveled but then, he always looked like he'd just gotten out of bed. His short blonde hair, parted in the middle, was tousled, probably from the convertible sports car he'd just bought, but his light blue PBA shirt was neatly pressed as were his khakis.

Rick's arrival was always heralded by the reek of cigarettes. He reached out to Alex and shook hands. Alex opened his mouth to speak.

"Don't talk to me. Not one damn word. Not one," Rick growled.

"Uh...okay. Why?"

"Because nothing you say to me is protected speech. I, unfortunately, can be subpoenaed to testify. I've got Gloria Maddox en route and she will take over as your attorney when she gets here. Until then, I'll fill you in on what to expect."

There followed a precise summation of what would be happening to Alex for the next couple of hours. It was not Rick's first post-shooting situation. He was thorough and professional, speaking in clipped tones, frequently pausing to be sure Alex understood him. As he was finishing his rundown, Deni entered the store. Short and slightly built, with light brown, almost reddish hair, a small, pert nose, and a no-nonsense manner, Deni pushed past the rookie with the crime scene log like he wasn't there, tersely giving him her name out of the side of her mouth as she scanned the inside of the store. She found Alex and nodded, walking toward him and Rick. As she approached, Rick reminded Alex, "Remember, not one word."

"Hey," she said, walking up the stairs to the office. "Are you all right? "

"Yeah, I'm fine. What's going on in the outside world?"

"They're going outside the department for a shooting team. Probably FDLE. Their ASAC is on his way here now. My guess would be he's assembling his team on the fly and they'll meet him here."

As if on cue, a tall, thin, angular stranger in a tailored gray, pin-striped suit walked through the door past the officer with the security log. He stopped briefly, speaking with Sgt. Hull who waved him through, pointing him toward Alex's position. He nodded to Hull and started into the store but didn't come directly toward Alex, going instead to the area of the shooting.

"I know him," Deni said." His name's Coburn. He seems to be squared away. At least, the handful of times I've met him, I've gotten that impression."

They watched as Coburn asked several questions at the scene and then walked toward them. As he approached, Alex noticed that Rick adopted a semi-defensive posture on Alex's right while Deni did the same on his left. Agent Coburn put on a friendly smile as he approached the three. He extended his gloved hand to Alex and Alex looked down at it, placed his hands carefully behind his back, clasping them together, then looked back up at the agent. "If you're going to be handling evidence, my hand is probably the last hand you want to shake," he said.

Chagrined, Coburn recovered quickly, looking at Alex as though re-evaluating him and introduced himself. "Probably so. I'm Agent Coburn from FDLE, as I'm sure Deni here has told you," he smiled at Deni. "I wonder if I might ask you a few questions."

Rick stepped forward. "No, I'm sorry, Detective Dorn won't be making any statements or answering any questions until his attorney gets here."

"And you would be...?"

"Rick Norton, PBA."

"Ah, well, then. I guess my questions will wait. Except one: Has anyone taken possession of your service weapon, Detective Dorn?", he asked. Alex shook his head. "I'll do that now, then," he said, holding out his hand.

"We could do it like that, Agent Coburn. Or, I could just drop it in the bag for forensics when they get here. That would minimize contamination and shorten the chain of custody. Your scene, your call." Alex waited for a response.

Coburn paused for a moment, considering. "I'll take your advice on this, detective. You won't be going anywhere before the arrival of Forensics?"

"I'm fairly sure that Sgt. Hull would have my ass in a sling if I tried," Alex answered.

"Good enough. If you'll excuse me?" Coburn smiled again and turned, walking down the steps and toward the bodies.

"I'll give him this; he's smooth," Alex said.

"Positively ophidian," Deni said.

Alex raised one eyebrow at her. "*Someone's* been taking college courses," he said.

"Some of us want to get ahead," she said, staring straight ahead, deadpan.

A few minutes later, forensics showed up at the front door and Coburn met them. He turned and pointed at Alex who raised his hand in response. One of the forensics guys was heavyset, wearing a tan jumpsuit. He carried a lot of equipment and looked relieved to set most of it down inside the store. His black, curly hair was matted with sweat and his jumpsuit stuck to him in places. He wiped his face with his sleeve after pushing his black-rimmed glasses back up onto the bridge of his nose. He took a moment to catch his breath. Then he opened one of the cases, selecting a sheet of cardboard and two plastic bags. Armed with these, he approached Alex's elevated position, lumbering up the stairs.

"Hi," he said. "I'm Alex. I'd like to collect your gun." He was still sweating profusely.

"Nice name," Alex said. "Your parents obviously had good taste. Mine did, too."

The tech smiled. "Could you separate the magazine from the weapon and take the bullet out of the chamber, please?"

The evidence tech did some fancy origami with the cardboard and a gun box appeared. It was like a magic show. Alex popped the magazine and racked the slide with his hand over the ejector port. He placed the gun in the box and secured it while the tech watched. The bullet and the magazine went into one of the plastic bags, the gun box going in the larger one. Alex the tech sealed both bags and wrote pertinent information on them before placing his initials and the date across the seal.

"One last thing," forensics Alex said, "I'll need a GSR swab from you. Are you right-handed or left-handed?"

"I'm a rightie," Alex said.

He produced a swab kit from one of his jumpsuit pockets and ran the cotton end over Alex's right hand. When he was done, he put it in a tube, sealing it with the same procedure.

After squaring everything away, he looked up at Alex. "Thanks. Excuse me." And with that, he went back to the boxes he'd schlepped in, securing the weapon and ammunition in one of them and the gun-shot residue evidence in another, then locking both. Alex watched as he went to the bodies and bagged their hands. He started taking pictures of the bodies, but Alex's attention was drawn to the front door once again as the chief and two captains walked in. *Great. His Majesty and his retinue have arrived.* Alex pictured beefeaters in royal livery blaring trumpets upon the chief's arrival. He was dressed in his class "A" uniform – long sleeves, tie, four gold stars adorning his collar on each side, service ribbons and medals over his right breast representing God-knows-what as Alex had never seen him do anything important. He was truly resplendent. *Christ. If he was a peacock, he'd have his tail feathers fanned out.* At least he didn't have on the coat he wore on formal occasions – The Monkey Suit.

Predictably, they walked over to the bodies first because, well, they're bodies. Sgt. Hull did yeoman's work, keeping them from crossing the inner perimeter. The brass kept edging closer to the tape and Hull kept running interference, firmly but politely blocking their way. After several minutes, Hull won the struggle, and the chief cast about until he saw Alex. He smiled.

Crap, here he comes. Captains towed in his wake. It's like a horror movie. Jaws, maybe. And there's no escape.

"Leave. Save yourself," Alex said out of the corner of his mouth to Deni.

"And miss this?" she said. "No way."

The chief made it to Alex's perch and climbed the three stairs to occupy the Forensics guy's former position, leaving his honor guard behind due to the crowded conditions in the office area. They looked perplexed, like remoras separated from their shark.

"I want you to know, Detective...," he struggled for a moment with Alex's name, "Dorn, that the department stands behind you a hundred and ten percent. Whatever you need in this time of trial, you just have to ask."

Yeah. Right, said Alex's inside voice. Outside, he said, "That's good to hear, sir. It takes a load off my mind."

The chief looked at a bit of a loss as to what to say next and Alex feared he might try to hug him. He'd seen him do it before, to other cops. His fellow officers had been merciless, afterward ... *Did he touch you? Did he get near your Danger Square? Did you need an adult?* That shit was *not* going to happen to him. He diverted the chief's attention by pointing out the useless camera system like it might be important. *Look! Squirrel!* It worked. The hugging crisis was averted.

After Alex's camera system show-and-tell, the chief looked at Alex's empty holster and smiled, like a light bulb went on over his head. He drew his weapon, holding it out toward Alex.

Alex looked at the gun the chief held as though he was going to grab it by the barrel and said, "I don't think that'll be necessary, sir."

"Are you sure?" the chief asked. "I don't want you to feel powerless or vulnerable."

Alex nearly laughed out loud. "I'm surrounded by thirty of my closest friends right now, sir. And they all have guns. I think I'll be fine."

"Very well, then," the chief said, re-holstering his weapon, with the air of a man that had made a magnanimous gesture. "Just remember, detective; my door is always open."

"Yes, sir," Alex replied. "I will. Thank you."

The chief turned and made his way to the door; the captains resuming their flanking positions. The chief paused at the door, checking his uniform in the reflection of the window. He adjusted his tie by at least a micrometer and brushed his hair back from his forehead. At last, convinced that his glorious appearance matched his exalted status, he strode forth to meet the press. He loved the media. And they loved him.

"What the Hell was that all about?" Deni asked.

"I dunno," Alex said. "I think he read it in a book somewhere or saw it in a movie." He shook his head. "What a putz." He looked up as a woman entered the store.

"Hey," Rick said. "Gloria's here. You'll need to brief her".

"That's fine," Alex said. He relaxed and found his center. It was going to be a long afternoon.

Chapter 5

"How long are you gonna be ridin' the pine, Alex? Making me do all your work and mine too?" Detective Chuck Rindall asked, idly stirring a white styrofoam cup of department coffee with a flimsy red plastic spoon. "Just so we're clear here...I ain't yo' bitch."

"You're everyone's bitch, Chuck. It's who you are. Is that midnight-shift coffee?"

"Well, let's see," Chuck said, holding the cup at arm's length He tilted his head to one side, regarding it critically. "It hasn't eaten the plastic spoon yet and, if I put the spoon upright in the middle of the cup, it doesn't stand up there by itself so I'd say...no, definitely NOT midnight-shift coffee."

"Good. Could you go get me a cup?"

"Aaagghhh! I really AM everyone's bitch!" Chuck slumped his shoulders in mock despair and shuffled toward the coffee pot in the next room. Alex smiled. Seniority had its privileges.

Investigations was a nondescript room decorated in shades of institutional light brown, or, as Bobby Hull had once put it, "it covers the spectrum from beige to *ecru*." Alex was pretty sure Bobby had to look up that last word. It was depressingly similar. There was only one entry, which everyone hated because it forestalled any quick escapes from admin types, trapping detectives like wolverines in a den. The desks were arranged in groups of four cubicles that formed a plus sign if you looked at it from above. Alex called them Veal-Fattening Pens. The dreaded "Detective Spread" that caused investigators to gain twenty pounds when they walked through the door. It was a combination of stress, easy access to donuts, being planted at a desk, and the fact you got to buy your clothes as a detective. If you gained weight, you could buy roomier clothes. Not patrol officers. The uniform was a harsh taskmaster and the Sam Browne belt, an unforgiving and implacable indicator of weight gain. Alex's zone partner had tried to wear his ballistic vest per the new chief's rules after a year of not wearing it. He'd waddled into read-off looking like a six-foot, five-inch, blood-filled tick; like if you poked him with a pin, he'd pop. Alex was already sitting down when Karl stopped across the table from him and asked, "Tell me the truth, Alex, does this vest make me look fat?" Alex took a moment to look Karl over and replied, "Why no, Karl, it's your big fat ass that makes you look fat." Karl grumbled and sat down at the read-off table. One of his shirt buttons popped off and shot across the room. Hilarity ensued.

Deni entered the room as Rindall exited it. Alex was Deni's usual partner-in-crime but, since his assignment to desk duty, she had been teamed up with Mike Pritchard, who was insufferably stuck on himself and more than a little misogynistic. He'd moonlighted as a male model for the last ten years but was doing that less frequently these days as his waistline thickened and his hair thinned. He wasn't the sharpest tool in the shed either. Pritchard had noticed Deni looked exactly like that girl from the movie *American Pie*. He had given her the nickname "Band Camp," a fact Deni didn't know. It was probably a good thing as Deni had sworn to find the perpetrator of that little deed and shove a clarinet up his ass.

"When you coming back, partner?" Deni asked, setting her briefcase down at her desk.

"You're the second one this morning who has asked me that. I'm starting to believe you guys miss me."

"Shit. I've got Pritchard. I'd miss you if you were a full-time drooling simpleton. Which you are, but only part of the time."

Alex chuckled, "Oh, I don't know. There are certain advantages to being a member of the rubber-gun squad. For example, I get to review reports and assign cases. And patrol just requested a CAP detective at a Sex Batt scene."

Deni's expression was guarded. "Crap. I know that look, Alex. What's wrong with it?"

"What's wrong with what?" Pritchard asked as he walked up behind Deni. He paused, taking a moment to brush back his wispy blonde hair, the front of which had been hairsprayed to the point the hairs moved as a single unit. She glanced back and then looked at Alex, rolling her eyes. Alex stifled a laugh, hiding his smile with his hand.

"Well, let me read from the CAD notes...let's see…," Alex shuffled some papers until he found the right one. "Ah, here it is 'complainant stated that, when she woke up this morning, she had peanut butter in her hair and her pantyhose was on backward. She believes she was raped'. It just doesn't get more open-and-shut than that." Alex looked up with feigned innocence.

Pritchard guffawed. Deni regarded him with a sour expression, looking less than pleased. Pritchard doubled down. "Come on, Deni, I'll show you how a real man handles cases. I mean, after all, you've only had Dorn's example these last six months."

Deni rounded on Pritchard, eyes narrowed, voice dripping acid, "So, tell me, Mike, exactly what part of your penis do you use to solve crimes?"

Pritchard smirked and said, "Well, usually just the head. But for a complicated case, I might go half-shaft."

Deni's face was a mask of disgust as she moved past Pritchard, throwing her elbow into him at solar plexus height. It knocked him back, his breath shooting from his lungs with a *woof.*

"God, I hate you."

Pritchard recovered, chuckling and idly rubbed his sternum; then he looked back toward Alex with a grin, waiting for a good ol' boy affirmation. Alex grabbed a black marker and scrawled something across a piece of blank paper. He held that piece of paper up for Pritchard to read just as Rindall returned with Alex's coffee. Pritchard's eyes went wide and the color drained from his face. He held both hands up in a prayer position, silently mouthing the words "okay, okay" and turned to follow Deni.

"Hey. Here's your coffee," Chuck said, holding the steaming cup out for Alex. "What was all that about? What'd you write?"

Alex looked down at the paper and turned it over. On it were two words. Band Camp.

Chapter 6

Alex took a stack of reports into 'The Hole,' a back-office occupying an alcove in the building that was out of the normal traffic flow of Investigations. Detectives retreated to the hole when they had a lot of work to do and didn't want to be bothered with the normal office banter in the bullpen. It had also been known to host an afternoon nap or two and, legend had it, at least one romantic late-night tryst. Alex was dressed casually in a black polo shirt and khakis since he was still on light duty and figured he might as well be comfortable. He settled himself into a chair with his back to the wall, facing the door, and spread the reports out in front of him like a fan.

As he sorted through the stack of paperwork, Alex's mind wandered. He was concerned about his status after the civilian review board got done with his shooting. He'd heard through the grapevine their reactions weren't exactly positive. He worried he might be out of a job which, he firmly believed, his pregnant wife would find inconvenient. Not for the first time did he wonder whether his ability to create loci in the fabric of the universe and to return to that waypoint, like a salmon swimming up a temporal river to its birthplace, might be more of a curse than a gift. If he hadn't had the gift, then he never would have had the opportunity to get into the shooting. The universe would have flowed on, blissfully unaware there was even a chance of something else happening. It would've absolutely sucked for Carstairs, though, and for those kids, whether they realized it or not.

Alex sighed, thinking back to his discovery of the gift. He was fourteen years old and was experiencing a growth spurt that left him awkward and yet still chubby, with a thin, reedy voice that would drop into a bass with no hesitation and not a moment's notice. He'd also been suffering from an intermittent feeling of tightness between his shoulder blades. His parents had told him he was having typical "growing pains." With the benefit of hindsight, Alex later realized he was involuntarily creating waypoints as he pondered decisions. Without action, though, without the activation of that waypoint, the knot between his shoulders eased and disappeared within an hour. He was completely ignorant this held any meaning at all beyond mere annoyance.

The first incident happened during a school day. Alex had made up his mind to ask Jeanette Peters to the homecoming celebration. They had known each other since grade school and she had always been nice enough when they talked. Since she was one grade ahead of him, those times were less and less frequent, especially of late, as adolescence widened the gap. Still, he believed that nothing ventured, nothing gained, and decided he should at least risk the asking. Jeanette was pretty and blonde and slender and, frankly, the living embodiment of Alex's adolescent fantasies. As he rounded the corner of a hallway intersection, he looked up to see Jeanette talking to a girlfriend at her locker.

Alex straightened his shoulders. *There it was again. Damn! Right between the shoulder blades.*

He clearly and definitively resolved to ask Jeanette to homecoming. He felt as though he'd turned a corner. *This is what manhood feels like,* he'd thought, feeling a surge of confidence. He approached Jeanette and her friend, affecting a slight swagger, picturing himself as James Dean or maybe James Bond. Definitely a James, though. He pushed his glasses back up onto his nose and planted himself close enough for Jeanette to register his presence but not so close as to be intrusive. He adjusted his backpack across one shoulder, waiting for a break in the conversation. Time stretched until it became awkward. Alex shifted from foot to foot. He began to sweat. Jeanette seemed to know he was there but was studiously ignoring him. Alex felt his resolve weaken, but he steadied himself and broke into the conversation, finding the nerve to speak.

"Excuse me," he squeaked. It was at that precise moment his voice, like a traitor laying in ambush, betrayed him. He pressed on.

"Excuse me, Jeanette. I wanted to ask you if you...if...if you would go to homecoming with me?" Alex's voice rose and fell, seemingly malicious, with a mind of its own.

Alex closed his eyes and could still see the look of revulsion and horror that crossed Jeanette's face. She could not have looked any more disgusted had he asked her to eat a live slug. Alex was convinced that nothing more terrible could happen to him. He was wrong.

"I...uh...I mean, I...uh", Alex was trying to form some coherent thought, but nothing was happening. His brain had checked out and left him on his own. Then Jeanette started laughing. Her friend was laughing. People nearby were joining in. Alex felt as though he were the sole object of the world's derision. His vision tunneled, focusing on her face until it seemed like she would laugh like that forever. That he would hear it forever. He was trapped. He couldn't move. He couldn't think. He couldn't breathe.

Any decision was taken from him as a senior football player slammed into Alex from behind, knocking the breath from him. He fell forward onto his hands and knees, hot tears flooding his eyes. His glasses fell off, the lenses skipping across the sandy tile floor, coming to rest under someone's foot with a final crunch. His stomach knotted. He couldn't get air into his lungs. The spot between his shoulders was pulling, pulling. He could still hear her laughing. He would give anything...ANYTHING...if he had never asked her. If he could somehow take it all ba...

Alex felt like the universe slammed into him and then he found himself rounding the corner of the same hallway intersection. He was so startled he yelped and stumbled, barely catching himself. He felt like a coin that had been slotted into place. Jeanette looked up, focused on him briefly, then dismissed him. Alex kept walking, on autopilot, trying to gather his wits. He walked past her, sparing her a furtive glance, and then moved on to his next class. He had no idea what had happened. Why had he been granted a reprieve? Briefly, he considered a fairy godmother as a possible explanation. He also thought he might have experienced his first psychotic break. He made it into his next class and sat down at his desk out of habit. He was numb. As the world came back into focus, Alex noticed the tension in his back was gone. He mentally retraced his steps and realized it had disappeared the moment he...what was the word? Time traveled? Got a second chance? Whatever it was, he knew it had something to do with what he'd been feeling.

Alex flipped idly through the reports. He was looking at the papers, but not reading them. His eyes were unfocused, remembering those first few months.

It took three full weeks for Alex to replicate the incident in the school hallway. In the end, it was about manipulating internal states, *feelings*, more than anything. He found that, once he could do it on command, it was the easiest thing in the world. Like a kid who tries and tries to ride a bike but then, once he succeeds, it was like he always knew how to. Alex found he had limits. He could set a waypoint, a locus, and hold on to it for about two hours, give or take. And that was with him concentrating on it. Left to its own devices, the waypoint evaporated within the hour. He found he could set multiple waypoints but seemed to be limited to three. He'd set the first one and feel the tightness between his shoulder blades. Then the second one and the feeling of a knot between his shoulder blades would intensify, and it would seem like there was a *pulling* sensation. After the third waypoint, Alex felt like there was a rock embedded in his upper back and there was a definite *pull* there. Every time Alex attempted a fourth waypoint, there was a *snap* and a release of tension. It felt like a rubber band had been stretched to the point of failure, the broken end popping him in the back. It stung.

At first, Alex was afraid the *snap* had broken something, changed something permanently, and he couldn't get back to where he had been. He looked for changes in the world around him but found nothing different. Everything seemed normal. So he tried pushing the envelope on the waypoints, trying multiple times for the fourth locus. Every time, there was a *snap*, and he could not retrieve the previous decision points. And still, nothing seemed to change. That is, until the family Fourth of July get-together.

Alex's father loved to barbecue and he liked to do it for a lot of people. He took pride in his handling of the meat, picking through the offerings at an upscale meat market, marinating it the night before in a sauce that was his own special recipe, getting just the right mixture of charcoal and hickory chips, and carefully tending to it over the open flames. He was a master of the grill. That Independence Day, on a bright Sunday afternoon, his father had invited his brother and their kids over for dinner. Alex spent the afternoon swimming in their backyard pool with his cousins, Donald and David, until he heard his mother call out, "dinner's ready!" While Alex and the rest of the kids ate burgers and dogs, their parents had steak. Everyone was joking around at the table when Alex noticed his father was eating exclusively with his left hand.

"Hey, Dad, what's the matter with your hand?" Alex asked.

"Eh, nothing, son. What do you mean?"

"Dad, come on! You're eating with the wrong hand."

At this point, everyone had stopped shoveling food into their mouths long enough to stare at Alex.

"Ummmm...I'm left-handed, son. I always eat with my left hand," his dad had said, peering at him, his brows furrowed and a half-smile on his lips.

Everyone at the table had now stopped any pretense of eating and were staring at Alex as though he had grown an extra head out of his shoulder. Desperately, Alex cast about for some explanation for his behavior.

"Oh, yeah, I'm sorry. I got my left and my right confused. I think Donald held me under the water too long," Alex smiled crookedly, in what he hoped was an endearing manner.

It was lame, Alex thought, but it was a family gathering, and they bought it, at least to the extent normal eating and conversation resumed. *Thank God for normalcy bias.* Until that point, Alex's father had always been right-handed. He was now in a reality where his father was left-handed. It was a small but permanent change in his universe. He never again attempted to form a fourth waypoint.

It could have been worse. I could have made it into a universe where I was blind. Or my parents were dead. Or I didn't even exist at all. Hell, I barely made it as it was.

He was one of a set of premature twins. He'd made it by the skin of his teeth, but his identical twin brother, Alaric, had not. His mother mourned the loss, which made Alex's birthdays bittersweet affairs for her. More than once, he'd caught his mother alone in her room, crying on his birthday.

He'd often wondered what it would have been like to grow up with someone who was just like him. Someone he could relate to. A brother.

He'd experimented throughout his high school years with his newly acquired power. He tried it out under stressful and non-stressful conditions, finding he could snap back to a waypoint from the middle of jumping from a cliff into a lake, going from mid-air to the waypoint in a smooth transition. He'd also used it in innocuously selfish ways. He remembered trying to decide between two entrees on a menu during one of his family's infrequent outings. He finally set a waypoint and ate them both, enjoying each of them in different universes. He tried not to be too cavalier with the gift or use it to someone else's detriment. That would start a slide down a slippery slope, one he might not be able to stop. He realized he had to have a strict code or his gift could easily become his curse.

A quick knock on the door broke his reverie. *Shave-and-a-haircut.* It was Pritchard who opened the door, sticking his head in without waiting for a response.

"Hey! You okay back here? You're not touching yourself inappropriately, are you? I know how you married guys are when your wives get pregnant and you hit the P.C.O.D. ."

"P.C.O.D.?"

"Pussy Cut Off Date. Jeez! Don't make me explain everything. Hey, the Lieutenant wants to see you ... you know, when you get done," Pritchard leered and closed the door.

Alex sat for a moment and sighed, muttering to himself, "I don't blame you one bit, Deni. I kinda hate him, too."

Chapter 7

Alex made his way through Administration, a no-man's-land populated by people who don't deal with crime or criminals and who, in some cases, actually make it harder for those that do. His journey's end lay at the east end of the department, where the offices of the command staff were clustered, appropriately enough, in a circle. Patrol lay at the west end of the PD, with the sergeant's offices near the Read-Off Room and Investigations to the east of them. There was a doorway that made a very distinct demarcation between Patrol/ Investigations and Administration. Every once in a while, a captain would get lost and find himself in Patrol. Once, Alex even caught Chief Tremaine in Patrol. He looked frantic, like a man driving an expensive car who'd wandered into a bad neighborhood by mistake. You could almost hear him locking his car doors.

Tremaine had come to Bay City PD from another agency where he had risen in rank by attaching himself to his supervisor's ass like a lamprey. He turned out to be a disaster as a supervisor himself, having to be constantly transferred as he managed to piss off everyone who worked for him. How he ended up as Chief of Bay City was anyone's guess. Alex had pulled his jacket to see what kind of experience he'd had and it wasn't much.

I swear I have more time in pissing behind dumpsters on midnight shift than he has actual street experience. Maybe he has pictures of the mayor in a compromising position with a farm animal.

He threaded his way through the islands of administrative desks until he came to the door of the Professional Standards Lieutenant's Office. It was closed as were the blinds lining the inside of the windows. Alex set a waypoint, just in case something in this interview went south, and knocked sharply.

"Come in," Lt. Blakely called.

Opening the door, Alex stuck his head in. "You wanted to see me, sir?"

"Yes, yes...come in, Detective Dorn. Have a seat," he said, indicating waving at the chairs in front of his desk.

Alex took the chair and sat stiffly, his hands in his lap. Looking around the room, Alex was struck with the difference between the decoration of the lieutenant's office and the average patrol office appointments. His desk was mahogany, his executive chair made of leather. It looked plush and comfortable. The bookshelves were real wood, not particle board. It got more lavish the further up the chain you went. He fully expected Chief Tremaine to have a mink-lined chair and, possibly, a live eagle in his office. Blakely had come up through the ranks and had a solid track record at the Department. Still, Alex didn't fully trust him. Something seemed to happen to people over the rank of sergeant, like there were pods hidden in the basement somewhere. Blakely was a large man, one of the few on the department taller than Alex. He took off his reading glasses as Alex came in, setting them on the desk as a wave of cologne washed over Alex like an invisible tsunami. Alex leaned back in his chair, squinting and blinking. In response, Blakely leaned forward, interpreting Alex's reaction as mental, rather than physical, discomfort.

"Relax, Detective," Blakely chuckled. "I'm not here to rip you a new asshole."

"As long as I leave here with the same amount of ass I came in with, sir."

Blakely smiled and formulated a look of concern on his face, "How have you been, Detective? Since the shooting, I mean."

I didn't really think you were interested in my golf game, numbnuts. "Fine, sir. Just waiting to get the word to go back to work."

"Ah, yes. That's what I wanted to talk to you about," Blakely said as he reached for some papers on his desk.

Crap. Here it comes, Alex thought, settling into his seat, steeling himself for the worst.

"You're going to be loaned out to the FBI for some time. They have a multi-jurisdictional task force that's working in our area and I thought it would give you something different to do."

What the actual fuck?

"Soooo...I've been cleared to resume normal duties, sir?" Alex asked, still a little stunned, trying to catch up.

"What? .. oh, yes. You've been cleared. The shooting of the woman would come under the felony-murder rule. Even if she wasn't trying to stab her boyfriend to death at the time," Blakely sniffed.

Well, you could have led with that, asshole. Alex let out a breath he didn't know he was holding.

"I understood the civilian review board wasn't too happy with me, sir," Alex said.

The lieutenant was beginning to look distinctly unhappy, "Yes, well, that was another good reason to loan you to the Feds. Out of sight, out of mind."

Ah, so now comes the real reason...

Alex opened his mouth to say something but was cut off by Blakely. "Here are your orders, detective," he said, shoving the papers on his desk over to him. "Take the rest of the day off and report to the Anderson Federal Building tomorrow morning at nine o'clock. Now, if you'll excuse me, I have a luncheon engagement." Blakely returned his glasses to his nose and his attention to his computer.

Alex toyed with the idea of asking some more questions, just to be a dick, but decided it wasn't worth it. "Yes, sir. Thank you, sir," He said as he gathered up the papers from the desk. He stood and turned to leave but stopped at the door.

"Oh, and Lieutenant?" Alex asked. Blakely looked up from his computer screen and over his glasses.

"I'll try not to shoot anyone for a while," Alex said, closing the door as he heard sputtering noises. He stepped quickly out of the office area and toward the west end of the PD and its relative safety. *Well, at least it made me feel better.*

Chapter 7

Alex pulled into his driveway about one in the afternoon. His wife, an English teacher at the local community college, wouldn't be home for several hours. He heard the excited barking of his shepherd as he got out of the car. Then he heard Khan scratching on the inside of the door.

I'm gonna have to replace that door soon. He'd tried to break Khan of the habit, but nothing to this point had worked. Khan had scraped all the paint off and was now working on the wood. Alex sighed and shook his head.

He opened the door to see ninety pounds of fur-covered love staring up at him. Khan's tail smacked the side of a cabinet wildly, his face split with a lop-sided grin. Alex told him to sit and he did, reluctantly, his butt still wiggling frantically on the floor. Alex reached inside and got the leash from the peg by the door as Khan's tail wagging became frantic, a low whine escaping his throat. Finally, he opened the door wide and Khan shot through, pausing only long enough to leap and lick the side of Alex's face.

"Aagh," he said, swiping at the slobber, a broad smile on his face. Khan ran out into the yard and back, completing multiple orbits that led, inexorably, to the trail behind the house. Alex's property backed up to state land and was undeveloped except for a series of hiking trails that had been cut at the time of the CCC and maintained only sporadically since. Alex finished wiping dog saliva from the side of his face and caught up to Khan, placing him in a sit and hooking up his leash. He loved watching the fluid grace of his shepherd at a run. Every movement perfect. Zero wasted motion.

Man and dog set off down the trail, their routine well established. Khan sniffed everything interesting and stopped frequently to mark his territory. Alex followed behind, thinking about whatever the day had brought him. He turned, looking at the back of his house. He loved the house, having remodeled it to include the Asian touches he enjoyed. It was large without being ostentatious, but it still looked like it would cost too much for a thirty-one-year-old police officer. And it would be, were police work his only source of income. He supplemented his police salary with another activity: gambling.

I guess it's not really gambling the way I do it. He made at least one trip a year to Las Vegas, playing mostly blackjack and roulette. He'd set a waypoint just before the hand was dealt or the wheel spun and then, when he knew the outcome, snap back to the waypoint and play accordingly. He never won too much at any one time or place and made sure he lost occasionally. He also frequented the dog and horse tracks, using the same system.

The nail that sticks up is the nail that gets hammered flat, an old Japanese proverb. Through careful winning, he'd accumulated a healthy financial portfolio that was owned through a series of holding companies. He had thought of becoming filthy rich but the idea of money for money's sake bored the crap out of him. He enjoyed his job immensely. Besides, most rich people he'd met had been assholes.

Certainly, don't want to take that chance, he thought, grinning. Khan coursed back and forth in front of him, pulling on the leash now in anticipation of arriving at the finish of their usual mile walk.

"Sit!" Alex snapped and Khan planted his butt on the ground. Alex knelt, unlatching him. He stood, watching him run to the house, his ears up and his tail switching back and forth like a banner. He checked his watch. *There's still time for a decent workout before the wife gets home.*

He checked the mailbox, finding several pieces of mail. He went through it as he walked up to the door, sorting the bills from the junk mail and throwing the ads in a recycling bin just outside the door, under the carport. Khan was busy putting his nose on the doorknob and then looking at Alex as if to say, "Look, dad! I found it! It's right here! The doorknob!" He opened the door and Khan pushed through, going directly to the back bedroom, checking each bedroom on his way before returning to the kitchen. Alex followed him through the door, tossing the mail on the kitchen counter as he passed. He stopped and filled Khan's water bowl from the sink in the green, marble-topped island counter that separated the kitchen from the dining area. He set the bowl down and Khan fell to, lapping up the water in great slurps, spilling water on the tile, splattering the wall. Alex walked down the hallway to the master bedroom and Khan abandoned the water bowl, following on his heels, slobbering water on the oak floors as he did so, leaving a trail. Alex sighed and scratched Khan's head as he came even with him. Khan threw his shoulder into Alex's leg. *I'll have to mop that up. The perils of wood floors.*

He opened the door to the master bedroom where Khan helped himself to the bed, gaining it in a leap that flowed into a tight turn as he lay down to face Alex, still drooling water and panting. He stripped off his newly regained service weapon, a Glock .40, and placed it in the small, flat biometric safe on the nightstand. The safe read his index fingerprint and popped open immediately. It was the perfect combination of secured and yet accessible. He threw his clothes onto the closet floor and grabbed his *Gi* and *Obi* from their hangers. Putting on his pants and carrying his jacket and belt, he walked back down the hallway to a hardwood-floored room adjoining the Japanese-style garden in the backyard. Khan followed him but sat at the entrance. He knew it was strictly invitation only.

"Sorry, boy," Alex said as he shut the door in his dog's face. Alex could hear him pad away in the direction of the kitchen, toenails clicking across the floor.

Alex turned and took a moment to appreciate the view of his garden through the floor-to-ceiling sliding glass doors along the back wall of the *dojo*. He loved the bamboo and arched bridge over the small stream. He opened the sliding glass doors so he could hear the water move over the rocks. The sound never failed to soothe him.

Originally, the room had been a large bedroom that Alex had converted into his private studio. Mirrors covered half of one wall with a rack of Okinawan weapons on the other side. Between them was a small *dojo* shrine called a *Kamiza*. It consisted of a shelf about shoulder-high containing a picture of Alex's sensei and a small vase with a Japanese *Ikebana* flower arrangement. It was virtually identical to the one at his sensei's dojo.

Pulling on his jacket and tying the black belt around his waist, Alex knelt down, assuming a position on his knees with his legs tucked under him, his right big toe over the left, and his butt sitting on his calves. *Seiza*. Resting his hands, palm down, on his thighs, Alex took a moment to let the thoughts and worries of the day melt away from him. He focused on trying to have no thoughts at all.

When he felt sufficiently relaxed, he bowed and got to his feet. He started with a well-rehearsed series of push-ups, sit-ups, arm swings, and leg stretches to loosen up. Then he ran through *kihon,* the basics, including blocking, punching, kicking, and striking. Breaking a sweat now, Alex started punching the *makiwara,* a two-by-four that was secured to the floor, tapering at the top with a small pad on the end. Most people thought the primary use of the *maki* was to toughen the knuckles and inure them to impact and, though it did an admirable job of that, the main purpose of the board was to test your technique. If your stance wasn't stable or your wrist wasn't straight, the *makiwara* let you know with immediate and painful feedback. He worked through backfist, hammerfist, *shuto,* palm heel, and forearm conditioning, slamming into the *maki,* making it sing. He proceeded to the heavy bag to work kicks. He started with front kicks, impaling the heavy bag, making it jack-knife around his foot and not just swing back. He did the same with side-kicks, back-kicks, knee-strikes, and roundhouse kicks; working all of them as he began sweating in earnest. He finished with one of his favorite street techniques, the elbow strike. The elbow was a cold, hard, unforgiving weapon he'd used on many occasions to end a fight.

Still breathing hard, Alex looked out the sliding-glass doors at his garden and decided to relax and take a break. He pulled the front of the *gi* top out of the belt, allowing it to dangle loosely, untying the sides of the jacket and letting it fall open in the front before walking out the sliding-glass doors to his garden. He walked down the path of flat, irregular rocks to the bridge, feeling the cool smoothness of the shadowed stones on his bare feet He stopped in the middle of the arch, putting his hands on the railing and leaning over to look at the water. A small waterfall near the house fell into a pond sheltering several *koi*; from there a stream flowed from the pond over river rocks to a small pool that had its own population of domesticated carp. The water was then pumped back to the waterfall behind him but the entire water effect was arranged so that it looked completely natural. Alex had worked on it for months. The koi pond was beneath the window to his study, located between his *dojo* and the master bedroom. He liked looking out his window, watching the *koi*. His favorite was a large white-and-orange mottled male he'd dubbed "Sensei."

He kept a small bag of food pellets on his desk that he would throw to them, watching them roil the water to get to the nuggets. He took a deep breath, surveying the garden with a critical eye. *Have to work on that bamboo; it's getting messy.* He finished peeling the rest of his sodden *gi* top out of his belt and walked back inside. He threw the jacket into the corner, going to the center of the room facing the mirrors.

Alex rolled his shoulders and cracked his neck before starting his *kata,* the dance-like forms of traditional karate. He worked through *Gekisai, Seisan, Seiyuchin, Saifa, Shisochin, Seipai, and Kururunfa* from Goju Ryu. He did the three *Naihanchin* kata, *Bassai, Kusanku, Wanshu, and Chinto* from Shorin Ryu. The only sounds were the sliding of his feet on the hardwood floor, *sui-ashi,* and the punctuated breathing as he exhaled on a punch or kick. He finished with *Sanchin* and *Tensho,* both dynamic tension katas that used hard-style *Ibuki* breathing. Alex's wife said it always reminded her of the sound effects in those old black-and-white movies that showed two "dinosaurs" hissing at each other and getting ready to fight. Alex was a traditionalist in the martial arts world and that, increasingly, made him something of a rarity. Mixed Martial Arts had captured the American imagination, with its contest-oriented approach and its emphasis on winning. Alex thought of the matches as human cockfights and, though they were fine for others, they weren't his cup of tea. There was a young cop who'd heard of his hobby and, with six months of MMA training under his belt, decided to tell him how useless he thought traditional karate was. Alex had been studying several systems of karate since the age of fourteen. The rookie's cocky diatribe irritated him and he'd finally asked, "So let me get this straight. You think a martial art that was founded in the back alleys and battlefields of Asia and honed through centuries by uncounted masters, is somehow less authentic than you dressing up in spandex and rolling around on a padded floor?" The conversation had terminated abruptly.

Glancing at the clock, Alex realized it was time to start dinner. He looked wistfully at the medieval-looking weapons on his wall. His *Kobudo* practice with *Bo*, *Sai*, *Kama*, and *Tonfa* would have to wait for another day. He retrieved his sweat-soaked gi top from the corner and draped it over a free-standing bag with a wet, soggy sound. The bag looked like a person with no arms. A Body Opponent Bag. BOB for short. He placed his belt around Bob's neck and shoulders, the jacket clinging to his rubber head.

"Sorry, Bob," he said, and left the dojo, turning into the kitchen.

Chapter 8

Alex finished cutting up the meat and vegetables for the kebab he intended to grill, then threaded the various pieces onto skewers and lowered them into the flat pan of teriyaki marinade resting on the marble-topped island counter. He opened a small can of pineapple juice and poured it into the pan. *The secret ingredient.* He read through the mail he'd thrown on the countertop earlier until he heard his wife's car pull up in the driveway. Khan started whining and turning in circles at the door, looking back at him expectantly. Covering the pan, he went to the door and put his hand on the doorknob as he looked down at his dog with disapproval. He shook his head.

"I think you love her more than me," he said. "Traitor." Smiling, he opened the door, Khan bounding out to the driver's side of the door, standing on his hind legs and propping his front paws on the car, peering into the window at Eve and leaving nose prints on the glass. She laughed and told him to sit. Reluctantly, step by step, he backed away from the door and sat on his haunches, panting, his tongue lolling out of the side of his mouth. She opened the door cautiously, maintaining eye contact with Khan the whole time as she got out.

Eve looked up and saw Alex standing in the doorway. She gave him a wide, brilliant smile. Then she turned her attention to Khan who had stayed in a perfect sit, waiting for his fair share of petting. Eve bent forward at the waist and grabbed his face in both hands, bringing her face close to his, saying, "Have you been a good boy? Is Khan a good boy?" Khan's tongue answered her question with a swipe intended to cover her face from chin to hairline but Eve turned her face at the last instant so he got mostly ear. Eve laughed, standing up and wiping the side of her face. She shut the car door despite Khan trying to stick his nose into the car. She opened the rear door, fishing her briefcase out of a backseat crowded with folders of paperwork as well as several stacks of books, and walked up the slight incline to the house, Khan trailing behind her.

"You know, a more chivalrous man would have run out of the house and opened my door for me, especially since I'm carrying your offspring," she said as she approached the door.

"True, but I was busy making dinner and had delegated that chore to my manservant, Khan."

"You made dinner? Pray tell... what feast awaits me?"

"Kebabs on the grill. Beef and chicken with green and red peppers, onions, tomatoes, and mushrooms."

"Oh, you are soooo forgiven. I am starving. To death. Literally," she said, canting her face to one side as Alex kissed her, simultaneously putting his right arm around her waist and taking her briefcase with his left hand. Eve's hand slid behind his neck, cradling him there as she made sure he was thoroughly kissed.

Pulling back, Alex's eyes were wide in surprise at the passion of the kiss. "Wow, I need to make dinner more often," he said.

"You're just lucky I'm so hungry. Otherwise, I think I'd have my way with you on the living room couch. Right now."

"Is it my imagination or have you actually gotten hornier since you've been pregnant?"

"Oh, it's not your imagination, Buck-o. And you better enjoy it while you can because, before you know it, I will be a whale that waddles everywhere and needs help getting up off the couch," she said.

Alex set the briefcase down, his arms encircling her waist as he looked deeply into her eyes. "To me, you will always be the most beautiful woman in the world." She smiled back at him and they kissed again. Pulling away, Alex looked at his wife's slim figure, rolling his head from side to side, making a show of appraising it.

"Besides, you're barely showing so I'd say we've got awhile."

"Well, that's good because I'm not looking forward to having to pee every ten minutes." She slipped from his grasp like an eel, her movement fluid from years of ballet. She walked toward the back of the house, Alex admiring her the whole way.

"I'm going to take a shower. I've had a hard day trying to beat the proper use of the English language into college kids," she called back over her shoulder. "And stop looking at my ass."

"Not a chance," he called back, smiling.

Alex placed the rice cooker on the table, thinking about how fortunate he was. His wife was a beautiful woman - smart, educated, funny. She was about five feet six inches tall with a slim build she kept toned through dance workouts. She had some Native American ancestry, accounting for her high cheek bones, easily tanned skin, and jet-black hair. Having those ancestors didn't explain her startling blue eyes, set in her otherwise dark features. When Alex had asked her about her eyes, she'd shrugged, saying, "There must be a Scotsman lurking in my genes somewhere." Alex knew he was a decent-looking guy with a strong, masculine face and an imposing physicality at over six feet tall and two hundred pounds. His close-cropped dirty blonde hair and green eyes had gotten him his share of dates but, as his cop friends were quick to tell him, Eve was out of his league. *Yep. I definitely married up.*

Alex started the rice cooker and placed the kebabs on the indoor grill, thinking back to the first time they'd met as the meat sizzled and sputtered, filling the room with a savory aroma. He'd stopped at a bar near the college to meet with cops from the training division of the University Police Department. They'd met there to discuss a joint training exercise. The bar was an upscale sports bar with televisions placed strategically around the room, mounted on the wall near the ceiling and all turned on to various sports programs. The waitresses were all dressed as referees, as were the bartenders. One of the University cops knew the owner, so they'd gotten a semi-private room off to the side. They had commandeered a pool table to spread paperwork out when Alex looked up to see Eve walk through the door and take a seat. She was wearing tight jeans and a black silk shirt. Alex thought she was the most beautiful woman he'd ever seen. He stood stock-still, a sentence half-said, and simply stared with his mouth hanging open. The other cops looked at him curiously, then followed his gaze to where Eve was being joined by a friend.

That was when the ribbing started. Cops are merciless with their own. This was no exception.

"You think you can get **that**, Alex? Are you blind? Do you have a fever?"

"You are fighting out of your weight class, man. Besides, she's one of these stuck-up college bitches. You'll get exactly nowhere with her. Zip. Nada. The big goose egg."

Alex heard these comments like fading background noise. The saying that you never get a second chance to make a first impression wasn't exactly true in Alex's case. He took a moment to set a waypoint, feeling the familiar tug between his shoulder blades, and set off to introduce himself to the future Mrs. Dorn. He approached and introduced himself five separate times. He was shot down every time. After each unsuccessful attempt, he reset at the waypoint and tried again. He began to worry he'd never find the right approach. On the sixth attempt, he closed on the table from a slightly different angle. Eve turned to talk to him and her purse, slung on the back of the chair, fell off, and hit the floor. A book popped halfway out, letting Alex see the title. Gravity's Rainbow by Thomas Pynchon. Despite his best efforts, Eve turned him down again.

He retreated to the pool table. The cops heaped generous amounts of ridicule on him for his failure. From their point of view, it was the first time it had happened. Alex dug his smartphone out of his pocket and began googling Gravity's Rainbow.

"What are you doing, man? You think there's an app for that, too?" said one of the college cops, slurring his words slightly.

"Shut up and let me work," Alex said, scrolling through information on the book. Unfortunately, it was an extremely long, dense piece of literary genius. He didn't have much hope of understanding it at a level that would engender a conversation in the next ten minutes. He *had* read, or tried to read, a book by Samuel R. Delaney, *Dhalgren*. At about page 300, he'd given up. Deciding on the M.O. for his next approach, Alex *pulled* on the knot between his shoulder blades, feeling himself snap back to the reality that existed just before the first time he'd approached Eve.

He walked to the table where Eve and her friend were sitting and smiled at them both. Eve turned, and with the same frigid glare he'd encountered before, said, "Yes?". She later told Alex she was used to getting hit on in bars and just wanted to talk to her friend. Frankly, she was annoyed when he'd walked over.

"Excuse me, I'm trying to settle a bet; which do think is the more complicated novel: Thomas Pynchon's *Gravity's Rainbow* or Samuel R. Delaney's *Dhalgren?* Take your time; I'm in no hurry." That said, Alex crossed his arms and waited for her response.

Eve raised one eyebrow, gauging him and his request. "And the people you are betting with are...those people back there?" she said, indicating the group of cops behind him, disbelief evident in her voice. Alex glanced back and noticed the two drunker ones weren't even trying to mask their interest in his progress. They couldn't have been any plainer if they'd been cartoons with their eyes bugged out and their tongues hanging out of their mouths.

"Well, yes, it was either them or a group of shaved monkeys. I'm not sure there's a difference at this point. So, which do you think...?"

Eve measured him for a moment and then said, "*Gravity's Rainbow* was, I think, more complicated but *Dhalgren* was more...ummm...chaotic. Have you read either of these books?" she asked, tapping the fingernail of her index finger on the tabletop, regarding him skeptically.

"Well, not Pynchon's book but I did get 300 pages into *Dhalgren* before I was overcome by an irresistible arson impulse. I'm still on the run from the law. I'm afraid it took two fire stations to put the book out".

Eve laughed and smiled at that. *Score!*

"I did make it all the way through Korzybski's *Science and Sanity*, which, by the end, had me doubting my own."

Eve smiled again. *God, I love her smile.* She asked, "And that book is how many pages long?"

"A shade over 900. I use it now when I work on my car and I can't find a jack stand," Alex said, putting out his hand. "Hi, I'm Alex."

"Eve," she said, placing her hand in Alex's. It was warm. "And this is my friend, Ginger," she said, nodding to her companion, Alex glanced at her and gave her a brief smile. "I'm afraid we're just getting together for a little while to talk about some work matters".

"It's the same with me. I have to get back. I was wondering if I might get your number and give you a call some time? Maybe take you out to dinner?"

The air seemed solid with anticipation to Alex as she weighed her decision, seconds passed like hours as she stared into his eyes. He was barely breathing. Eve abruptly broke eye contact, making her decision and reaching into her purse for her wallet. She pulled a card from it and, turning it over, wrote a number on the back.

"That's my cell number," she said. "I'm busy with midterms next week but after that, I should be free." She smiled as she slid the card across the table. Alex's body blocked the view of his actions from his fellow officers as he palmed the card.

"So, you're a teacher. What subject? English?" he asked.

"Yes. How did you know?"

"*Gravity's Rainbow.* Why else would you torture yourself like that?"

"Ah," She said, "And you? What do you do?"

"Well, let's see...six feet two inches tall, 200 pounds, a bad haircut, no appreciable taste in clothing...I'm afraid the conclusion is inescapable: I'm a cop. Does that make a difference?"

"Not at all," she said, "I look forward to hearing from you."

"And you will. I hope you both have a great evening. It was nice to meet you, Ginger," Alex said, nodding at Eve's friend, the woman who would be her maid of honor.

Alex made his way back to his party with the card still palmed in his hand.

"How'd it go, man? You gettin' some, or what?"

"Nah. Struck out. But she was very nice about it. You can't win 'em all."

"Ain't that the truth," drunk-boy said, throwing his arm around his shoulders as Alex quietly slid the card into his pocket. The rest of the evening was a blur for him as he tried to concentrate on the particulars of the exercise while his thoughts kept turning to Eve.

*   *   *

Khan bumped him in the groin with his nose as he stood in front of the grill, crudely snapping him out of his reverie. He bent over at the waist and grunted.

"Nice, Khan. I gather you're telling me the kebabs are done? Did you want to try one?". Khan seemed to nod his head in agreement, turning around to sit about two feet from Alex.

"Okay, here ya go," he said, gingerly stripping off a piece of beef from a skewer and throwing it toward the dog. Khan lunged, snapping the piece of meat from out of the air. It disappeared down his gullet in two quick swallows.

"You know, you might want to take time to taste your food," he said. Khan smiled, as all German Shepherds smile, wagging his tail appreciatively and sitting in anticipation of another treat.

"Nope. That's all there is, greedy boy."

"I hope there's some for me," he heard Eve say behind him, as she slid up and placed her arms around his waist, molding her body to his back.

"What are you doing? Practicing your ninja skills? I didn't even hear you," Alex turned around inside her arms and hugged her to him.

"You need a shower, mister," she said, disentangling herself and taking a seat at the table, "but we need to eat first. And then you can get a shower. And then...well, then I have plans for you." She regarded him with a decidedly lascivious expression. It sent a shiver up Alex's spine.

"Sounds good to me. The rice is already on the table," Alex said, bringing the kebabs with him as he set them down between them as they sat down. As they ate, Alex made his big announcement. "Well, they gave me my gun back," he said.

"Really? That's great, hon" Eve said, reaching out and placed her hand on his forearm. "I know how much it's bothered you not to be working as a detective."

He looked into her smiling face, feeling the love that had only grown deeper during their three years of marriage. "I'm going to be 'on loan'," he said, making air quotes, "to the FBI."

"Wow. The big time."

"Yes. The FBI. Famous But Incompetent. I'm so lucky. I think the Lieutenant is getting me out of the loop for a while because of all the publicity about the shooting," Alex looked at his food with a sour face.

"Maybe that's best, babe. At the very least, you'll get to do something new." Eve said, looking hopeful.

"Maybe. I just hope this isn't for show. I'm not gonna be their butt boy."

"Oh, no. You're taken. You're MY boy toy. Just wait until later," she leered, pumping her eyebrows up and down like a villain in an old movie – like Snidely Whiplash.

Alex laughed. And, as it turned out, being a boy toy wasn't all that bad.

Chapter 9

The next morning Alex stood outside the Anderson building, early for the 0830 meeting. In front of the building, there was a broad concrete walkway that held a decorative fountain as well as some landscaping, which include massive, decorative concrete balls, each of which stood about waist high. They were staggered in front of the door. Bollards, they were called. Decorative and large enough to stop a suicide bomber's car. They'd been added after 9/11. He debated setting a waypoint for a few moments and decided to err on the side of caution. He'd gotten into the habit of setting them early on in his career. As a rookie, he'd set one as soon as he and his field training officer got a call on the radio. His FTO, George, told him he was the only rookie he's ever trained that had never gotten lost on the way to a call. *Oh, if George only knew.* He'd gotten lost plenty of times, but none George knew about. After he got out on the road on his own, he'd gotten 'sloppy' and most times hadn't set a waypoint at all.

That changed one night on a routine prowler call. K9 was busy so Alex was solo on this one. *No biggie.* These calls usually turned out to be a raccoon, or a neighborhood cat, or, most frequently, nothing at all. The complainant was a woman known throughout the department as a "frequent flyer," calling the police for pretty much anything that annoyed her. Including a solar eclipse. Alex had gotten out of his car and was carefully picking his way through the overgrown yard in the darkness, working his way toward the back of her residence. The house was dark except for thin slivers of light peeking out from behind drawn shades that were covered with layers of aluminum foil. He opened the gate of the rusty, four-foot chain link fence and remembered she was something of a hoarder. Her backyard was filled with a large number of useless objects, many of which were at ankle-breaking height. He sighed and set a waypoint before turning the corner into the backyard. As he rounded the corner, something slammed into his belly. He felt a searing pain in his gut, just below his vest His breath left his body in a rush, his knees buckling. His assailant grabbed his right shoulder and smashed him against the brick wall. As he hit the wall, his head bounced off it. He saw stars. Alex cried out in agony as his attacker pressed his face up against his own. Alex could smell his unwashed body and rancid breath, feel his unshaven face pressed against his skin. He pulled back slightly, staring into Alex's eyes, grinning as he twisted the knife. His left hand clutched the attacker's shoulder as the pain tore through him, making him gasp. He tried to reach for his gun but the suspect's left arm pressed his right arm back and he wasn't able to get to it. Alex fought through the pain and terror and focused with every ounce of his will and *pulled* on the knot between his shoulder blades. He found himself turning the corner of the house, back to the reality that existed just before the attack. Gasping, still carrying the pain of his gut wound in his head, he dropped all of his bodyweight into a downward block with his right forearm. His right ulnar bone smashed across the suspect's radius with a dry, snapping sound. The suspect screamed as his arm broke and the knife dropped from his hand. Alex continued his forward momentum to shoulder the suspect back, then exploded with every drop of adrenaline-fueled strength in his body, striking his attacker in the side of the neck with the same forearm that had just broken his knife-arm. He ragdolled into the brick wall, smacking the back of his head and dropping like a wet sack of meat. Alex stood over him for a second, bent over, placed both hands on his knees, and vomited on the suspect.

*   *   *

Lesson learned, he thought, as he entered the building, unconsciously rubbing where he'd been stabbed. Alex found the field office listed as being on the ninth floor in the lobby directory. Looking around, he wondered about security and decided he wasn't impressed. He took the elevator up to the 9th floor and stepped out into a solid, transparent cube. It looked like it was made of ballistic glass an inch thick and was bounded on all three sides and the top. It ran from wall to wall in the short hallway entrance and had its own air supply with a conduit pumping in cool air. There was a door directly in front of Alex, a card reader to the right of it on the transparent wall. He tried the door. It was locked.

"Yes? Can I help you?" came a woman's voice from a speaker in the ceiling.

"Detective Dorn to see Agent... let's see," Alex fished through his jacket pocket to find his notebook. "Ah, here it is...Agent Stormant?"

"Thank you. Someone will be with you shortly." The voice sounded professional and thoroughly disinterested.

Within a few moments, a deeply tanned man with a starched, white shirt came out of one of the offices. His sleeves were rolled halfway up his forearms and his tie was loosened so that his top button could be unbuttoned. He nodded at Alex, smiling as he walked over. He was shorter than Alex and looked to be in good shape with dark hair in the standard Fed haircut. He was carrying a Beretta 92F on his right hip and two extra mags on his left, and his badge was hooked onto his belt just in front of his holster. He took a card attached to a lanyard on his belt and put it on the card reader. As the locking mechanism disengaged with an audible thump, the agent pulled open the door with his left hand and extended his right to Alex.

"Hi. Sorry about the hamster cage. It's a pilot project. Post 9/11 world and all. I'm Agent Stormant. Call me Don," he said. His handshake was firm and he looked Alex in the eyes as he talked.

"Hamster cage?"

"Yeah. That nickname got tacked on pretty quick. Until the bugs got worked out, agents used to get trapped in there all the time. The record is three hours." Stormant grinned. "If you'll follow me." He turned and started down the hall.

"You ever think about putting an exercise wheel in there? Maybe one of those bottles with a drinking tube?"

"There were suggestions like that. I thought we should put down a layer of sawdust for droppings."

Alex smiled. He was starting to like this guy. They continued to talk as they walked past open office doors on each side of the hall. Alex could see agents hunched over computers as they passed.

"What happens if someone gets out of the elevator who doesn't belong here?"

"You mean, like a terrorist?"

"Something like that."

"We can flood the hamster cage with O.C. in a matter of seconds. Not enough to kill you but more than enough to make you wish you were dead." Stormant stopped by a door, motioning him inside. "Ah, here we are. We're just about to start the briefing."

Alex entered the room and saw five people around an oval table. There were two guys there from the Sheriff's department he knew but didn't much like. There was a detective he knew from the Town of Hampstead, Joe Esposito AKA 'The Walrus,' and two guys he thought were FDLE. Alex nodded to them as he walked into the room, going around the table toward Esposito. Stormant moved to the head of the table by a laptop and projector as Alex pulled up a seat by the Hampstead detective

They nodded, smiling at each other and Joe squinted out of the corners of his eyes in both directions, leaned over, and whispered; "Who'd you piss off?"

"It'd be easier to ask who I didn't piss off. What about you?"

"Arrested the mayor's son. Little dirtbag was pawning stolen goods. Apparently, the mayor believes his family is above the law. Surprise." Joe shrugged his massive shoulders.

Stormant cleared his throat and hiked one hip up onto the table behind him. "Hi. I'm Agent Don Stormant with the FBI. I want you to know that, just because I'm with the FBI, it doesn't automatically mean I'm an asshole." There were appreciative chuckles from around the table. "I started my police career as a patrol officer in Washington, DC. So I know what it's like when the Feds move in and you feel like you're being marginalized. It's happened to me before and I can assure you that will not happen here. The reason we reached out to your various agencies is that we are stretched pretty thin. The truth is that a lot of our staff has been tasked with things involving terrorism, as you might imagine. That leaves fewer and fewer agents to work on criminal matters that usually fall under the FBI's jurisdiction. And we've found we can kick only so much of that crap back to state agencies. By utilizing local resources, we can multiply our effectiveness while taking advantage of your knowledge of the area. So, without further ado..."

Stormant looked at the screen and turned on the projector with the remote in his hand. It showed the computer's desktop environment on the screen behind him. He moved the mouse to a file labeled "PP" and clicked on it.

"The agency is currently working on a series of high-profile thefts that all involve the same perpetrator, an Unsub we call "Peter Perfect". We call him that because he never makes a mistake." A rueful smile crossed Stormant's face. "At least, he hasn't so far."

The projector began showing a video of a man moving quickly and confidently down a hallway. He was wearing all dark clothing with a ski mask and carrying a small bag slung over his shoulder. At one point, he looks directly at the camera, reaches into the bag, and pulls out a can of spray paint. He reaches forward with the can in his hand and the picture goes dark. There appeared to be no hesitancy in his movements and no wasted motion.

Stormant stopped the playback, looking around the room. "That camera was hidden. By professionals. We have no idea how he knew it was there. At first, we suspected an inside job, but we worked over everyone with any knowledge of the location with a bag of oranges. And got nothing for our troubles. Okay, okay...we didn't really beat anyone with citrus fruit but we did put them through the wringer. Polygraph, PSE, interrogation by the Behavioral Unit...the works. Everyone checked out clean."

"This same sort of crime has occurred all the way down the eastern seaboard. Usually jewelry, money, bearer bonds. Things that can be converted into cash relatively easily. And...Yes?"

One of the Sheriff's detectives raised his hand. "How come we haven't heard anything about this until now? There's been nothing in any of the media, at least that I've seen."

Stormant stepped forward, pointing at the detective, "Good catch. Why hasn't there been more in the press, or, frankly, much of anything at all? The answer is that Peter here has been stealing from people that would find it embarrassing, for one reason or another, to have it known that they had been stolen from. We believe there are cases out there involving Mr. Perfect that have gone unreported. Also, this is all relatively recent. You are one of the first task forces to work on this case."

Stormant moved back to the laptop. A map of the eastern part of the United States filled the screen. Dots began appearing on the map, starting around New York and working their way south, stopping at the Florida-Georgia border.

One of the FDLE agents let out a low whistle. "My, my, he has been busy, hasn't he?" he said.

"You could say that," Agent Stormant said dryly.

"Ever get close to him?" from the same FDLE guy.

"Not even a whiff," Stormant said as he walked around the table and picked up a box.

"We estimate losses to be in the millions. And that's just what we know about," Stormant said. He placed a small, white cardboard box on the table in front of the deputies, shaking it slightly so the contents rattled. "Pass this around. Each of you pull out a thumb drive. On it is everything we know about Peter Perfect. Let's see, today is Thursday...take the weekend off to work on this and we will meet Monday morning at 0900 to work on an Ops Plan. Wait a minute...I have a deposition that morning so let's convene at 1300 hours. Any questions?"

No one said anything. As the box made it around to Alex, he pulled out a drive and put it in his pocket.

"Okay, then. See you all Monday. I'll walk you out," Stormant said, as he shut down the projector. There was a rustling sound as everyone gathered their belongings. Joe leaned over to Alex and said "Great. Now when my wife asks me what I'm doing, I'll have to tell her I'm goin' out lookin' for Peter."

"That's alright, Joe. We've all known you were gay for years now. It's about time you came out of the closet."

"Really?" he said, scratching at the overgrown mustache that gave him his nickname, "What gave me away?"

"I think it was the 70's porn 'stache, man."

Joe stroked his mustache with one hand. "I don't care. The 'stache stays. What's for lunch?"

"Whatever you're buyin'. Let's get out of here."

Chapter 10

It was early Friday afternoon and Alex had spent the better part of the morning working through the case documentation on Peter Perfect. He'd tried to find commonalities in Petey's M.O. - time, date, day of the week, method of entry, tools, etc..., but nothing stood out. It was like each job had been tailor-made, each crime specifically engineered for that particular scenario. He rubbed his face, his elbows on the dining room table, printouts from the material on the thumb drive strewn across it. Most successful career criminals found a method that worked for them and then implemented that method on suitable targets. This went against the grain. Besides, there was something about the few snippets of video on the Unsub that bothered Alex, but despite racking his brain six ways from Sunday, he couldn't quite put his finger on it. Alex got up from the table, almost falling over the German Shepherd rug/ death trap had been waiting patiently for just this opportunity to rise into a sit and trip him. He stumbled a few steps and looked at the dog disapprovingly.

"Jeez, Khan, what? Are you trying to kill me?"

Khan's only reply was a lopsided grin as he cocked his head to one side, trying his best to understand what Alex was saying. He laughed and grabbed Khan by both sides of his head and neck and roughed him up. Khan responded by leaning his whole body into Alex's legs as Alex bent over and switched to scratching his chest and side. Straightening, Alex rolled his neck and shoulders to loosen them up, deciding to work on some *iaido* to clear the cobwebs from his brain. He let Khan out into the fenced side yard and grabbed a fresh white gi and belt from his closet as well as a solid black *hakama*, a full, flowing, split skirt used in *iaido* as well as *aikido* and some other martial arts. He walked down the hall to the dojo, bowing as he entered, and put the *hakama* aside. He began his warm-ups in just his *gi* bottoms, feet bare on the floor. After he'd worked up a sweat, he put his *gi* top on, tying his *obi* around his waist and then putting on the *hakama*. Grabbing a *bokken*, a wooden sword, off the wall rack, Alex did some *suburi*, practice cuts, cleaving the air. Each slice made a distinctive whistling sound. He worked back and forth across the floor until his shoulders, arms, and wrists began to ache.

He replaced the *bokken* on the rack, going to one knee in front of a black, lacquered, rectangular box along the wall. Alex removed the top with both hands and set it aside. He took a moment to admire the *katana*, the samurai sword, that was lying on a red silk bed. The *saya*, or scabbard, was black lacquered wood, the carefully layered paint and polish making it shine. As he picked it up with his left hand, he looked at the *tsuba*, or guard, separating the blade from the handle. The dragon motif worked into the metal was both subtle and artful. Though the blade was of normal length, about thirty-one inches, the handle, or *tsuka*, was built to his specifications and was fourteen inches long, about two inches longer than usual. The extra length allowed for Alex's longer reach and also allowed him to transmit more cutting power to the blade. The handle's black braid was laid over real *same,* ray skin. The *menuki* on the handle were small, decorative dragons, serving to index the user's grip and orient his hands properly.

Alex reached up to the handle and pulled the sword out several inches, looking critically at the *hamon*, or temper line, created when the master swordsmith forged the blade. It ran from the handle of the sword to the *kissaki,* or point. It was a thing of beauty and had cost Alex most of the profit from a Vegas trip. He knew it was worth it every time he opened the case. The edge was razor sharp and he felt it was surely the equivalent of any sword carried by a samurai in medieval Japan. Maybe not a Masamune - a legendary Japanese swordsmith about whose blades it was whispered that a leaf, riding the current of a fast-moving stream, would halve itself effortlessly upon contacting the sword's edge – but close. Alex had never tested his blade like that. Not yet. Snugging the sword into the scabbard and gathering up the *sageo*, the restraining cord, Alex went to the center of the dojo and sat in *seiza,* on his knees, sitting back with the backs of his thighs on his calves. Centering himself, he held the sword level in front of him with both hands at forehead height.

He then performed *To-rei,* holding the sword in front of his forehead, palms up and level, and bowing his head to show respect both for the maker of the sword and for his practice. He then put it on the floor in front of him with the hilt to the left, sitting back on his heels. After a few moments, he placed his right hand, palm down, in front of him followed by his left hand so the two hands formed a triangle with the thumbs and forefingers. He then bowed, touching his forehead to the floor between his hands.

Sitting back again in *seiza,* he retrieved the sword with his right hand at the top of the sheath and rotated it one hundred and eighty degrees, placing it through the *hakama* and under the obi on his left side, edge up. He maneuvered the sword until it felt comfortable there. He secured the *sageo* to his belt, sitting back for a moment with his hands on the tops of his thighs. Abruptly, his right foot came up as his whole body rocked forward and then came down so he was in a kneeling lunge position. Pushing off with his right foot, Alex came to a standing position with his left hand resting lightly on the scabbard of the sword just behind the guard.

Alex began working through standing kata – *Tsuigekito,* Pursuing Sword. *Shato,* Angled Sword, *Zantotsuto,* Beheading Stroke, *Tatekito,* and *Kotekigyakuto.* He worked each form with precision and extreme concentration, each one beginning with *nukitsuke,* the sudden drawing of the blade with the purpose of killing or controlling the attacker. Immediately prior to the lightning-fast draw of the blade, Alex's left thumb pushed against the guard, freeing the blade from the sheath. Some forms ended with one attacker and some went on to deal with multiple assailants. At the conclusion of each form, there was *Chiburi,* a ritual shaking movement to remove blood and bits of flesh from the blade before sheathing it, and then *Noto,* the sheathing of the blade. Each time, the blade was returned by feel, with the back of the blade running along the web of Alex's left hand between his thumb and forefinger until the *kissaki* dropped into the *koiguchi,* the scabbard mouth. At that point, Alex fed the blade into the sheath until the last six inches; then the sheath was moved forward to cover the blade. The last thing done was the left thumb came over the guard, finishing the form by pulling the blade into place.

Each time, Alex strove for the state of *zanshin,* remaining mind, the state of continued spiritual and mental alertness after an offensive action is taken and the swordsman returns to *kamae,* or posture. *Zanshin* must be maintained so the swordsman is ready for any further attack. Alex's karate sensei referred to it as "staying in the dance" when completing a kata. Like many Japanese martial arts concepts, it is difficult to explain but easy to recognize once you experience it.

Back and forth, Alex worked the forms. His feet slid across the dojo floor bare millimeters above it. The Japanese phrase he'd had drilled into him was *ashi no ura ni hanshi ichi mai,* meaning there should only be room for one thin sheet of rice paper between the samurai's foot and the floor. Alex lost himself further and further to the process of the forms. There was no conscious thought, no analysis, no ego. Only the movement.

Alex's last form ended with him staring at the mirrors on one wall of his *dojo*. He completed the ritual shaking of blood from his sword and returned the blade to its sheath. His mind was empty. He was in complete *zanshin*. The sweat ran down his face and off the end of his nose as he looked at himself in the mirror without feeling he was, in any way, connected to the image. The realization came to him both quietly and in a rush. He knew what bothered him about the video of Peter Perfect.

He moves exactly like me, he thought. *Like me.*

Chapter 11

The rest of the weekend passed uneventfully, with Alex never able to let go of that single thought: *he moves exactly like me*. His mind chewed the thought up into a thousand pieces, spreading them out like a jigsaw puzzle, trying to put the puzzle back together so it made sense. There always seemed to be a piece missing. At any rate, his brain was perfectly capable of working on a problem without his help, frequently coming up with solutions to knotty investigations at three in the morning. *Sometimes, I feel like I just get in the way. Consciousness is way over-rated.* It was still distracting, making him less than attentive. That was brought home when he and Eve were out to dinner Saturday night at their favorite Italian restaurant. He was on auto-pilot, absently working his way through his Caesar salad when his wife brought him up short.

"Did you hear what I just said?" Eve asked.

"Hmmm? Oh, yeah, of course," Alex covered as he unsuccessfully tried to review what was just said.

"Really? Because I just said I felt the baby kick and that it felt like a sidekick, karate-boy," Eve fixed him with a penetrating stare, her head cocked to one side and her mouth twisted into a half-smile expression, half-grimace.

Alex quickly ran through the mental calculus and decided honesty was, by far, the best policy here. "I'm sorry, baby. This case I'm working on with the Feds has me preoccupied. I don't want to screw it up and have me and the department look bad. I guess it's more pressure than I thought it would be. Plus, it's coming right on the heels of the shooting and that doesn't help," Alex said. That last part was a blatant play for sympathy and Alex hated himself for it. But only briefly.

Eve's expression softened. "I understand. Look, if it's too much, you could ask for leave and just stay away from the whole police-thing for a while. You've got plenty of sick and vacation time," she said, "and besides, that would also allow you to worship me as I deserve to be worshiped. After all, you're the one responsible for my impending, balloon-like shape".

"I seem to recall you were a more-than-willing participant in those activities," Alex said.

"I'm sure I don't know what you mean. I am sweet and innocent. As pure as the driven snow," she said, with fake indignation and an arched eyebrow.

The rest of the dinner went without incident and he managed to keep any further distraction to a minimum through the weekend. On Monday morning, after kissing Eve goodbye, Alex mulled over his options. He didn't have to be at the FBI meeting until 1300 hours. That left the morning free to do some research. He thought about going over the files on the thumb drive but decided he'd rather poke himself in the eye with a sharp stick. Reluctantly, he decided to do some research into his ability to shift realities. However unlikely, it seemed like Peter might possess something like this. It would, at least, account for his ability to avoid mistakes. He'd always wondered if he was the sole person on this earth born like this.

When Alex initially discovered his "gift", he'd spent a considerable amount of time trying to work out the mechanics of how it was possible. He'd looked through books from the public library on the subject and found they fell into one of three camps. The looney tunes, woo-woo books that talked about psychic powers, astral planes, and the like. Other than an occasional tidbit of information, Alex found them to be a dead end. Then there were the science books that dealt with parallel universes and quantum physics. Alex only had the math background to understand the popularized versions of the science involved. This still did not explain, with any clarity, how he was able to bend the universe to his will. The third category concerned books that sounded scientific but were, in fact, simply more cleverly disguised woo-woo. Given his choices, Alex decided his best bet was to find someone who could explain the science. Enter Dr. Eisenshenk.

Alex's parents were thrilled when he expressed an interest in auditing classes at the university while still in high school. His father was a mechanical engineer by training and experience who worked on drilling rig design. His mother was a college graduate with a degree in sociology. How they'd gotten together still amazed Alex, though they seemed to complete and complement one another. His mother used to refer to his father as "Left Brain," on occasion. Lovingly, of course. At any rate, they were both quite happy and proud that Alex was taking the initiative to further his academic career.

Alex had researched the professors and curriculum at the college, deciding Dr. Eisenshenk would be his likeliest source of information. Eisenshenk was a professor of physics and taught most of the curriculum that dealt with theoretical physics and quantum mechanics. Unfortunately, the prerequisites for his classes were a lot of courses with PHY and MAT in front of them. Steeling himself, Alex spent the summer with his nose buried in one book or another. He worked through basic physics and calculus by dint of sheer determination. He also had his father there for any questions and there were more than a few. His father was ecstatic, envisioning Alex following in his academic footsteps. The disappointment would come later.

After jumping through the necessary bureaucratic hoops, Alex was able to sign up for one of Dr. Eisenshenk's classes on quantum mechanics, a selection that mystified the college administration and his parents alike. But, since he wasn't receiving an actual grade, both just shrugged their shoulders, convinced that the difficulty of the material would overwhelm him and he would reconsider his choice.

Alex's first class was in the evening, beginning at six PM. He got there early and watched nervously as other students filed in. At sixteen, he had already achieved his adult height and weighed a respectable one hundred and eighty pounds.

He was grateful he did not look completely out of place in the class, having dressed in what he believed to be his most collegiate clothing, khakis and a light blue polo shirt. The class was held in an auditorium with tiered seating that faced a blackboard and projector system. An attractive girl sat down to Alex's left and smiled at him. *Things are looking better already.*

The door next to the blackboard opened and a tall, stooped old man walked in. He was wearing a tattered green sweater over a white shirt, black tie hanging loosely around a thin neck, wrinkled grey trousers, and scuffed leather shoes. He was barely managing to carry a shifting armload of books on top of a bulging briefcase. He made it to the table next to the lectern before the books began to slide out of his arms onto the tabletop. He took a moment to steady the pile before looking up at the class. His thin face was strong, dominated by a large, hooked nose and an unkempt goatee. His dark eyes were sharp and alert, roaming around the audience like a hawk looking for prey. Alex could have sworn the professor's gaze lingered on him and he involuntarily sank lower into his chair.

As Professor Eisenshenk turned toward the blackboard, Alex thought he heard an audible sigh of relief from the students. He took a moment, smoothing his thinning gray hair and running his right hand over the goatee that framed his mouth, finally placing an index finger over his lips as though considering his next move. He picked up a piece of chalk and wrote "QUANTUM MECHANICS" on the board. He put down the piece of chalk and turned to face the students.

"How many of you have at least a partial understanding of quantum mechanics?" he asked. His gravelly voice filled the auditorium without the use of the microphone. *They must teach that in Professor school somewhere,* Alex thought, and smiled.

Several hands went up, but Eisenshenk narrowed the focus of his attention to Alex. *Crap! Was it the smile? That's it! Dammit!*

"Are you smiling because you know something, young man, or do you just find me amusing?" Eisenshenk asked, skewering Alex with his gaze, pinning him to his seat

Alex could feel people pulling away from him the way antelope pull away from the slowest of the herd, the one the lion selected as his prey. He could almost hear them thinking. "glad it's not me."

He swallowed hard and said, "N-no, sir." He didn't trust his voice to say anything more.

"No sir, what? No sir, you don't know anything or no sir, you don't find me amusing?" he asked.

"E-either one. Both. Sir." Alex managed to squeak out.

"I'll accept that you don't know anything, young man, but I, for one, find myself vastly amusing," Dr. Eisenshenk said, and there were smatterings of nervous laughter throughout the auditorium. Alex felt the pressure of his gaze lift from him. He managed to draw a deep breath.

The professor placed his hands on the lectern, bowing his head."To those of you who believe you have some idea about quantum theory, let me tell you a little story. Wolfgang Pauli and Werner Heisenberg, he of the uncertainty principle, had just given a presentation on the non-linear field theory of elementary particles at Columbia University. After the presentation, Pauli looked out at the audience. They had broken up into small groups and were in earnest discussion."

Eisenshenk raised his head, looking at the audience. "After a while, he became nervous and approached one of the groups of physicists, asking if they thought the ideas presented were too 'crazy.' The response was 'Oh, no, no. We are agreed your theory is crazy. The question that divides us is this: is it crazy *enough?*'. So if you thought you knew something about quantum mechanics, I assure you that you do not. And the admission of ignorance is the beginning of knowledge."

That was Alex's introduction to Dr. Eisenshenk. At the end of the class, he screwed up his courage and approached the professor as he was sorting papers and stuffing them into his briefcase.

"Professor Eisenshenk?" Alex asked, trying to keep the tremor out of his voice.

"Hmm? Yes? What is it?" Eisenshenk looked up distractedly.

"I just wanted to introduce..." Alex started.

"You're Alex Dorn. A high school student who is auditing my class on quantum mechanics," the professor interrupted, snapping his briefcase shut and fixing him with a steely glare. "What I want to know is this. Why?"

Before Alex could think to devise an interesting and erudite response, the words came pouring out. "Because I have questions and I want answers."

Eisenshenk seemed to consider that for a moment, finally saying, "Your answer has the advantage of appearing to be truthful. Alright, Mr. Dorn, you can stay. Don't cause trouble and don't ask stupid questions in class. If you have a stupid question, see me *after* class."

With that, he heaved his assorted books up under his arm and trudged to the doorway. He looked back over his shoulder at Alex and said "Well?" jerking his head in the direction of the door. Alex hurried to open the door. Eisenshenk grunted his thanks and left the classroom.

Alex smiled at the memory. Eisenshenk had an irascible persona he utilized to the fullest in the classroom. Outside the classroom, he was a much more approachable and likable person. He and the professor had become friends and Alex suspected Eisenshenk had, in some strange way, adopted him.

Well, it's time to go see my adoptive father.

Chapter 12

On the way to Dr. Eisenshenk's residence outside of town, Alex called him on his cell to confirm that he would be home. The phone rang a dozen times and Alex took the phone away from his ear and moved his thumb over the disconnect button when a familiar voice answered.

"Hello."

"Hello. Professor. It's me, Alex."

"Well, of course, it's you, Alex. I recognize your voice. I'm just retired, you know. I'm not completely senile. Yet."

Alex chuckled. "It's good to see that retirement hasn't changed you. Listen. I have some questions and was hoping I could drop by."

"Since when haven't you had questions? I AM gardening now, but I suppose I can fit you into my busy schedule," he sighed.

"Thanks. I'll be there in about ten minutes."

"Time is an illusion, Alex. I'll see you when you get here," and with a click, the line went dead.

Alex turned his phone off, putting it back on his belt. Wistfully he remembered a time when it was possible to be unreachable. Then Satan invented pagers and it was all downhill from there. He settled into driving, enjoying the journey to the professor's place. The professor lived outside the city limits, where there was far less traffic and far more nature. Occasionally, you could glimpse deer along the edge of the road, poking their noses out of the dusty palmettos and twisted scrub oak, gauging the safety of a mad scramble across the roadway. Armadillos, possums, and the occasional raccoon provided mute roadway testimony that mistakes were costly.

He saw the driveway to the professor's place and turned in, spotting the bright yellow house a quarter of a mile away. It was well off the road. There was a screen of Australian pines between the road and the professor's front yard that served to further dampen the traffic noise. He saw Eisenshenk in the middle of his front yard among the profusion of flowering plants that served as his lawn. The professor loved butterflies and had planted a host of perennials and annuals to attract them, getting a fair number of the hummingbirds that migrated through the area into the bargain. He was bent over when Alex approached but stood up when he heard the car and waved. His long, tan sleeves were pushed back on his forearms and a broad straw hat covered his balding head. He wiped the sweat from his brow and stretched, arching his back with his hands on his hips, just above the waistline of his khaki pants.

Alex waved back, grinning. He thought of the professor as a father figure, more so since he lost his parents in a traffic crash five years ago. The professor's wife, Tova, came out onto the front porch of the Cracker-style house, smiling and waving at him. If the professor was tall, thin, and irascible, his wife was, physically and emotionally, his opposite. She was a shade over five feet tall and looked like a cherub. She had a surfeit of positive energy that she bestowed on anyone and everyone in her presence. It was impossible not to like her.

Alex parked the car halfway down the driveway and walked over to the professor, extending his hand. Eisenshenk shook it, his grip still strong.

"So, Alex, you've come to see your old professor, eh? Are things that slow at the police department?"

Immediately, Eisenshenk's face fell. He grabbed Alex's forearm and peered into his face. "I am sorry Alex. I forgot about the shooting. How are you doing? Are you well?" he asked, his face creased with concern.

"I'm fine, Professor. They've thrown me to the FBI to work on a case, so I'm staying busy."

Eisenshenk reached out and placed his hand on Alex's upper arm and squeezed.

"Good, that's good." He released Alex's arm and turned toward the house, taking his straw hat off and fanning himself with it, his wispy hair plastered to his skull. He put the hat back on and rolled down his sleeves, covering the numbers tattooed on his forearm. Alex knew what they meant. The professor had never spoken of them and he had never asked. "Come. Let us get out of the Florida sun. It will cook your brain if you let it."

As they approached the porch, the professor's wife, dressed in a long blue gingham dress, came to the bottom step and threw her arms around Alex in a bear hug. When she released him, she held him at arm's length and said, "Alex! It's so good to see you! How have you been? How is Eve? Have you picked out a name for the baby, yet? Is she having morning sickness?"

Alex laughed at the rapid-fire questions. "Good, good, no, and no. In that order."

Eisenshenk looked exasperated. "Tova, let the boy get in out of the sun. Would you like something to drink, Alex?"

Tova turned so she still held Alex's arm, leading him up the steps. "How about some ice tea? And I made some of those oatmeal cookies you like so much."

"Well, you know I would never turn down anything you baked, Miss Tova," Alex said. She beamed a brilliant smile at him and released his arm, hurrying off to the kitchen.

"Let's go into the study. She will no doubt track us down there," the professor said as he turned to walk down the hall and Alex followed. Like all Florida "Cracker" homes, this one was made of wood, in this case, cypress. It was elevated off the ground a little less than three feet and had a wraparound porch. There was a centrally located attic fan drawing fresh air into the house from all directions, and the windows were positioned for maximum cross-ventilation. This house was built before air-conditioning, constructed so the owners could survive the Florida summers without it. The houses constructed more recently in Florida were designed to be livable only with air-conditioning. Every year hurricanes caused power outages, turning the expensive homes into sweat boxes. Alex had to admit to a certain perverse satisfaction in watching people abandon their McMansions because staying in them had become untenable during the regular storms that arrived like clockwork.

Eisenshenk's library was a simple affair with a roll-top desk covered in papers, two chairs, a small coffee table, and three walls covered floor-to-ceiling with bookcases that were overflowing. He motioned for Alex to take a chair, sitting opposite him with the coffee table between them.

"So, tell me, what brings you to my humble abode today?" the professor asked, leaning forward and placing his elbows on his knees, his fingers clasped between them.

"Our old friend, the multiverse, Professor," Alex said.

Eisenshenk laughed, leaning back in his chair, a smile wreathing his face. "Ah, Alex, this has been an obsession of yours since the first day you sat in my classroom. You remember that day?" he asked.

"Of course I do. I still have nightmares about it. Sometimes, I even wet the bed."

Eisenshenk raised one eyebrow, "I wasn't that bad, was I? Don't answer! It was a rhetorical question." Eisenshenk sat back, looking thoughtful for a moment, idly pulling at the goatee on his chin. "Let's review what we know, Alex, and forgive an old professor his habits, but this may seem like a lecture."

Alex settled in, smiling, "I'm used to it professor. I'll survive."

"Yes. I'm sure you will. Enjoying it, though, that's another matter. So, we have various theories concerning a multiverse. There's the beyond-the-horizon multiverse in which universes exist that are nearly like ours or vastly different but are separated by such fantastic distances they never, ever interact. You are interested in that theory, perhaps?" the professor asked.

Alex knew Eisenshenk was aware that he was not. But he was perfectly willing to let him play the part of professor once again. It was a role he had played for decades, and Alex knew he must miss it terribly. He shook his head.

"Ah, so not that one. Perhaps the fecund universe theory where the quantum gravity effects inside a black hole spawn another universe isolated by the black hole from the universe in which the black hole lies? Black holes were all the rage once, you know," Eisenshenk said as he looked at Alex expectantly.

Again, Alex shook his head.

"So, we have two down. I'm not even going to bring up the oscillating big bang theory because no one believes that old thing anymore. It was popular for a while, though."

"I was hoping you wouldn't," Alex said.

Tova appeared through the door with some ice tea and cookies on a tray. "Now, Edward, you aren't subjecting Alex to more schoolwork, are you? He must have had enough of that from you when you were teaching," she said as she smiled at Alex.

Alex reached over and grabbed a cookie, "No, Miss Tova, he isn't boring me at all. I asked for this, if you can believe it."

"Well, I'm not sure I can, but I will leave you two alone. You'll be staying for lunch, Alex?" Tova asked with a hopeful look on her face.

"Yes, Ma'am. If it won't be a bother," Alex replied.

"No. No bother at all," Tova said, looking enormously pleased as she bustled out of the room.

Alex turned to find the professor with his chin in his hand, regarding him with a jaundiced eye. "What?" He asked.

The professor sighed, "Never mind. Where were we? Oh, yes. There's the ekpyrotic universe, where two branes separated by an extra dimension collide and create new universes. This is very popular with string theorists. Hmmm...?"

"Uhm, no."

"Well, we are running out of options here. How about the bubble multiverse, where the inflationary hyper-expansion of the cosmos has pocket universes spread throughout it? String theorists like this one too."

"No. No, I'm afraid not."

The professor let out an exaggerated, theatrical sigh. "I'm afraid all we are left with, then, is the many-worlds multiverse. That is if you're sure I can't entice you with a nice faith-based multiverse?"

"Yes. Quite sure."

"Well, then, we would normally begin with the Copenhagen Interpretation, but, since time is limited, let's proceed right to Hugh Everett, though Everett himself never used the term 'many-worlds multiverse'. That was later done by Bryce DeWitt. But I'm getting ahead of myself."

"Hugh Everett was a Ph.D. student at Princeton when he proposed a Ph.D. thesis called 'The Theory of Universal Wavefunction'. His idea, in a nutshell, was that every time a decision is made, every time an individual decides to go left instead of right, the universe, for want of a better way of putting it, splits in two. In one universe, that person went left, and in the other, right. This eliminates the idea of a wave-function collapse as we find with Schrodinger's paradox. You'll recall his poor kitty cat was trapped in a box and exists in a super positional state, both alive and dead, until you open the box and the observation forces the wave function to collapse. Then you see either a live cat or a dead one. Everett's idea was that the wave function of the universe exists in an infinite-dimensional Hilbert space. This huge, unimaginably complex wave function evolves smoothly, containing all possible outcomes, and preserves probability. There is no collapse. Both outcomes exist, but we can only perceive one. You can never perceive the superposition state due to decoherence. You are either on one side of the decision or the other."

Alex leaned forward. "So all universes are equally real." It was a statement more than a question.

"Absolutely."

"Can you travel from one universe to another?"

"You do all the time. Every time you go fishing instead of hunting."

"No, no. That's not what I meant." Alex stopped for a moment, frustrated, considering how to ask his question without sounding crazy.

"How about a hypothetical question?" Alex asked.

"I'm a theoretical physicist, Alex. Hypothetical is what I do. It's all I do. Fire away."

"Let's just say, for the sake of argument, an individual had the power to go hunting and then change his mind, and go fishing. But not from where he is, from where he was when he initially made the decision. He could essentially go back to the point in time when the universe split and take a different path. What would that look like?"

"I don't think thermodynamics would let you do it, Alex, but, to the traveler, I think his experience would be like someone who changed their mind at that time. The first time."

"What happens to the universe where he decided to go hunting? Does it cease to exist?"

"No. I wouldn't think so, Alex. I think it would go on as before, part of the great cosmic wave function, as it were."

"How different are these universes likely to be from each other? Is the traveler likely to end up on a frozen world trying to breathe chlorine?"

Eisenshenk laughed out loud. "You've been reading too many science fiction books...but, no. I don't think that's likely."

"Why not?".

"Think of it this way. Take a million sheets of paper, spread out side-by-side across an infinite gym floor. Now comes an Ink Fairy..."

"Ink Fairy?"

"Is this my explanation or yours?" Eisenschenk cocked one eyebrow.

"My apologies, Professor. Proceed with your Ink Fairy," Alex grinned.

"Yes, as I was saying...this Ink Fairy has an infinite can of ink and she bounces merrily along spreading this ink all over the sheets of paper. Some sheets get a lot of ink, some get only a little, some are nearly black and others all white. The sheets of paper nearest each other get similar amounts of ink. Get the picture?"

"Got it. Go on."

"You then take all these sheets of paper and bind them together. Paper and ink being what they are, there is a transfer between the sheets of paper. Pieces of paper near to one another are likely to be very similar. Sheets that are distant from one another may be quite different. So it is with universes in the multiverse. Does that answer your question?"

"One of them anyway."

Tova appeared at the doorway again, delicious aromas wafting into the room with her. "I hope you are both finished and hungry. Lunch is ready."

Alex smiled with anticipation. He'd never eaten at the professor's house when it wasn't good.

"I think I'm more hungry than I am curious now, professor. What do you say we have lunch?"

"I'd say that's a fine idea."

Both Alex and the professor got up from their seats and headed for the door. Alex didn't catch the puzzled look Eisenschenk gave him as they walked out of the study.

Chapter 13

Alex ran into The Walrus, AKA Detective Joe Esposito, out-side the Anderson building just before 1300. Joe moved his considerable bulk well, betraying the muscle under-girding the gut hanging over his belt. He reminded Alex of a more muscular John Candy with thinning black hair and a mustache completely hiding his upper lip. Joe carried a cup of coffee from a convenience store, his mustache flaring away from his lip as he blew on it to cool it down.

"You know, Joe, they'll probably have coffee up there for us," Alex said.

"They're feds. I don't trust 'em," Esposito replied, his eyes narrowing suspiciously.

They went inside to the elevator bank, joining the two county detectives as they waited. They nodded to each other stiffly, like dogs meeting for the first time, wary. There was a certain degree of rivalry between the county and municipal agencies. Deputies seemed convinced they were the premier law enforcement agency in the county and thought of city cops as, well, lesser. The elevator doors opened and several lawyer-types carrying briefcases and talking on cell phones got out. Alex slid in first so he would have his back to the elevator wall. The doors whispered shut and one of the county detectives punched their floor. The deputies looked at each other and then faced front, silent. The stillness grew in the elevator car.

"Sooooo, you guys got any hot ideas about our suspect?" Alex asked suddenly, with an eagerness in his voice he didn't feel.

The two county detectives looked at each other again, as if gauging how much information they were able to part with. Alex looked back and forth from one to the other, making it as uncomfortable as possible until, at last, one of them said, "We have our crime analyst working on the information. She hasn't gotten back to us yet."

"So, did you give her copies so you could keep the original data to look through yourself, or what?"

At this point, Alex knew he was being a dick. Both county detectives fidgeted. Alex waited, a pleasant smile on his face. His ill will toward the county went back to a homicide case he worked that eventually involved them. He caught the case after a patrol unit found a dead body in the trunk of a car parked in a K-mart parking lot. It was an obvious body dump and the primary scene could have been anywhere. Alex and his lieutenant practically begged the county to take the case based on jurisdiction. With no suspect and no crime scene, the solvability of the case approached zero. The county declined. Forty-eight hours later, with very little sleep, Alex had a suspect and a crime scene that was about fifty feet into the county. The lieutenant made Alex contact the county even though he, like most detectives, had been bonded as a deputy. After looking over the case file, the county decided that, since it was their jurisdiction, they would magnanimously take the case off his hands. Alex had been a ball of seething anger at the time. His heavy bag had taken a brutal beating.

"Uh, no, the Captain wanted it done by crime analysis."

"Oh, I see," Alex said, turning away from them dismissively. He was in full 'Dick Mode.' Out of the corner of his eye, he saw Joe hiding a smile behind the combination of his mustache and coffee cup. The elevator doors opened up, all four of the detectives stepped into the hamster cage, and the elevator doors slid shut behind them.

"I wonder if this thing is going to catch on," Alex wondered, looking around the ballistic plexiglass enclosure.

"If it doesn't, they can always fill it with water and use it for an aquarium," Esposito said.

Alex turned and stared at him. "You know you're just begging for a walrus joke, right?" he asked.

"Fuck you. And I mean that in the nicest possible way," Joe answered pleasantly. He was completely aware of his nickname.

A tall, blond woman, her hair pulled back from her face and dressed in matching dark blue blazer over a crisp, white blouse marched toward the cage, her back ramrod straight, a professional smile on her face that didn't quite reach her eyes. Her heels tapped an even rhythm on the floor. She held her card up to the card-reader on the outside and the lock disengaged. The door swung open slightly. She turned and began walking away.

"Follow me to the meeting room, gentlemen," she said over her shoulder. Alex and Joe were the first through the door and into the office.

Alex nodded as Joe looked over at him and whispered loudly, "She doesn't know you." Alex smiled.

Behind him, one of the county detectives said, "I do admire their taste in staff here," and the other chuckled inappropriately.

In front of Alex, the woman pivoted abruptly in a military about-face, forcing him to stop suddenly, a bit too close. Her eyes were narrowed to slits. "I'll be sure to let the staff know that, detective. I should have introduced myself. I'm Agent Jones," she said. Alex felt the temperature of the room plummet. He could swear he saw his breath. She stared at them for a full five seconds, then executed another about-face and continued. He wondered how she could do that in heels without breaking an ankle.

Alex looked over his shoulder at the sheepish County detective who refused to meet his gaze. "Thanks for that," he said.

Agent Jones stopped at the door to the conference room and motioned them inside. She smiled at Alex and Joe; then her lips tightened into a line for the deputies. The FDLE agents were already there and Agent Stormant was talking to one of them at the front of the room. Joe and Alex sat in the same seats they'd had during the previous meeting. Alex looked toward the back of the room and spotted the coffee maker, steam rising from the full carafe.

Alex nudged Joe in the ribs. "Look, Joe. Free coffee," Alex grinned, rising to get a cup to kill some time, even though coffee wasn't his favorite beverage. As he sat back down, he made a show of stirring the coffee in front of Joe.

"Bet it sucks," Joe said, taking a sip from his cup.

Alex looked around the room, sizing up the occupants. After a moment, he decided he would try to partner up with Esposito. They got along well, sharing a similar sense of humor. *I don't think I would enjoy being in the car for eight hours with one of the dicks from the county. And that's not a colorful euphemism for "detective."*

The room settled down, Agent Stormant clearing his throat to start the meeting. He flipped on the projector and the screen filled with the Peter Perfect folder already open.

"So, you've all had time to take a look at what we have in the way of information on our Peter Perfect. Any ideas?" he asked, looking expectantly around the room. The silence was only broken by people shifting uncomfortably in their chairs.

Well, here goes. Alex spoke up. "He didn't seem to have anything in the way of a pattern. M.O., target of theft, type of premises, time of day, day of the week...all varied widely. Additionally, he didn't seem to have any quirks or discernible peculiarities. Except he doesn't make mistakes."

Stormant turned toward Alex. "That's exactly right, detective. Anything else?"

"Well...I think he might be involved in some form of martial arts," Alex said, trying not to sound lame. There was an immediate snickering from the county detectives and curious looks from FDLE. Even Joe looked at him with what he assumed was a frown under the mustache.

"Oh, great. We're looking for Bruce Lee. Or his ghost," one of the county detectives said, making a predictable "karate chop" motion with his hand. Alex managed a tight smile, feeling his ears go red.

"What makes you say that?" Stormant asked, looking genuinely interested.

"The way he moves. Just his general body kinematics, really," Alex stated.

"Kinematics," Stormant repeated. "Hmmm…do you have any expertise in this field?"

"No formal training," Alex said, "But I have been involved in the martial arts for eighteen years."

"Black belt?" asked Stormant.

"I have *dan* rankings in a couple of arts," Alex answered.

"That's interesting," Stormant said, turning to look at the screen. "The reason that's interesting is that it is the first piece of new information we've had on Peter for a while."

Stormant widened his attention to the whole group. "Detective Dorn is correct in his first statement. There is no discernible M.O. In fact, the only real M.O. here is that there is none. And that is unusual in and of itself. Peter seems to craft each operation exclusively for that crime. So the question is this: how do we catch him?"

"Do we have any idea where he will surface next?" one of the FDLE guys asked.

"Not really," Stormant answered. "We're basing our current operations on the notion that he's headed south and sticking to the coast but, frankly, we're pulling that out of our collective ass. He could show up in Chicago or Los Angeles. But with what little we've got, the bureau has decided, essentially, to cast a wide net, to enlist local aid – that's you poor, unfortunate souls – and reconnoiter possible targets before any crime being committed. There are meetings similar to this one being held in other FBI satellite offices as we speak. All of these meetings have the same basic directive: try to find out where he'll strike next. Rather than staying a step behind him, we're going to try to get out in front of him."

Stormant turned back to the screen and closed the Peter Perfect file. He opened another file, a map of Bay City, the surrounding jurisdictions coming crisply into view. Agent Jones began passing out folders to the seated law enforcement officers.

"As you can see from the materials Agent Jones is passing out, we have divided the area up into sections for each team of two. We have Agents Lowry and Blair from FDLE, Detectives Harn and Belton from the county and...," Stormant looked expectantly at Alex and Joe.

Alex spoke up. "I'll team up with the Walr...um, with Detective Esposito," he said.

Alex felt more than saw Joe pivot in his chair to face him. "Dude. Seriously? I'm right here." Alex refused to look in Joe's direction. The two county guys stifled their laughter. Barely.

Stormant looked from Alex to Joe with a half-smile on his face. "Well, good. I'm glad we've got the team assignments settled. In your packets, you'll find the parameters for the reports you'll be generating. We expect you to identify specific targets in your area and then develop an OPS plan for hardening those targets or, preferably, setting traps for Peter so we can catch him or, at least, get a lead on who he is. You are all experienced law enforcement officers and investigators. Take the week to see what you can come up with and we will reconvene here at 0900 hours next Monday," Agent Stormant instructed as he turned off the projector. "Any questions? No? Fine, see you next Monday."

Finally, Alex pivoted in his chair to face Joe. "Sorry man, it just came out. I couldn't look at you. I would have cracked up," he said, a grin splitting his face.

Joe leaned forward, hunching his shoulders conspiratorially, lowering his voice. "You know what a walrus and I have in common, Alex?" he asked.

"No."

"We both like a tight seal," he said with an evil smile.

"You will never know how hard I am trying NOT to get an image of that in my mind, Joe," Alex closed his eyes, shivering in mock horror. They both got up and followed Agent Jones toward the exit, talking as they walked.

"Ah, too late. You're stuck with it now. You'll probably have nightmares," Joe said with a self-satisfied smirk on his face. "So, your place or mine?"

"For what? Are we dating now? I think you are taking this partnership waaaayyy too seriously."

"No, asshole. We need to go over how we're going to approach this project. Your department or mine?"

"Oh, let's do mine. It's closer. We can use the planning room. It's usually empty," Alex said.

"As long as there's coffee, Alex. And don't think I won't come up with a nickname for you. Let's see...Bruce Lee? Too obvious. Let me think." Joe appeared to ruminate for several seconds and then snapped his fingers. "I know! Grasshopper! Perfect!"

"What? Like the old TV show with David Carradine as Kwai Chang Kane?" Alex asked.

"Exactly," he said, looking smug.

"Great," Alex said.

Agent Jones opened the hamster cage to let them out. They were the first pair of investigators there. The elevator opened immediately when he pressed the button.

Joe's eyes narrowed, thinking. "Come to think of it, do you know what your porn name would be?" he asked.

"I'm sure you're going to tell me. Get in the elevator," Alex said as he held the door open.

Joe got in the elevator and turned to face him, "Asshopper," he said with a smile.

Alex stopped at the door to the elevator, holding the door open with his palm as he leaned in and inspected the inside of the car. Then he cocked his head, listening.

"What are you doing?" Joe asked.

"Just seeing if the elevator could bear the weight," Alex said, stepping inside and turning to face the closing doors.

"You're such an ass-" And the doors closed.

Chapter 14

Alex drove to the PD with Esposito trailing him. He badged the card reader at the secured parking gate and the six-foot-tall section of chain-link fence topped with razor wire rolled back in a jerking stop-and-go fashion as the chain slipped on broken sprocket teeth. *Wonder when THAT will get fixed?* Alex chose a parking spot on the backside of the lot where the afternoon sun would be partially blocked by the building and Joe found a space three over. Alex got out of his car, moving immediately into the shade to wait for Joe. They approached the building together, Joe trailing and already starting to grumble and sweat. Alex decided to use the side door closest to booking so they could take the stairs to the second floor without having to check through the front desk or go through admin. The front of the department was decorated with a large sign that read "BAY CITY POLICE DEPARTMENT" as well as a flagpole flying the American flag and a xeriscaped garden using native Florida plants. It was meant to impress citizens as they entered.

The door Alex approached was a dull gray, reinforced metal security door with a badge reader near the latch side of it; both set into a red brick wall. As they approached the door, Alex moved to badge the card reader as Joe reached for the door handle. The door burst open, striking Joe in the forehead. It knocked him back, his arms windmilling for balance until he fell onto his back, his short, stocky legs flying up in the air. A huge, wild-eyed biker with long, dyed blonde hair rushed through the opening, his left hand still shoving the door. He tried to orient himself, squinting in the strong sunlight and momentarily disoriented. He was wearing a denim vest emblazoned with his colors, filthy jeans, a set of silver handcuffs swinging from his right wrist. Only his right wrist. He was a 1%-er. A real biker affiliated with a gang, not one of the weekend warriors on their fifty-thousand-dollar Harleys pretending to be "outlaws" on Saturday and Sunday and then went back to being bankers and lawyers on Monday.

Still partially blinded, he ran to his right, colliding with Alex, and moved to shove him aside. Alex grabbed him by the vest to prevent himself from falling and dragged the suspect with him. The biker staggered a couple of steps, desperately trying to peel Alex off him as they reeled off the curb and onto the parking lot. Alex burrowed into his chest, holding him close, fighting for footing. When the suspect failed to get Alex off him, he started throwing looping punches, trying to hit Alex hard enough to make him let go. The first few strikes glanced off the back of Alex's head, hurting but doing no real damage. Alex waited until the biker threw a right hand and then he ducked, pushing the biker's arm up and over his head and quickly sliding under, taking the suspect's back. He grabbed the suspect from behind, using the vest for hand grips at each shoulder, and, raising his right foot high, planted it violently in the back of the suspect's right knee. It drove his knee to the pavement and buckled him backward. Releasing the vest, Alex grabbed the biker's hair with his left hand, cranked his head to his left shoulder, and smashed him twice on the side of the neck with hammer fist strikes. The side of his fist made a dull, meaty sound as it hit. He felt the suspect shudder and twitch as he snaked his right arm under the suspect's chin until his Adam's apple was nestled securely in the crook of Alex's elbow. Alex snugged his right hand into the crook of his left arm, putting his left hand behind the suspect's head. The suspect, who outweighed him by 75 pounds, struggled blindly to throw Alex off. Alex fell onto his back, pulling the suspect with him. He hooked both of his ankles in at the front of the suspect's upper thighs and *squeezed* his arms while pushing the suspect's head forward and arching his own back. The suspect dug his heels into the pavement and pushed back, driving Alex across the parking lot, scraping his upper back along the rough surface for ten feet, shredding his coat. Alex held the pressure on the hold until the suspect passed out. His body turned to jelly abruptly and his arms fell to his sides.

Joe had regained his feet and stood over Alex as the biker went unconscious. "Need any help?" he asked.

"No, no. I'm fine. Thanks though. Really."

Three young cops flung the door open and ran out, almost knocking Joe down for the second time. The first officer pushed Joe to one side, snapping his ASP open and drawing his arm back.

Alex yelled, "No! He's out!" The young cop hesitated; the collapsible baton still drawn back. He was shaking with adrenaline, anticipation, and indecision. Alex reiterated his warning, "That's it! It's over!" The rookie cop reluctantly lowered his baton as Alex released the choke, pushing the suspect off him and rolling the opposite way to his knees. He took a second to catch his breath. He looked up at the three young cops standing there, looking back and forth from the unconscious suspect to Alex, unsure of their next action.

"You know, you really should handcuff him while he's sleeping," Alex said, still on his knees. "Trust me; it'll be easier. And make sure you double lock them."

The three officers, snapping out of their daze, swarmed the suspect like ants on a piece of melted sidewalk candy, all trying to secure the handcuffs themselves. Alex's FTO had once described this maneuver as "three monkeys trying to fuck a football". At the time, he thought it would make a great name for an exotic kung-fu technique. Eventually, they managed to get the cuffs on correctly as Alex noticed a red crease running down the side of Joe's face from the edge of the door.

"Man, does that hurt? It looks painful," Alex asked.

"I'll live. Is this the way you always treat guests?" Esposito rubbed the side of his face.

"No, but you're special." Alex stood and turned to the three rookies with the prisoner now semi-conscious and standing. He was unsteady, blinking rapidly, trying to clear his head. "So, how did this clusterfuck happen?"

All three of the officers looked at each other, waiting for someone to go first. Then two of them looked at the third. He sighed. "Okay. Look, it was my fault. He was cooperative, even joking around with me and it was just a misdemeanor warrant. For traffic, for chrissakes. Anyway, I was un-handcuffing him in the holding cell area when he spun on me and caught me in the temple with an elbow and I went down. But he hadn't caused any trouble up until then. He seemed all right."

Alex leaned in, looking more closely at the officer's left temple. The area was already swelling. He was going to have a nice knot there. "OK, this is why we teach you in field training to take the cuffs off after they get into the cell. You know the procedure. Consider it a lesson learned. Oh, and don't forget to fill out an injury form. Also, run a thorough check on blondie here. I'm betting you'll find more charges on some of his aliases."

Alex started to turn away when the young cop grabbed his arm. Alex looked down at the hand on his arm and the rookie immediately released it. "Sorry. Uh, Do I have to? Fill out a form, I mean? I don't think it's that bad..." He looked hopeful.

Alex turned back to face him. "Yes, you do," he explained, slowly and deliberately. "Because you don't know how bad it is. It probably is nothing. But you don't know that. If you start having problems a month down the road it'll be too late. Workman's comp will tell you to kiss their ass. The department will tell you the same thing. I've been screwed by this so learn from my mistake. And if you're thinking you can bury this embarrassing little incident? Forget it. Not only do you have several witnesses but I have to fill out a use of force form. And that's going to be a problem because I choked him out."

"But he's fine," the young cop blurted. And he was right. Not only was the suspect conscious, but he was also now causing trouble, struggling with the two officers holding him and telling them that they could do new and interesting, if anatomically impossible, things with their genitals.

Alex sighed. "That's true. But the lateral vascular neck restraint has been ruled deadly forced by CJSTC. Never mind..." Alex stopped, shook his head, realizing he was spinning his wheels. "Look, you write your report, I'll write mine. If I'm lucky, they'll overlook this since the bad guy is physically okay and they don't want me back in the spotlight after the shooting. A man can dream, anyway."

Alex started to turn away, paused for a moment, and then turned back, continuing, "And while we're here, let's talk about the fact that you were about to club an already senseless man who was incapable of resisting." The young cop, Johnson according to his name tag, looked away. "Can you give me a good reason why?"

Johnson's brow furrowed. He was thinking furiously, trying to come up with a legal, defensible reason for his actions. "Well, he'd already committed a felony when he clocked me and he was still resisting...".

Alex raised his hand and sighed. "No, he wasn't. He was out. Look, we're professionals. We don't get the luxury of being personally offended. We don't get to play catch-up-ball after the suspect is in cuffs. It doesn't matter how much they've resisted. It doesn't matter if your ass has just been handed to you and your uniform is in tatters. We don't exact revenge. Because we are... what?" Alex cocked his head, cupping his hand to his right ear, leaning toward Johnson, who looked miserable.

"Professionals," he muttered.

"That's right. Professionals. Now go write your report. And make it good because I'm going to request a copy to write my supplement."

Alex looked at Esposito and nodded toward the door. Joe waited until Alex badged the door and opened it for him.

"Once bitten, twice shy?" Alex asked as the three young officers followed them with the suspect still trying to fight. They made an abrupt right turn into booking.

"Can't be too careful around here. By the way, you've got dirt all over your back. And I think there's a couple of tears in your coat. OK, I'm not gonna lie, that coat's wrecked."

"Nice. There goes my clothing allowance," Alex said. "I'm just gonna stop by my desk to check on things."

"Lead on. I'm getting paid by the hour."

Alex led Joe through the PD to the Investigations Section. As soon as he cleared the door, Deni spotted him and started in.

"OOOH, look! It's Mr. Important! Mr. I'm-Working-with-the-Feds-Now! So what causes you to grace our humble office with your august presence, Oh Mighty One?"

Alex looked around. He could see Pritchard grinning at him and he could see the back of Chuck's head. He looked like he was typing. Dave Brown was still on vacation. Jensen and Crile were on the other side of the room.

"Anybody else got anything? Come on, get it out now."
Alex paused. "Nothing? Good. And yes, the rumors you've
heard are true. I have, indeed, been assigned to work with
the *Federales* for an unspecified amount of time. If it makes
you feel any better, I was not chosen for my expertise; nor
for my astonishingly good looks. Not even for my phenom-
enally tight abs. No. I was chosen because Admin wanted
me gone for a while. Apparently, I am something of an
embarrassment."

"Hell, Alex, we could have told them that," Deni said.
"And is that Joe in the doorway, tagging along behind you?"

"Yes, Deni. Yes, it is," Joe said, moving around Alex. "You
gonna continue to sit there on your fat ass or are you gonna
come over here and give me a hug?"

Alex raised an eyebrow and looked from The Walrus to
Deni.

"Oh, get your mind out of the gutter, Alex. Joe and I have
been friends since the academy," Deni said as she crossed the
space between them and hugged Esposito. It looked like a
bear hugging a small child.

"Oof, I think you've gained a few pounds, Joe."

"It's not my fault; it's my wife's. She keeps cooking. And
I'm weak."

"Hmmm..." she said, looking at him skeptically. "So what
are you guys doing here? And, by the way, what the Hell
happened to your coat?"

"I had an impromptu judo match in the parking lot."
Deni crossed her arms and looked even more doubtful, if
that was possible. "Look, don't ask. We were going to use

the planning and training room to work out just how we're going to approach this project we've been given. Why don't you come on up and we'll go over it with you? I'd like to see what you think."

Deni sighed. "OK, let me finish this email and I'll be right up." Deni went to her desk, sat back down, and began typing.

Alex looked over the paperwork on his desk and then booted up his email. There didn't seem to be anything earthshaking in either category, so he closed his terminal, grabbed Esposito, and headed upstairs to the training room. The room looked like they had recently used it for defensive tactics; the tables were lining the walls and the mats were still on the floor. The department's BOB dummy was in the center of the room. They moved it to one side and cleared the mats from a section of the floor. Joe and Alex grabbed two tables and shoved them together. Alex commandeered the laptop that was usually used for the projector and set it up on the table. They had just finished setting up when Deni came through the door.

"So, what's all this about, anyway?" she asked.

Alex and Joe took turns detailing the particulars of the Peter Perfect assignment. They used the laptop to run through the information on the thumb drive, explaining what they knew as they went along. The folder with their assignment in it lay next to the computer.

"Whew!", Deni said. "Looks like you've got a big bag o' nuthin'."

"Yeah," Alex said. "Pretty much. Any ideas?"

"Nope. Not a one. What's your assignment look like?"

Alex opened the file Agent Jones had given them. As he looked through it, he realized they'd either gotten the plum of the assignments or the worst of the lot, depending on how you looked at it.

"Looks like we drew most of downtown. In the financial district. I guess I'd call that a target-rich environment," Alex said.

"I think I'd call it getting the most work," Joe grumbled.

Deni looked up at the zone map on the wall and back down at the folder. "Joe's right. You got screwed. Fortunately for you, I might have some free time I could use to help you out."

"I thought you were jammed. Speaking of which...how did that sexual battery turn out?" Alex asked.

"Pretty much how you'd expect, considering the witness. She had that thousand-yard-crazy-stare. During our interview, she locked onto me and started talking about how vampire snakes were eating her brains. So I looked her dead in the eyes and said, 'You know, Detective Pritchard here is our department expert on the occult.' She said 'Really?' and her focus shifted to Pritchard. I selected zone 5, extended, and escaped. Pritchard was caught like a fly in molasses. I wandered freely around the scene while he tried desperately to disentangle himself from her."

"Well done," Alex grinned. "And nice 'Top Gun' reference".

She pantomimed tipping her hat. He and Deni liked to trade movie references back and forth. He was pretty sure she could recite "The Untouchables" verbatim.

Alex looked back at the map. "So, since we have the proverbial shitload of things to cover in our area, why don't we subdivide our assigned area into three sections. I think that's the only way we can hope to cover all of it in a week."

"A week?" Deni said. "They don't want much, do they? I guess all things are possible to the man who doesn't have to do them."

"I think that's on Chief Tremaine's Coat of Arms. Except it's in Latin. You know, all classy-like."

Deni smiled. "I'll take The Hook. It's a smaller area and I used to work it in patrol, so I'm familiar with it." The Hook was a small peninsula that jutted out into the bay and was home to some of the very-most expensive real estate attached to the financial district.

"Sounds good to me," Joe said. "You wanna start this afternoon or hit it fresh in the morning?"

"Eh, let's start tomorrow," Alex said. "I think we've had enough excitement for one day."

"God, I was hoping you'd say that. It's lasagna night at my house. And my wife makes fresh bread when there's lasagna."

Deni eyed Joe skeptically, "You are right, Joe. It's all her fault. How could you resist that?"

"What am I? A rock? Jeez!" Joe said, looking exasperated.

Alex gathered up the folder and looked at Joe. "Do you want to keep this crap or shall I?"

"Oh, you do it. By all means. Did I mention it's lasagna night?"

"You might have. I'll walk you out, so you don't lose your way. Unless you dropped breadcrumbs on the way in...?"

Alex said as the three of them walked out of the training room.

"No, smartass. I did not drop breadcrumbs on the way in. Besides, considering your department's reputation, they'd probably already been eaten by someone. Tell me, why's your department so fucked up, anyway?"

"We prefer to think of it as a friendly and delightful pastiche of departments." Joe's look of disbelief at that answer caused Alex to chuckle. "OK, basically it's been added on to so much over the years that it kind of resembles Frankenstein's monster. There are rumors of a Minotaur in the lower sections. We occasionally sacrifice a rookie to appease him," Alex said as they opened the door to the stairwell and began to walk down the steps.

"They say that they are planning to build a brand new department in the next couple of years and abandon this one. I don't believe it."

"Yeah. I wouldn't, either. Well, I'll see you guys tomorrow at what? Nine?"

"Works for me. How about you, Deni?"

"Yeah, I'm good. See you, Joe. Say hi to Rebecca for me."

"Will do. See you guys tomorrow," Joe said, opening the door to the parking lot, causing everyone to squint into the afternoon sun.

As the door closed, Deni said, "Got a minute?"

Alex looked around. "Is this a stairwell conversation?" The stairwells were the only places they were sure there were no cameras or mikes.

"Yep. I've been hearing scuttlebutt that you're still in the cross-hairs."

"Even after being cleared?"

"Yeah. Someone upstairs still has a hard-on for you."

"Great. I just choked a guy out in the south lot. Nothing like giving your enemies ammunition. Why don't I just load the gun for 'em, too?"

"Why'd you choke him? Never mind, I'm sure you had a perfectly good reason. I just thought you should know about IA."

"Thanks. Any specifics?"

"Nope. But when I know, you'll know."

"Thanks, Deni," Alex said. "Guess I'll call it a day, too. Go home and switch the trauma plate from the front of my vest to the back".

"That's the spirit, partner," she said, giving him a wink and a punch on the shoulder. "See you tomorrow."

"Yeah. And thanks again," Alex said. He turned and opened the door to the parking lot, letting the heat and light wash over him. It felt purifying.

Chapter 15

When Alex got home, he found a note on the fridge from Eve saying she had a late meeting and wouldn't be home for dinner. She'd already been home in the afternoon, grabbed a snack, and went right back to the campus. He was disappointed at first, then remembered it was Monday night.

Kali night.

Every Monday night, a loosely organized group of Alex's friends gathered on the municipal tennis courts in the north part of the city and practiced Kali, a Filipino martial art that uses sticks, knives, and machetes. The usual practice weapon was a twenty-eight-inch rattan stick that was lightweight and springy on impact so mistakes only resulted in bruises, not broken bones. And there were a lot of mistakes. In actual fights, the sticks were made of hardwoods like *bahi* or ironwood, a wood so dense it won't float. Alex had heard from other practitioners that some old-timers preferred to fight with machetes because the wounds would heal cleanly, but the broken bones suffered from an ironwood strike could be a lifelong and crippling memento of the fight.

Alex brightened up considerably at the thought of hitting his friends with sticks. He had always thought it strange that physical violence created a bond between men, but it seemed to do just that. He looked at the clock, deciding he had enough time to take Khan for a run. He realized he was trying to take his mind off recent events - the shooting, the new assignment, the imminent porking from the department – but physical exertion had always been a panacea for him. It took him out of himself and freed up his mind. He put on a pair of sweats and a t-shirt, laced up his running shoes, and did a few stretches. At this point, Khan was whining at the door and spinning with gyroscopic intensity.

At least the house won't flip over. Alex rubbed Khan's head while he leashed him. They started on their usual route, but he went a different way today, causing Khan to question Alex's mental state and pull in the opposite direction. But, as he was still outside running, Khan was willing to let this transgression pass and soon fell back into a comfortable trot by his master's side. Alex intended to run the power line right-of-way. Its high-tension lines aimed in a straight line toward the back of his house before making a ninety-degree turn southbound. Alex was grateful they didn't pass directly overhead. All the popping and buzzing would have disturbed the peace and serenity of his garden and threatened his sanity.

As he and Khan cleared the treeline, he looked to his left, up the swath of mowed grass under the power lines. It sloped gently upward to a crest about a half-mile away. At the top, he could see a figure in a hoodie scanning the area of his house with binoculars. The man looked toward Alex and Khan, seemed to focus on them, then turned and went back over the crest of the hill.

"Come on, boy," Alex said to Khan, picking up the pace. He wasn't a world-class runner by any means, but he thought he could do a half-mile, even uphill, in four minutes or less. Given what he knew, Alex was only curious. There are lots of reasons someone could be on the ridgeline with binoculars. Birdwatching, maybe. But it made him uneasy that the back of his house was also in the line of sight.

Paranoid much? Well, you know what they say: if you're not paranoid, you don't have enough information.

Alex made it to the crest, out of breath with his legs burning from the strain, in time to see a dark green SUV turn onto a service road and disappear behind a screen of trees. Bending over and putting his hands on his knees, he stopped to catch his breath. He eventually straightened up, pausing for a few more breaths before kicking Khan loose to explore. He walked in small circles with his hands on his hips, still blowing hard.

Probably nothing. I gotta get a grip. "Come on, Khan. Let's go home." He started walking down the right of way to his house with Khan coursing in front of him back and forth through the tall grass, always checking to see if Alex was behind him. *Maybe someone will hit me hard enough in the head tonight that it'll knock some sense into me.*

Chapter 16

On his way to the tennis courts, Alex picked up a friend of his. Lee insisted on a side trip through the drive-thru of a fast-food restaurant. He needed to refuel. Lee was shorter and thinner than Alex but ate enough for two of someone his size.

Alex continued on to the tennis courts after picking up the food, looking at Lee suspiciously. "Really? Food? We're going to be working out in twenty minutes."

Lee didn't even slow down, shoving fries into his mouth in handfuls. "I have a shrew-like metabolism," he said, around the food. "If I stop eating, I'll die."

Lee had introduced Alex to the Filipino martial arts. He'd studied several systems before meeting Alex and they'd become good friends over the last several years working out together. FMA was so different from the Japanese and Okinawan arts that there was a good deal of "unlearning" to do. Footwork was a problem early on. The Filipino footwork was all based on triangles and there weren't any real stances, at least, not like there are in karate.

One day, Lee had had enough. He laid three sticks on the ground in the shape of a triangle with the base facing him.

"OK, I'm going to show you this one last time. When I swing a forehand angle one strike, it travels from my right shoulder diagonally down. You will shift your right foot over to the point of the base of the triangle and bring your left foot back to the apex. I'll then reverse direction and swing an angle two which travels from my left shoulder diagonally downward. You will do the mirror image of what you did for angle one. Those are the only two angles I'll use. If you get hit, it's not my fault. It's yours. It's because you're too slow or you didn't do the footwork right. And remember: hurting is helping."

What followed was thirty minutes of footwork with Lee swinging progressively faster. *I got hit a lot but at the end of that half-hour, I had the footwork down cold. Pain is an excellent teacher.*

They parked at the recreation complex and walked back to the tennis courts, lugging their duffel bags filled with equipment. The courts were green squares enclosed by a twelve-foot high, chain-link fence and illuminated by bright, low-sodium lamps on thirty-foot poles. Occasionally, they were bothered by actual tennis players but, for the most part, they had plenty of room to work out. Several of the regulars were already there and, after the usual exchange of bad jokes, they partnered and worked on *sinawali* to warm up. The pairs of FMA practitioners hit each other's sticks in an almost hypnotic pattern of strikes, each mirroring the other. The sticks were moving in and out, cracking together with rhythmic intensity, weaving a tapestry of motion out of thin air. As they worked the exercises, they honed basic strikes, positions, body mechanics, and footwork.

After *sinawali,* they worked on drills that brought out attributes like speed, power, timing, and sensitivity. The Five Count Drill, Break in, Break Out, Hubud — all flow drills that worked the movements back and forth until they were second nature. Tonight they also worked on *Contra por Contra,* Counter for Counter, where each person blocked whatever attack was thrown at them and then launched their own attack, which was, in turn, blocked and countered...ad infinitum.

Then, as the evening wound to a close, it was time for what they all enjoyed: full-contact fighting. This was a relatively recent development for the group. They used hard, thin Wiffle ball bats cut to size. It took a while to locate bats sturdy enough and several toy stores had badly bent Wiffle bats in their aisles to prove it. Although the bats were very light, they used no protective gear and, when you got hit, it hurt. A lot. Alex noticed one of the guys, Ralph, was putting on street hockey gloves.

"Why are you wearing those?" Alex asked.

Before he could answer, one of the other guys leaned in and said: "'Cause he's a pussy."

"Well, that certainly explains it."

Ralph colored, but continued putting on the gloves.

They fought two at a time with plenty of commentary from the peanut gallery. Alex started with Ralph, the glove wearer. They circled each other warily, throwing an occasional backhand strike that was used like a boxer's jab, to gauge distance and keep your opponent on his toes. The bats were held in the forward hands, constantly moving lest the opponent smack you in the hand and disarm you. Ralph liked to do a lot of twirling or *floretes*. Alex bided his time and, while his opponent was twirling his weapon, Alex lunged in and got in a good forehand shot that bounced off the top of Ralph's head and then hit his forearm, causing the bat to fly from his grasp. Ralph had two choices; close to *mano-mano or corto* range and tie up Alex's weapon, making it a hand-to-hand contest; or to run like Hell for his own stick. Unfortunately, he chose to do both. He started to close with Alex, then thought better of it and ran for his weapon. Immediately, Alex closed the gap and started whacking him across the back and shoulders. It was brutal and cause for general merriment among the onlookers. Afterward, as they watched two other guys fighting, Alex asked him, "Man, what were you thinking?"

Ralph winced and said, "I thought I should close with you but then changed my mind when I saw the bat out of the corner of my eye. It was a tactical error," he grinned.

"Well, at least you didn't get those new gloves ruined," Alex said. "I never hit your hands."

"No. Just everywhere else," Ralph said, wincing.

After an hour of beating the crap out of each other, and because the public park closed at 10 PM, they decided to break and go home. Alex was pleasantly tired and hungry. He decided to swing through a local burger joint to get some dinner after dropping Lee off at his apartment. Eating before working out had never worked out well for him. He learned that lesson as a teenager when he got to the dojo and found it locked. It looked like the class had been canceled. It hadn't.

It had just been delayed. Alex went next door to an ice cream parlor and had a hot fudge sundae. As he was leaving, his sensei caught him and motioned him inside for class. That night, he caught a front kick solidly in the solar plexus, the sundae ending up all over the mat. It seemed to take forever to clean up.

As he went through the line, he looked over in the parking lot and saw what was obviously an unmarked police car — a dark, 4-door Crown Vic with too many antennas. *Probably a Sergeant or Lieutenant. He should go somewhere else to do paperwork. He's too exposed. Oh well, not my circus, not my monkeys.* Alex shrugged and pulled up to get his food. As he pulled away and exited the parking lot, Alex noticed the lieutenant's car did, too. Alex loved to eat while he was driving and was working his way through the hamburger, listening to a story on NPR when he noticed the same unmarked car on his six. Alex checked his speed and he wasn't being followed for that. He was five under the limit. He was driving a department-issued vehicle, so he was pretty sure all his lights worked. He was about halfway home when he finished the last of the burger and decided to see if he was being followed. Alex made a series of random turns, alternating left and rights, but the car stayed with him. *So far, so good. Let's see how much they want to stick to my ass.* He slowed down approaching an intersection, timing a light so the unmarked car following him got caught. Then he made a left turn, in full view of the chase car, down a fairly narrow, brick-paved alleyway. He went halfway down the alley and parked the car, leaving it far enough away from the curb so as to block the whole alley. He got out, ran back to the mouth of the side street, and waited in the shadow of the building's corner. Within a minute, the unmarked car came around the corner at speed, clipping the curb, and was nearly on top of his vehicle before the driver realized his mistake. He screeched to a halt within inches of Alex's bumper.

The driver of the car was looking around, squinting into his rear-view mirror, when Alex tapped on the driver's side window. The driver looked over at Alex and dropped his head forward, slowly shaking it back and forth. After a moment, he reached for the switch on the armrest and rolled the window down. Alex bent over and looked inside to see two guys from Internal Affairs, Howard Reed and Quentin Malloy.

"I keep forgetting. Which one of you guys does Martin Milner play?" Alex asked.

"Oh, that's funny, Alex. We've never heard that joke before," said Reed. He was sitting in the driver's seat, a rueful smile on his face.

"I told you he made us," Malloy said, looking at Reed. Then he looked at Alex. "I told him you made us." It was like watching an old married couple from the fifties. A bad mash-up between the Honeymooners and Adam-12.

"Well, this has been fun guys but I gotta ask: why are you following me?"

Reed and Malloy looked at each other; then Reed looked back at Alex, both shrugging. "We don't know. We're just supposed to follow you and report anything unusual. That's it."

Alex stood in front of the driver's door, thinking, arms crossed, staring at the side of Reed's face. Finally, he decided,

"OK, here's what we're gonna do. I never made you guys and we never had this conversation. Saves you embarrassment and saves me having to deal with it. Sound good?"

The two IA detectives looked at each other and then looked at Alex and nodded in unison.

"Excellent. And, in the future, if you want to follow me, call me on my department phone and I'll tell you where I am. It'll save both of us a lot of time and trouble. Have a nice night, guys."

As Alex walked to his car, Reed rolled up his window. Malloy stared at Reed's profile and said, "Hmmmm....that went well."

Reed turned and looked at him. "Shut the fuck up."

Chapter 17

When he got home, Eve's car was in the driveway and the front porch light was on. Alex got out of the vehicle as the door opened and Khan bounded out of the door to greet him. As he stood up, Khan put his front paws on Alex's chest and licked his face. In this position, the dog was not much shorter than his master. Alex grabbed his neck ruff, pushing him off to one side, and walked to the house. He looked up and saw Eve standing in the doorway with her arms folded.

"I wish you wouldn't let him do that, "she said. "If he does it to me when I get all tubby and off-balance, he's gonna knock me on my ass."

"I wouldn't want that to happen. Of all asses on this planet, yours is my favorite."

"I'm serious. Everything is not a joke," she said, giving him her 'I mean business' look.

"Alright. I will keep him from jumping up. Has he done it to you lately?"

"No. Sometimes he jumps up near me though. It's a little scary. Looks like a whale breaching."

Alex folded her into his arms as her arms encircled his waist. "I won't let anything hurt you or little Alaric," he said.

She pulled back slightly so she could look him in the face, "You don't even know the gender of the child. 'Alaric' is going to be a funny name to hang on a little girl. Besides, don't you think it's bad luck, not to mention a little, well, creepy, to name your child after your dead twin?"

"As long as the baby's healthy. Hey! If it's a girl, how about 'Alarica'? We could call her 'Rica" for short," he said brightly.

"Did you get hit on the head especially hard tonight?" she asked, a look of concern furrowing her brow.

"Not especially hard. Just the usual," he said as they both went inside the house with Khan trailing them.

"Are you hungry?" Eve asked.

"No," Alex said, flopping down on the couch. "I caught a burger on the way home. But that does segue nicely into something I want to tell you about."

"Well, thank God for that. I didn't want to cook anything, anyway," Eve said, as she sat on the couch next to him, her legs folded and her knees tucked under her. "Please. Enthrall me with your tale." She propped her head up with her chin cupped in her palm, her elbow resting on the back of the couch.

Alex smiled, "Well, I was in the drive-thru getting the aforementioned burger when I noticed an unmarked car in the parking lot next to the burger joint. At first, I thought it was just a supervisor doing paperwork or maybe another cop who'd just gotten food and was trying to jam it down his throat before his next call."

"And it was neither of those things?"

"No. No, it was not. When I started back home, I noticed the same car in my rear-view. I did a couple of random turns and they were still behind me, so I set them up and trapped them."

"Who was it?"

"Reed and Malloy. From IA".

"They should split those two up. For their sake."

"I know, right?"

"So, what were they following you for?"

"They said they didn't know. Their orders were to tail me and report if I did anything unusual.

"Do you believe them?".

"I think so. I'm not sure they're smart enough to lie to me and get away with it. Besides, I had them startled and off-balance at the time. I am a little worried about something. IA has been unusually busy lately. They've been doing things like headhunting people's arbitrators, looking for excuses to jam them up."

"Arbitrators?"

"In-car video systems. IA has been going through their data dumps to find policy violations like...oh, not turning on your siren when you activate your overheads. That kind of chickenshit crap. Maybe they've been put on a quota system or something. I don't know."

"How did you leave it?"

"I told them the next time they wanted to follow me; they could just call me on my cell and tell them where I was. Make it easy for them."

"That's my man," Eve said, smiling warmly. "It doesn't sound like there's much you can do about it."

"Probably not. And besides, I think they're relatively harmless," Alex said. " 'Knowing where the trap is. That's the first step in evading it'. Name that book."

"Easy. Dune by Frank Herbert. Your favorite."

"Dang! The perils of being married to an English teacher."

Eve reached down with crossed arms and grabbed the bottom of her blouse. In one motion, her arms raised over her head, peeling it off. She wasn't wearing a bra.

"There are perils...and there are pleasures."

"Yes. Yes, there most certainly are," Alex said, smiling and staring raptly at her breasts

Khan, who had been lying on the rug in front of the couch, sat up, looked from Alex to Eve and back again, and then retreated to his kennel.

They both laughed. "I swear he's human," Alex said. "If he had thumbs, he'd close and lock it."

Eve grabbed Alex's head in both hands and turned his face toward hers. "Enough about the dog mister, there's me to attend to."

"Oh, yes Ma'am," Alex said. "With pleasure."

*   *   *

Later, as he lay in bed in the twilight between sleep and wakefulness, it occurred to Alex he hadn't told Eve about the guy on the ridgeline with the binoculars. He could hear her softly snoring beside him. *Ah well, wasn't important, anyway.* Then sleep claimed him.

Chapter 18

When the alarm went off the next morning, Alex swung his legs over the edge of the bed, sitting up and hitting the top of the clock to silence it. He was instantly awake. There was no dozing or hitting the snooze button. He had been this way all his life. Eve, however, rolled over, clutching the covers under her chin as she fell back asleep. Alex smiled. She relied on him to be her snooze button. Khan came over to him, put his head on the edge of the bed against his thigh, and looked up at him while his tail whacked the nightstand vigorously.

Alex scratched Khan behind the ears and said, "Come on, boy. Let's go out." Khan's ears perked up as he headed for the bedroom door, pausing at the doorway to see if Alex was following. Alex grabbed his shorts off the dresser and put them on as he walked to the door. Khan pranced down the hall toward the door to the side yard, his nails clicking on the floor. As Alex let Khan out, he looked at the sun barely cresting the horizon. He took a moment to smell the clear morning air and listen to birdsong. The dew was still on the grass. This was his favorite time of day. Everything seemed new. Possibilities were endless. Many people preferred sunsets, but they had always struck him as melancholy affairs, a brilliant, beautiful funeral for the dying day. Alex watched Khan run through the yard for a minute and then closed the door to attend to his husbandly duties which, in the morning, included the starting of the sacred coffee maker.

Alex checked the level of the water, popped in a coffee pod, and started the machine. For his part, he got two tea bags, threw them in a cup of water, and put it in the microwave. Although if forced to, he would drink coffee at work, he vastly preferred tea It was the consequence of having been partially raised by his Canadian grandmother. His grandfather thought the U.S. was too slow getting into World War One, so he went north and joined the Canadian Expeditionary Force. After losing a leg in the trenches, he convalesced in a Canadian hospital where Alex's grandmother was a nurse's aide. Either Alex's grandfather was gifted with a silver tongue or it was winter in Canada but, either way, he talked Alex's grandmother into fleeing the frozen climes of the great white north for sunny, sub-tropical Florida. Alex loved that story. Until Alex had learned to drink coffee, he had taken endless shit from his zone partners on the midnight shift for his unmanly choice of beverage.

Alex sliced two bagels, put them in the toaster, and went in to wake his wife. He circled to her side of the bed and kissed her gently on the forehead. Her response was to furrow her brow, frown, and snuggle deeper into the covers.

"It's time to get up, baby," Alex whispered. Eve murmured something that sounded both angry and petulant and scrunched her face up. Alex grabbed the covers and slowly pulled them off. Eve didn't give up without a fight for the covers, but it was a losing battle.

One eye popped open, regarding him with a baleful glare. "Is the coffee ready?" she asked.

"It will be by the time you get out there. Bagels are in the toaster."

"OK. I'm up," she said as she swung her legs out of the bed and stood up as Alex stepped back to give her room. Alex stepped forward to hug her briefly and kiss her.

"I love you," he said.

"I love you more," she answered.

"Not possible," he said. It was the same every morning.

Eve put on a robe as Alex returned to the kitchen to complete breakfast, stopping to let Khan in on the way. He prepared his tea with milk and sugar then took the hot bagels out of the toaster and smeared both with strawberry cream cheese. Eve was particular about her coffee and he had learned long ago it was best to just wait for her. He moved the food and his tea to the dining room table and sat down. The table was a single massive block of wood hewn into a piece of furniture sometime around the turn of the last century. The chairs dated from the same time and were handmade from the same dark wood. Not a single nail was used in their manufacture. They weren't fancy, but they were elegant in their simplicity. Alex had found the set in a second-hand store, buying them on the spot. Eve came out, made her coffee, and then joined him. Khan curled up at Eve's feet.

"Have you noticed how protective Khan has been of you since you've been pregnant? It's like he knows."

Eve took her first sip of coffee and groaned slightly, "Nectar of the gods. How do you think he'll react to the addition to our family?"

"He'll be curious at first. Then, once he accepts little Alaric into the family, he will love him as much as he does us. They'll be BFFs."

Eve demurred. Khan was her first experience with a large dog or as Alex referred to him, "a normal-sized dog."

"I hope so," she said. "So what's on your agenda today, FBI Guy?"

"I can't tell you. It's top secret. It's just between us FBI Guys."

"Ok, smartass, now really."

Alex sighed. "Joe and I are going to scout likely targets today and work up responses. Oh, and Deni's going to help some."

"Well, that sounds exciting and rewarding. I'll be delving into the mysteries of Shakespeare and Chaucer today to the delight, amusement, and edification of my captive college students."

"I should read more Shakespeare."

"Oh, it's not just you. Everyone should."

"I'll see if I can work that into my spare time. Speaking of spare time, I'm teaching a class tonight for sensei. He has a colonoscopy in the morning, so this evening he will be... indisposed, shall we say?"

"You could say that. You could also say he'll be shitting his brains out."

"You know Mrs. Dorn, you shock me with your use of vulgarities. It is unseemly for a college professor."

"You can go easy on the professor stuff. So I take it we'll be dining separately again tonight?"

"It appears so. We need to be less busy."

"'We' probably should have thought of that before 'we' got me pregnant."

"True," Alex said as he got up and collected his dishes. He always ate faster than Eve. "I have to go dress up in my FBI Guy suit now." He leaned over, kissing her.

"Ok, baby. Be careful today."

"Always. Alaric needs a daddy."

Alex walked out as Eve attempted a retort with a mouthful of bagel. *Timing is everything.*

Chapter 19

Alex got into the office early and went through some paperwork on his desk. There was an email from Lt. Blakely wanting an update on his activities with the FBI, so he spent twenty minutes doing that. By the time he finished, Deni was walking into the office.

"'Sup, Alex?" Deni said. "Any word from the IA rats concerning their interest in you?"

"Funny you should mention that," Alex said, looking around to ensure they were alone. "I caught Reed and Malloy tailing me last night. We had a short conversation and they pleaded ignorance as to why they were assigned to shadow me."

"And no one got an ass-kickin'? What? Were you in a good mood or just tired?"

"A little of both but, mainly, it's better the devil you know than the one you don't. I know these guys, their capabilities, and how they work. If I burned them, IA would simply assign someone else. Hell, maybe someone from outside the department that I don't know. That could be a bigger problem."

Deni stroked her chin, regarding him with mock seriousness, "Well played, sir, well played."

The phone on Alex's desk went off, the red interdepartmental light blinking angrily. Alex hit the button, putting it on speaker.

"Detective Dorn."

"Good morning, Detective," said a voice Alex didn't recognize at first. "This is Officer Carstairs on the front desk. There's a Detective Esposito here to see you?"

"Hey, Carstairs! How's the arm?" Alex asked.

"Getting better, sir. Thanks for asking. I never got a chance to thank you for...you know...the shooting."

"I accept checks, money orders, and credit cards. Or you could just walk Joe back to Investigations so that I don't have to move my fat ass."

"Yes, sir. We're on our way." The line went dark.

"Sir? Wow. You must be more impressive than I thought," Deni said.

"I am more impressive than you can possibly imagine," Alex said. Deni rolled her eyes.

A few minutes later, Carstairs came in with Esposito.

"Hey Joe," Alex greeted Esposito. "Carstairs, how long you gonna be stuck on the front desk?"

"For a while, sir," Carstairs replied, holding up his arm with the cast on it. "Still got this on. Then it's physical therapy. Unfortunately, it's my gun hand. They're thinking nine months to a year." Carstair's mouth twisted into a rueful smile.

"Oh, I wouldn't worry about it. On the front desk, that time will fly by. Just kidding."

Carstairs smiled at the shared joke, "I've been told. And speaking of which, I'd better get back. I'm sure there's a lost property call there with my name on it."

As Carstairs left Investigations, Joe looked at Alex. "That the kid whose life you saved in the supermarket?" he asked.

"Yeah. Right place, right time," Alex answered.

"I'm thinking you could get your house painted for free," Joe said, with a shrewd, speculating look on his face.

"Not with that arm," Alex said as he looked around. "So, shall we get to the matter at hand?"

"Fine," Joe said, sounding wounded. "Can I at least get a cup of coffee?"

"Sure," Alex turned. "Deni, you want a cup?"

"OK," she said. "Why don't I meet you guys in the squad room. Read-off's over and we could use their map. Save us a trip upstairs and possible exposure to command staff personnel."

"Darlin', you had me at 'stairs,'" Joe said, hitching his belt up under his belly.

Alex and Joe met Deni in the squad room where she was standing in front of a map of the city with the zones outlined in magic marker.

"Still want to go with the same plan?" she asked as they walked up behind her. Alex handed her a cup of coffee.

"Yeah. You're gonna work The Hook while Joe and I split the rest of the district. Unless either of you has a better idea or a modification?"

Both Joe and Deni shook their heads.

"I need to be done by five. Anyone else have any obligations?"

Deni piped up, "I'm just working this until lunch because, unlike you guys, I have an actual job to do."

Joe turned to Alex. "And what do you have, Romeo? A hot date?"

"I wish. No, I obligated myself to teach the classes at my karate school." Alex didn't elaborate on the reason.

"That stuff ever come in useful on the job?" Joe asked.

"Yeah, but probably not the way you imagine," Alex said, thinking for a moment. "I'd say its greatest impact has been in my attitude and my mental state during crisis situations. You know how a lot of cops get into trouble either over-reacting and beating the crap out of someone or under-reacting and getting their asses kicked?"

Joe nodded.

"The mental side of karate has changed me over the years so that, when I'm faced with a clutch scenario, I do something I call 'drop into the pocket'. And that's just my term. I lower my center of gravity, calm my breathing, and center myself. In Japanese, it's called *fudoshin*, 'immovable mind', and it's saved my ass more than once. Funakoshi wrote *Dojo nomino karate te omou na* – 'Don't think karate is only in the dojo.' It was one of his dojo precepts. If I never do another *kata,* never throw another punch or kick, karate will continue to impact my life for as long as I live." Alex said, realizing he was lecturing but couldn't help it.

"Well, that's deep, Grasshopper," Joe said as Deni snorted a laugh. "But have you ever *used* it?"

"You mean other than yesterday?"

Joe nodded.

Alex thought for a moment, "Okay, I've got an example. I was out on patrol, I think my second year, and had a call of two drunks hanging out around an all-night Stop-n-Rob. I saw these two guys propped up against the wall and stopped my cruiser so they were right in the headlights. When I approached, one guy comes off the wall and starts doing some crazy, fake, kung-fu routine, flailing his arms around and making weird noises. I waited, picked my shot, and dropped him with a reverse punch to the solar plexus. He went down like a ton of crap. Then the other guy comes off the wall and I turn to face him as the secondary threat. But he keeps his hands in his pockets and semi-staggers over to where his friend is lying on the ground in a fetal position, leans over, and says, 'See? I told you that karate shit wouldn't work'."

Joe guffawed; Deni smiled. She'd heard it before. After allowing Joe a few moments to recover, she said, "Let's get a move on. How about we use TAC Channel One as our common frequency?"

Joe pulled his radio out from the clip carrier on his left side and looked at the top of it. "That's on bank three?" he asked.

"Yep," Alex said as he and Deni were both adjusting their radios. "He lifted the radio to his mouth. Radio check."

He could hear his voice come out of both Deni and Joe's radios. "Delta two-eight to dispatch, TAC Channel One."

"Go ahead, Delta twenty-eight," came the reply.

"Myself, Delta Five Nine, and Detective Esposito from Hampstead PD will be on this channel until further notice. Mark our status as a special detail."

"Copy that, Delta Twenty-Eight. The channel is yours."

"All set, then?" Alex asked. Both Joe and Deni nodded. "Good. Joe, why don't you ride with me? Deni's gonna bail about noon. She'll need her own ride."

Joe thought for a moment. "Sounds good to me. I've always enjoyed being chauffeured. Besides, it's your city. You know it better than I do."

"Aaaalllrighty then, let's saddle up," Alex said as he headed for the doorway, Deni and Joe in tow. They met Pritchard coming in as they were going out.

"Where you guys headed?' he asked.

"Secret squirrel stuff," Deni said. "We could tell you but then...".

"You'd have to kill me," Pritchard finished the old joke. "Hey, you don't wanna tell me, don't." He looked like he was going to pout.

Alex inserted himself into the exchange. "We'll be downtown in the financial district doing glorified security surveys for the Feds, Mike. We'll be on TAC-1 if you need us."

On most days he swore he used his hostage negotiation skills more in the department than outside it. Before he got into Investigations, he was on the midnight shift where intoxicated people always seemed to take themselves or someone else hostage. As the only negotiator on Mids, Alex always got the call. He was good at talking people out, not in small measure due to his ability to backtrack any mistakes he might make in the negotiation. Unfortunately for the assault team guys, many of whom were on days or afternoons, he usually talked the suspect out about the time they were at the department at 0300. They'd be suiting up in their SWAT gear, testosterone pouring from their ears and puddling around their ankles when they got the call-off. The third-straight time it happened, the assault team leader had threatened to shoot Alex himself. Alex told him he was suffering from "blue trigger finger" caused by "Assaultus Interruptus." The response was epic. The assault team leader had been a Chief Petty Officer and Navy Seal before beginning his second career in law enforcement. After a time, Alex relaxed and began to admire the skill at which he wielded profanity. Really, he was an artist.

"Got it. Thanks," Pritchard turned around and walked into the office.

Deni glanced at him sideways as they walked down the hallway, "Really, Alex, did you have to mollify the big, dumb bastard?"

Alex sighed, "Do you ever walk by a big pile of shit and NOT step in it, Deni?'

"Sure, but it's been a while. Besides, you haven't had to work with that misogynistic idiot like I have."

"True. You know...you could always kick a complaint up to IA about his behavior."

"That's not how I roll, Alex. You know that," she said, looking vaguely insulted. "If it gets bad enough, I'll just de-nut him myself."

"Good luck finding 'em. They're probably hiding under his micro-penis."

Deni laughed, "True. Kinda gross, but true."

Joe looked from Alex to Deni, "I'll say this. It's always entertaining here."

Alex opened the door, and they emerged into the already hot parking lot. Deni headed one way, Joe and Alex the other.

"See you guys at lunch," she called over her shoulder.

Chapter 20

Alex and Joe climbed into the Crown Vic and drove toward the financial district. Alex was not as familiar with downtown as he might have been. He had always worked the poorer sections of the city and the bar areas. He enjoyed staying busy and had always felt he could do more good in those areas than in the more affluent portions of the city. Besides, rich, entitled people irritated him. The drive to the downtown area took about ten minutes. Joe settled in on the passenger's side watching the scenery.

"I like coming to the big city," Joe said. "Makes me feel like the country mouse."

"Or walrus," Alex said.

"Watch it, Asshopper."

"Shhhh! I need to keep that porn career on the DL, Joe."

"OK, far be it from me to stand between a man and his paycheck. How long 'till we get there?"

"What are you? Twelve? We'll get there when we get there. Don't make me stop this car."

Joe grunted and sunk further into the seat. The scenery changed gradually from lower to upper-middle class and then to shopping areas — less pedestrian traffic and more parking lots. The financial district announced itself suddenly, the architecture going vertical in an instant, a clear warning expectations had changed. Steel-and-glass structures with marble facades surrounded them. The cars on the street showed a decided preference for the high-end; Lexus, Mercedes, and the occasional Lamborghini comprised much of the traffic. One of Alex's friends in the department who worked in this area regularly used to say that driving a Chevy here was probable cause for a stop.

Joe roused himself, forcing his body into an upright posture. "So, how we working this, chief?"

"Well, I figured you'd take the car and work south and I'll hoof it and work north."

"God bless you, son. Me and my poor, abused feet are forever in your debt."

Alex pulled into a parking area and popped the trunk. He got out and went to the back of the car, meeting Joe there. He got a messenger bag out, looking around before he took the H&K MP-5 out of it and stowed it in the bottom of the trunk. He got out a metallic clipboard and some paperwork and loaded up the bag. He turned to Joe and handed him the keys, "Don't get jacked. I don't want to have to explain losing that MP-5."

"What? Around here? No one's going strapped in this neighborhood. They might steal your retirement here but it will all be perfectly legal and backed with the approval of the bank's lawyers."

"Sadly true. Sooooo… these two lawyers were walking down the street and a beautiful girl walks past them. One lawyer looks at the other and says, "I'd sure like to fuck her". The other one looks puzzled and says, "Really? Fuck her out of what?"

Joe grinned. It was on. "You know what's black and white and looks good on a lawyer? A pit bull."

Alex's turn, "What's the difference between a lawyer and a prostitute? When you die, a prostitute will stop fucking you."

Joe's turn, "What happens to a lawyer when he takes Viagra? He gets taller."

Alex laughed at the last joke. "I hadn't heard that one before. OK, enough. I'll be heading north. Meet me back here at noon, which will give us…" Alex looked at his watch, "Two hours."

"Roger that," Joe said, with a sloppy half-salute, "See you then."

Alex threw the bag over one shoulder and started walking north. He passed by three buildings before stopping in front of the impressive marble edifice bearing the name and logo of Murman Investment Banking and Financial Services. He leaned back, looking at the building looming over him. *This looks promising.*

He pushed through the old-fashioned revolving door and was immediately relieved by the cooler air on the other side. He took a moment, luxuriating in the air conditioning, feeling the sweat on his back dry, while he looked around. The lobby was done in black marble with lighter veins running through it. The floors, the walls…even the security desk from which the armed guard was regarding him with narrowed, suspicious eyes was marble. Alex walked directly toward the desk, the guard watching him the entire way.

Alex smiled and extended his hand to the guard who appraised him openly. He was about six feet tall, muscular with a thick neck and broad shoulders. His carriage was ramrod straight. *Ex-military,* Alex thought. He did not offer to shake hands.

"Can I help you, sir?" he asked. His name tag said, C. Jenkins.

"I hope so. I'm Detective Dorn, BCPD," Alex said, as he reached into his back pocket and produced his credentials. "I'd like to speak to the chief security officer."

At the production of his badge and ID, the guard's demeanor changed. He relaxed, the tension easing out of his shoulders.

"That would be Mr. Petrelli. I'll see if he's in," the guard said, picking up the phone and punching a button.

Alex turned to look at the entrances from the guard's perspective, noticing that he had good lines of sight on all approaches. Behind him, he heard the guard.

"Hello, Angela? Is Mr. Petrelli in? There's a detective from BCPD here to see him." There was a pause. "OK, I'll send him up."

Alex turned back around to the guard.

"If you'll take the elevator to the sixth floor, detective, Mr. Petrelli's assistant, Angela, will meet you there."

"Ok, Thanks, man," Alex said and extended his hand again. The guard shook it with a smile.

"I hope you weren't offended when I didn't shake hands at the beginning there," the guard said.

"Not at all. You didn't know who I was. Caution is always a good thing in this business. Ex-military?" Alex asked.

"Four years Marine Corps, sir."

"It shows. Thanks again."

"You're welcome, sir."

Alex smiled to himself as he walked to the elevators. The guard was standing a little taller now. It took so little to spread good will he wondered why people didn't do it more often. He got into the elevator and pushed the button for the sixth floor. He was alone in the car. Well, kind of alone. There was a camera installed in the ceiling he was sure was being viewed by the guard at the desk. The elevator doors opened and a short, woman in a severe, no-nonsense black dress and wearing a very prim, plastic smile greeted Alex.

"Detective? I'm Angela, Mr. Petrelli's assistant. If you'll please follow me?" she said and turned without waiting for a reply.

"Could you give me some idea what this is about, detective?" she said, over her shoulder. "Mr. Petrelli is just ending a teleconference and has somewhat limited free time on his schedule today."

"I'm here to discuss your security. It shouldn't take too much time," Alex answered.

Angela stopped at a door and motioned Alex through. "Well then, your wait shouldn't be long. Mr. Petrelli will be with you shortly," she said as she closed the door. Alex could hear her heels tapping down the hall as she left. Alex found himself in a small waiting room with comfortable seats along two walls, a door, and a series of plaques on the other two. He glanced over the plaques; they seemed to extol the virtues of Murman Financial in general and Mr. Petrelli in particular. He was at the end of the wall when he heard the door open behind him and a deep baritone voice spoke.

"Ah, yes. The wall of shame. Every time I feel bad about myself, I just walk in here. Or go to Walmart. Have you seen that website, People of Walmart?"

Alex turned and saw a trim, middle-aged man about his height, with a dark blue pin striped suit. His hair was dark and thinning and his mouth was famed by a goatee. He wore steel-rimmed glasses.

He reached out his right hand. "Hi. I'm Dennis Petrelli."

Alex shook his hand. Petrelli had a firmer grip than he would have thought for an office worker. "Detective Dorn, BCPD. And yes, I've seen the website. I kinda think that people dress up like that on purpose now just to be on the internet."

"No one ever went broke underestimating the intelligence of the American public. That was H. L. Mencken; most people think it was P. T. Barnum. Come into my office and tell me how I can help you today."

Alex stepped into a well-appointed office dominated by a huge mahogany desk with two chairs in front of it. Petrelli stepped behind the desk. "Please, have a seat," he said, indicating the chairs in front of the desk with a wave of his hand.

Alex sank into the leather executive seat and regarded Petrelli. "I'm here to discuss your security with you but, first of all, let me say I applaud and appreciate you hiring veterans.".

"Claude? He's a good troop. He was one of my men during the invasion of Iraq. Solid as they come."

"So you haven't always been a desk jockey?" Alex asked.

"Oh, God, no. But I have to admit; this is easier than humping a ruck in the sandbox in full battle rattle. Pays a helluva lot more, too."

"I bet. So, could you tell me about your security here at Murman?"

"First, let me ask you why is the BCPD interested in such things? We've been here for years. Why now?"

"Fair question. I'm attached to the FBI right now and we're looking at the security of multiple businesses in the financial sector."

"Does this have anything to do with a series of places like Murman Financial that have been hit in the last year or so?"

Alex paused, mildly surprised, "Yes, it does. You seem well informed."

"News travels fast in the upper echelons of the security biz. I've known about this for six months. The FBI is just now getting to it?"

"They're spread a little thin right now. Which is why I'm here. I'm a local resource they're using to try to get ahead of this thing. Whatever it is. The U. S. Marshals do the same thing with fugitive sweeps. Using locals enhances their operational capabilities. A force multiplier."

Petrelli nodded, "Sounds about right. So...we here at Murman have a state-of-the-art security system that begins with, as you have seen, our personnel assets. Our security staff are all veterans who are qualified experts with their weapons and are certified in Taser technology as well as OC spray. And if it came down to physically handling someone...well, you've seen Claude."

"I'm sure he's more than capable".

"Our CISO is top-notch..."

"CISO?", Alex asked.

"Chief Information Security Officer. Jan Tomlinson. She makes Anonymous quake with fear. Just kidding, but she is tops in the field."

"Do you anticipate cyber-attacks?"

"Always. Information is, frankly, the thing we guard most here. Oh, we have money and a vault because we are, after all, a bank. But the most valuable stuff we have is information. If you don't believe information is more important than money, just ask one of the people who got their information exposed when Ashley Madison got hacked. That had to be a nightmare for a lot of folks."

"I see your point. Information is power. And power and wealth have a very close relationship. So how do you guard the data?"

"Without getting into the particulars, we have a system that allows card holders access with redundant biometric scans – fingerprints and retinal patterns – with multiple Chinese Walls as mandated by the Financial Services Authority."

"You're losing me. What are Chinese Walls?"

"The term comes from the Great Wall of China. A little bit more than eighty years ago, the government mandated that the people who make investment decisions should forever be separated from people who have access to undisclosed material information that might influence the decision-making process. This does not always work as advertised, hence the term 'insider trading.' In the old days, that meant physically separating people. These days, it means separating their access to data."

"Makes sense. So we've covered personnel and cyberspace. What is your physical access control like? How many entrances and exits do you have?"

"There is access through the front, the way you came in. And there's a back entrance that's seldom used by anyone but employees. There is a third access point that runs down a narrow alley and hits another alley running between this building and the one next to it at right angles. That would be the alley joining the two streets that face the front and back of the building. This is a confidential entrance we use for more high-profile customers."

"Okay, what sort of automated systems do you have in place?"

We have the usual – pressure plates, infra-red electric eyes, conventional motion detectors, etc... Now we have the newest thing out there. A tomographic motion alarm."

"I'm not familiar with that term either. Starting to feel a little slow here."

Petrelli laughed, "No need to feel that way. It's brand new. The sensors are mounted inside the walls. They send out radio waves the other sensors pick up. Anything that comes into that mesh-like field sets off the alarm. Like a rock dropped into a still pond. It's foolproof."

Alex smiled wryly, "And they said the Titanic was unsinkable."

"True. But we've tried every which way to defeat it. We even hired expert safe-crackers. No one even got close."

"Anything beyond that?"

"Everything is monitored with HD video 24/7. And our vault is a Mosler. Doesn't get any better than that. You know, when the *Enola Gay* dropped the bomb on Hiroshima, the Teikoku Bank was three hundred feet from Ground Zero. They had a Mosler vault. Of course, the bank ceased to exist but the money and documents inside the vault? Not a scratch. The Mosler company used it for years in their advertising until we became friends with Japan and they thought it was a little, you know, insensitive."

"Yeeaahhh...I can see that," Alex said. "Anything else?"

"No. I think that's about it. Oh, one more thing. If the alarm is activated, gates made of cold-rolled steel drop into place in multiple locations, effectively trapping the would-be robber."

"That would be great. Do our job for us."

"I think that's the extent of it. If that will be all then, Detective Dorn?" Petrelli stood up and started around the desk.

"I believe so. Thank you for your time and the information," Alex said as he stood up and shook hands with Petrelli.

"Glad to be of help. Angela will see you out."

Chapter 21

Alex nodded at Claude on the way out, receiving a smile and wave in return. As he got out on the street, he checked his watch, finding he had about an hour until lunch. He swallowed, cleared his throat, and realized that he was parched after the talk with Petrelli. He looked up and down the street for someplace he could get a soda without paying an arm and a leg for it. Halfway up the block on the other side of the street, he saw a little news stand that looked like it might sell diet sodas. Alex jaywalked, hoping the pricks from Traffic Safety weren't working pedestrians today. He sprinted across the four lanes of traffic without becoming part of the front end of a luxury vehicle and pulled up at the newsstand.

The front was open and Alex went inside, passing a heavyset man at the register who had his back turned, stocking cigarettes. The inside of the shop was thick with the smell of paper and pipe tobacco He made his way to the area behind the magazine racks and found the soft drink coolers. Alex opened one of the doors, appreciating the wash of cold air before selecting a Coke Zero. He got in line behind two people and waited his turn. As he got up to the register, the owner looked at him with surprise and said, in a thick Brooklyn accent, "Hey! What are you? A quick-change artist?"

Alex was taken aback, "What are you talking about?"

The man behind the cash register began to look annoyed, "You're going to tell me you weren't in here fifteen minutes ago wearing a green shirt and buyin' a copy of one o' them karate magazines?"

Now Alex was more confused because that was something he might do. "I'm telling you that I just came here from across the street and I've never been in here before in my life."

"Hey, I don't forget a face, pal. That was you! What are you trying to pull?" he said, stabbing at Alex with a big, meaty forefinger and turning red in the face.

The situation was spinning out of control. He pulled aside his coat to show his gold badge and gun. "I'm not trying to pull anything here. Why don't you tell me what happened?"

The sight of the badge had a calming effect. "Just like I said; you was in here about fifteen minutes ago and bought a karate magazine. Black Belt, I think. Yeah, that was it. Then you said, uh, 'have a nice day' or somethin' and walked out. Come to think of it. Your hair was longer. The fuck. What were you wearin'? A wig?."

"Look, I don't know what to tell you. Maybe everyone has a double. Can I just get this drink?" Alex asked, handing over two dollars.

"Yeah. Sure," he took the money automatically and handed back the change. "He sure did look like you, though. I mean *exactly* like you."

"Which way did this guy who looked so much like me go when he left?"

"Umm, pretty sure he went left. North. Toward the park."

"Great. Thanks for the drink."

"Sure. No problem. Hey, you catch up to him, you'll see I'm right. You two look like freakin' twins."

Alex frowned a little at the mention of twins as he left the store. He stopped for a moment and considered his options. *Fuck it, might as well go look for my twin*

He started toward the park, scanning both sides of the street as he walked. He took his time as his supposed double had no idea Alex was trying to find him and so had no reason to hurry or conceal himself. He stopped at each store to give it at least a cursory glance through the window, fully aware there was a fine line between missing him along the way and letting him get so far ahead that he loses him. Alex considered calling Joe or Deni but, really, what did he have? A guy who looks like him, in the opinion of a newsstand owner? Hardly probable cause. Besides, this felt personal. *Solo it is.*

Alex worried his double might have crossed the street and gone into one of the other stores but then, further up the block, he saw a cop from the Traffic Safety Unit writing someone a ticket for jaywalking. *Nothing if not predictable. Odds are he stayed on this side of the street with the traffic Nazis out in force* He continued up his side, approaching Washington Park, a green space in the middle of the concrete jungle that was downtown. It was about two blocks by two blocks and developers had been salivating over it for years. Thus far, the city fathers and the environmentalists who hectored them constantly had kept it out of their greedy clutches.

As he crossed the last street separating him from the park, Alex looked both ways, deciding the park was his best bet. He thought maybe his "twin" would like to read his new copy of Black Belt in the shade of a spreading granddaddy oak. It sounded like something he would do, anyway. He cut through the center of the park, looking both ways, checking each person for even a faint resemblance to him. He passed a small amphitheater on his left when he glimpsed a flash of green to his right as it disappeared behind a large sign announcing some kind of construction. Alex picked up speed, coming around the other side of the sign, only to nearly run over a woman in a green blouse pushing a baby stroller. She looked up, startled, and Alex, caught in mid-stride, side-stepped her, muttering an apology as he moved past.

Asshole! Rookie mistake! Focus!

He stopped, taking stock of his surroundings. After a moment, he went back to the point of departure from his path through the park and continued from there. He took up the search again, scanning in both directions, evaluating each person and rejecting them all out of hand. Shortly, he reached the other end of the park and paused, looking back. He had cut a more or less diagonal path through it. He should have been able to see anyone matching his description in the park along that route unless he missed them through some fluke or bad timing. He thought about continuing the search along his original path but the trail was rapidly getting colder and the rule of thumb was: the further you get from the point of origin, the less likely you are to find the suspect. At least, with no definite path. Alex looked at his watch. *11:20. Not that much time left before our meet-up for lunch.*

In the end, lunch was the deciding factor and Alex started back through the park. As he passed the amphitheater he detoured to look behind it. Alex walked around the building and came face-to-face with his absolute twin in a green shirt and jeans, sitting with his back to an oak tree, reading a magazine. Although the news stand owner had warned him about the close resemblance, Alex was completely unprepared for the reality. He came to a stop, astonished, with his mouth hanging open for a couple of seconds before it began, of its own accord, to form the word, "Wha...?".

Alex's double was under no such spell. He came to his feet in one smooth, fluid motion, sprinting away from Alex at top speed. Alex slung the messenger bag behind him and started after his doppelganger, but the bastard had a head start and at least a small advantage in that he was in jeans and a shirt and not wearing a coat and tie and carrying a messenger bag. Not to mention the sidearm, spare clip, and radio. Fortunately, Alex was wearing soft-soled leather shoes as opposed to the hard leather-soled shoes that many in Investigations favored. His twin was slowly pulling away from him, heading toward the Washington Bridge. Alex thought about his radio but still didn't want outside interference. Or other cops to witness his stupidity if this turned out to be nothing more than some nervous guy that looked like him.

As Alex made the foot of the bridge, he saw his twin was halfway to the center, passing stationary cars at a dead sprint. Alex looked to his left and saw a large ship cutting through the channel, aiming for the bridge. The bridge tender had already dropped the barriers and was raising the bridge. The ship's horn cut through the air with a deafening blast. Alex could see the metal lattice portion of the bridge beginning to rise and his quarry running right at it. Alex could feel his thighs and calves burning now as he started up the arched portion of the bridge, trying to put on a little extra speed, his breathing coming in ragged gasps as his mark reached the drawbridge. He started up it, slowing, showing the effort it cost him with each step, reaching the top just as Alex reached the bottom. His double jumped across the gap between the opposing sides of the bridge, catching the edge of the other side on his midsection. He swung his legs over the bridge until he was lying on it and hanging onto the edge, with only his face over the top, looking back toward Alex.

Alex finished his uphill sprint and made a last, desperate leap, catching the edge on his side and pulling himself up until he could see over. Across the widening gap, he stared at his twin, both of them breathing hard. Alex was still astounded. There was no difference in their faces. Hair length was the only thing that distinguished them.

His twin regarded him across the gap and smiled. Between gasps, he said, "So, how's *your* day going so far?"

Alex stared back, "Who the fuck *are* you?"

"Who do I look like?"

The ship's horn blew again.

Alex's twin looked down. "Well, gotta go. I'll be in touch."

"Wait!" Alex yelled, but it was too late. His twin slid out of sight. Alex let go of the edge and slid down to the base of the nearly vertical span, stumbling backward at the bottom, almost going ass-over-teakettle. Running back to the bridge tender's kiosk, he yanked on the locked door and then banged on the window.

"Lower the bridge!" he yelled.

The bridge tender was not amused. "Fuck off, asshole, before I call the cops."

Alex took his wallet out and smashed it against the window, badge first. "Just do it!" he screamed.

The tender recoiled from the glass, his eyes as big as saucers, "I can't! See the superstructure on that ship? It would cost millions in damage if I lowered the bridge. You gonna pay for that? The city gonna pay for that? And there's another ship lined up right behind this one. They can't just stop on a dime, ya know. That bridge is staying up for at least five more minutes."

Alex stared at the bridge tender, seething. He slowly realized there was nothing more he could do and, casting one last look at the raised bridge, started walking toward land, ignoring the puzzled stares of motorists along the way. The entire time he walked to the rendezvous point his brain spun in circles. He couldn't find a reasonable explanation for what he had seen. No matter what scenario he came up with, he wasn't satisfied. He was still trying to work things out when he saw Joe standing outside his car.

"Hey, you're ten minutes late and you look like shit," Joe said.

Alex snatched the keys out of Joe's hand, "I'm not gonna talk about it."

Chapter 22

Alex always kept a spare shirt and pants in his trunk, neatly pressed and in a box. He did this in case he got his clothes dirty in the field. Usually, if he had some idea things were going to be on the active side, he'd wear BDU pants and a polo shirt. Alex had only planned on being in people's offices today, conversing in air-conditioned environments, not running pell-mell through downtown, and trying to scale a raising drawbridge. He thought his only problem would be remaining awake during their security presentations. Instead, he ended up chasing himself. Literally.

He opened the trunk and got out the spare clothes. He took his coat off, threw it in the trunk, and then stripped off his shirt. A group of college-age girls went past at that moment, one of them yelled, "Ooh, Baby".

"I wish they'd stop doing that to me," Joe said. "It's annoying. I'm more than just a pretty face."

Alex laughed convulsively. He put his hands on his knees and belly laughed, shaking his head from side to side, releasing the tension that had built up inside him. He was in a sour mood and Joe's comment was just what he needed to put it in perspective.

"Hey, it's not *that* funny," Joe said, putting on a hurt face.

Alex laughed harder. When he straightened up, he wiped a tear from his eye. "Thanks, I needed that."

"That's what she said."

Alex grinned and put on his new shirt, buttoning it up.

"You're not going to change your pants out here too, are you?" Joe asked.

"Nah, I'll save it for wherever we eat. Speaking of which..." Alex picked up his cell phone and hit a number. Deni picked up immediately.

"Thank God. I'm starving here. Where do you guys wanna eat?" the voice on the other end sounded hungry and annoyed.

"Not around here. Too pricey. Let's hit the Mexican place on third."

"Got it. Enroute." The line went dead.

"Mexican? In this town? You sure like to live dangerously," Joe said, hitching up his belt. "Your funeral, compadre."

Alex and Joe got in the car and they headed out of the financial district over the Washington Bridge.

"I'm no authority on the topography of your city but wouldn't it be faster to go the other way for third?" Joe asked.

"You want to hear how I screwed up my clothes or not?"

"Oh right, yes. I'm all ears. Do tell."

"Okay. I was working down the street after I got out of Murman's financial. Interesting place, by the way. We'll have to discuss it at lunch," Alex said as he looked over at Joe.

"Go on. Get to the good stuff," Joe said, eyeing him impatiently.

"So I spot this guy I know has a misdemeanor warrant and might be involved in some burglaries on the east side. I hail him, in a friendly manner, and he takes off. Like a rabbit. Naturally enough, I follow him. He makes it over the bridge but, due to a passing ship, I do not. I almost made it and that's how my clothes took a beating."

"See? Running. That was your first mistake. Most of the problems in the world can be traced directly to running. So, did you face plant or what?"

"More like slid down the drawbridge. It wasn't pretty."

"So we're going this way...?"

"To see if we can catch sight of him. Look for a guy about my height and weight, wearing a green shirt and jeans."

"Color hair?"

"About like mine. A little longer."

Joe looked at him. "Sure you weren't chasing a guy with a mirror?"

"Just keep an eye out. I don't think we'll see him. He'll probably have gone to ground."

Joe grunted. The rest of their drive was uneventful despite their best efforts to locate Alex's twin. There were three false alarms but eventually, they pulled into the parking lot of the restaurant without finding their suspect. Alex was partially relieved. *I'm not sure how I'd explain the resemblance.*

Rosarita's was a long, low, dull red structure with white trim and a white sign with the name of the restaurant dead-center over the front door. A porch lined the front with white rocking chairs strategically placed along it for use by waiting patrons. Deni was parked directly in front of the entrance. She stood at the rear of her car, arms folded, leaning against the trunk, staring at them through aviator sunglasses. She barely waited for them to get out of the car.

"Do you have any idea how hungry I am? What took you so long? And what on God's green earth happened to your pants?" Deni said as she spit the questions at them, rapid-fire.

Alex walked past her, going inside with his spare pants in a box under his arm. "Talk to Joe. He'll explain everything. And Joe, get some nachos in her before someone here dies."

Alex walked into the restaurant, nodding to the hostess. "My friends are behind me. They'll be getting a table. And they'll be getting the chicken nachos. Large. Trust me on this."

He walked to the back of Rosarita's, moving carefully between the tables as his eyes adjusted to the dim lighting. He found the bathroom in the back and opened the door, finding that he was, mercifully, alone. He locked the door, stripped off his pants, and put the fresh ones on. He was washing his hands when he stopped and looked at himself in the mirror. *Who was that guy? How did he know who I was?* Alex felt a twist in the pit of his stomach as he began drawing conclusions he didn't like. *Peter Perfect moves like me. This guy could be my twin. He's in the financial district while I'm surveying businesses to see how vulnerable they are to Peter. This guy HAS to be Peter. And he's my double. How is that possible?* Alex grabbed the sides of the sink, gripping them so hard his arms shook, the veins in his forearms popping out. Slowly, steadying himself, he inhaled and forced the breath out. All the way out. *Ibuki* breathing.

He felt himself calm down. *OK. There's nothing to be gained by throwing out wild and baseless theories right now. Keep it to myself and see what I can do with it.* He felt better having made a decision. He finished up, taking one last look in the mirror.

"Alex 'Through the Looking Glass.' Screw you, Lewis Carroll," he muttered, as someone banged on the door. Alex jerked the door open just as the guy outside was about to hit it again. He froze. Something in his eyes caused the man to blanch and back up against the wall. "All yours," Alex said, forcing out a smile as he walked past.

Alex looked around the restaurant until he found Joe and Deni. She was working on a pile of cheesy nachos and a big bowl of queso as he pulled out his chair.

"So, the karate kid got his ass whipped by a bridge today," she said, a huge smirk on her face. "I wish I could have seen it."

"Call him, Asshopper," Joe said. Deni looked at him sideways. "No, really," he insisted, "he's getting used to it."

Deni turned back to look at Alex. "Asshopper? Really?"

Alex shrugged. "My porn name. Joe gave it to me. He thinks I've got the looks to be moonlighting."

"Ah, well, depends on how much you need the money, I guess."

The waitress arrived and took their order. They made small talk about their respective departments through lunch. At the end of their meal, Alex took stock of the half-full restaurant. It didn't seem overly busy. He asked the waitress if they could stay for a bit and talk about business.

"What kind of business?" she asked.

Alex badged her, explaining that they were working on something and only needed about a half-hour. She brightened noticeably, "You can use the banquet room. It's quiet and out of the way. No one will bother you there."

"Thanks," Alex said. "Where...?"

"Follow me," she said, leading the way.

"You know, my brother is in the police academy right now," she said, over her shoulder, smiling, pride evident in her voice.

"What's his name?" Alex asked.

"Miguel Santos. We call him Mikey. I can't wait to tell him about this," she said, very excited.

Alex thanked her and promised he would keep an eye out for her brother. She gave them all another wide smile and left them at the entrance to the banquet room. Alex had only done Murman Financial, so he started. After describing the tomographic motion detection system in place there, both Joe and Deni crossed it off the list as being too difficult. Peter was Perfect, after all, but not suicidal. They ran down the list of institutions Deni and Joe had visited – three for Deni, two for Joe, ranking them according to their vulnerabilities and probable payoffs. After they finished, Deni got up.

"Well, thanks for lunch guys, but I gotta run. Still wish I coulda seen you wrestle that bridge to the ground, Alex."

"Asshopper! How many times do I have to tell you?" Joe teased.

"Give it up, Joe. It's not gonna take. Not like your Walrus. By the way, shouldn't we be spraying you with water at intervals to keep your skin moist?" Alex asked.

Deni laughed, "You two boys have fun."

"Thanks, Deni. See you at the office," Alex said.

"Bye, darlin'," Joe called.

Alex looked at Joe, "You know, you're the only one she'd take that from."

"It's my natural charm. You want to see if we can hit a few more of these places before we call it a day?"

"Might as well," Alex said.

Chapter 23

Alex and Joe worked the next three hours in the financial district, compiling four more target profiles between them. They met at 4 o'clock, compared notes, and agreed there were several possible soft targets for their unsub. Alex tried to keep focused on the work but his brain would not stop throwing out explanations for his newfound twin. Alex had even started thinking about his "gift" and how that might play into this. He had always assumed he was the only person in the world who could backtrack through quantum reality.

Could he be me, somehow? Could I, by some exotic twist of quantum weirdness, get myself an evil twin? Alex was deep in thought as they drove back to the station. Without warning, Joe's sausage-like fingers were in front of his face as he snapped them.

"Hey, you still with me? If you're gonna be driving, I insist on you being conscious. It's kind of a thing with me."

"Yeah," Alex said, glancing over at Joe. "Sorry. What were you saying?"

"Well, I *could* have said I wanted to dance the hula naked at your next birthday party, for all the attention you were paying, but what I *did* say was 'what time do you want to meet tomorrow morning?"

"Nine is still good for me if you're OK with it."

"Nine it is. Bring donuts this time. No bagels. Those are for old people and rookies watching their waistline."

"You're not watching yours?".

"Watchin' it get bigger every day," Joe sighed. "No, I'm afraid we crossed the Rubicon on that issue sometime back."

"Never too late. You could start coming to karate."

Joe looked sideways at him as if to say, "are you shitting me?"

"Do you guys teach Sumo? 'Cause I think I could have a shot at the local title here."

"*Yokozuna?*" Alex laughed. "I can see that. You'll have to grow a topknot, you know, just to look authentic."

"How do you say 'walrus' in Japanese?"

"*Seiuchi.*"

"Hmmm," Joe mused, then, in a ring announcer's voice, "Now entering the ring, the Great Seiuchi! I like it!."

Joe looked at Alex, "You think women would throw me their underwear?"

Alex grinned, "Oh, without a doubt. You'd be covered in 'em."

"Wait," Joe said, suddenly suspicious. "How did you know what 'walrus' was in Japanese, right off the bat like that?"

"I looked it up some time ago," Alex said as he pulled into the lot next to the department where Joe's car was parked. He stopped at the back of Joe's car.

"Figures, you bastard," Joe said, getting out of the car. He turned around and put his meaty forearms on the roof of the car and looked in. "Don't forget. Donuts," he said and spun on his heel.

Alex watched Joe walk toward his car. For such a big guy, he still managed to move pretty well. Alex pulled into the secured parking driveway, badging the plate on the driver's side. The RFID chip in his wallet shook hands with the PD's computer and decided between themselves that Alex was good enough to get in. The gate ratcheted open and he drove in, parking in his usual spot.

Alex walked into Investigations to find a bridge built of office supplies spanning his cubicle. It was quite good, considering what they had to work with. Markers and legal pads formed the bulk of the structure with paperclips and scotch tape used to firm it up. Under it were the words *Mr. Miyagi's Bridge.* Alex marveled at the workmanship.

"Hey, Bridgeman!" Pritchard shouted.

"I take it Deni can't keep a secret?" Alex said, looking over at Deni's cubicle as she slowly rose out of her seat and peered over the partition. She had a smirk plastered across her face.

"Apparently...I cannot," she said.

Several of the detectives gathered around now and hilarity ensued. He took it good-naturedly as he had, on many occasions in the past, dished it out. He sat down at the desk and turned on his computer.

"I am going to leave this here as a testament to what a half-dozen morons can do if they work together. You are all very, very special. And I mean that in the educational sense of the word." The other cops laughed, slowly dispersing back to their cubicles, most of them packing up to go home.

Alex was clearing out his emails one by one. Before the age of email, most of this material would have been on paper in the form of memos. Thousands of trees were slaughtered needlessly to print out crap that Alex and most of the other cops threw out immediately. Email slowed deforestation by at least fifty percent. Most of the mail was intra-departmental but, as he worked his way down, one email looked to be from outside. The title on the email queue read "A Friend".

Alex punched it up, reading it in stunned silence. *Hello — We met today at the bridge. I trust you know who this is. We need to meet again, under better circumstances. Public library, main branch, second floor, north side of Reference. There's a secluded area and won't be the subject of casual observation. 1100. - Alaric.*

Alaric. The name of his dead twin. This was getting weirder by the second. *This is impossible. Yeah. Impossible. Like being able to backtrack any decision you make. Fuck,* I'm *impossible.*

Alex felt a cold sweat break out on his forehead as he thought it through. *There are only two explanations. One is that this is an elaborate hoax by someone who has access to all kinds of information about me that's confidential and had someone wear an "Alex" mask to impersonate me. Also had it coincide with the FBI Peter Perfect investigation...or...somehow, someway, Alaric crossed over from a universe where he didn't die. Occam's razor militates for the second choice. If not for my "gift", I'd have to go with option one.*

Alex closed his desktop and pushed away from the computer, wiped his palm across his forehead, and sighed. *When I said "Evil Twin" universe, I didn't mean it literally.*

He grabbed his messenger bag and walked to the door, giving Deni a nuggie on the way past her desk. "Hey!" she yelled, grabbing the top of her head.

"You deserved it," Alex said, walking on without turning back to look. *I have a karate class to teach. Maybe that, at least, will be fun.*

Chapter 24

Alex went through his usual routine when he got home. Khan looked at him disapprovingly when he did not retrieve the leash for a run. Sometimes he wondered who trained who.

"Sorry, boy, not today," Alex said as he let him out into the side yard.

He grabbed a protein bar from the refrigerator, the cold making it marginally more edible. Walking to the bedroom, he got his black dojo bag from the closet and threw it on the bed. He stuffed a crisp, white *Gi* and black *Obi* in it and, after thinking for a moment, added an extra *Gi* top. He took the bag into his private dojo and looked at the weapons on the wall. Advanced belts were doing *Kobudo* tonight, practicing with ancient Okinawan weapons. He took a pair of *Sais* off the wall and placed them in the bag as well as a pair of *Tonfa*. As an afterthought, he tossed in a pair of *Nunchakus*. *Nunchakus* were commonly called "numb chucks" by teenage boys the world over. Alex hated the term. He thought it sounded like an anesthetized rodent. Still, they had been enormously popular since the seventies when Bruce Lee used them in his movies.

He thought about bringing one of his *Bo* staffs, but they were six feet long and kind of a pain to transport. He'd appropriate one of the spares at the dojo. He checked his bag. The *Sais* were his favorite weapon, heavy, forged steel truncheons with leather-wrapped handles. They looked like short swords with two tines on to either side of the "blade", which was a rounded piece of steel with no edge. He'd read stories of the weapon's origin that didn't seem reasonable; that they were farm implements used by the plucky Okinawan farmers as weapons during the age of the Japanese samurai. The fact there were nearly identical weapons in China called "Iron Rulers" cast considerable doubt on that, at least in Alex's mind, but the myth persisted.

Alex's *Tonfa* were made of twenty-four inches of round hardwood with a handle four inches from one end. In the '80s, an enterprising cop had modeled a police weapon called the PR-24 on the Okinawan *Tonfa,* and then marketed it to police agencies. Alex's own department had gone to the PR-24 for a time but had then transitioned to expandable batons. Alex kept his PR-24 on the floor of the cruiser between the driver's seat and the door. It had come in handy more than once.

Alex let Khan back in and wrote a quick note to Eve on a piece of scrap paper on the bar. *Back after class, Love you and little Alaric.* He barely finished the note when he realized he'd written Alaric's name. He held the note up and thought about tearing it up and writing another. He chewed his lip, mulling it over. He put it back down on the bar. *Doesn't really make any difference.*

He locked the door in Khan's disappointed face and walked to his car, where he opened the door and threw the bag into the back seat in one swift motion. Departmental SOP stated that he could use his car to go to a "health facility to maintain an appropriate level of fitness". That's the *dojo* – a health club. As he drove, he thought about the classes he'd be teaching. From five-thirty to seven would be the mixed class, mostly beginners. A lot of basics and some *kata* – limited sparring. The next class ran from seven to eight-thirty and was technically advanced, including green belts at 6th *Kyu* and above. From eight-thirty to nine-thirty, there were only advanced ranks and would involve weaponry. That class could run to ten, depending on who was there and how much fun they were having. Alex was feeling better already.

When Alex arrived at ten after five, several students were waiting at the door. He always took it as a good sign if a student cared enough to be early. He was always early. He parked his car and got his bag out of the back. As he approached the door, the students, three green belts, and a white belt, bowed. *Sensei* ran a strict and very traditional school. Alex returned the bow and unlocked the door. He held it while each of the waiting students entered, one by one, bowing as they crossed the threshold. One white belt stooped as he entered and gathered up mail on the floor under the mail slot. He turned and handed it to Alex with a short bow. Alex smiled and nodded. *Good habits, learned young, last a lifetime.*

The dojo smelled musty, having been closed all day with the windows shut. Alex started up the air conditioners, two ancient, wall-mounted units that made noticeable whirring noises. The building was an old concrete block structure that needed repairs. Alex and several of the black belts had helped *Sensei* put in the wooden floors and painted the walls the current pale green when he first got the place. Alex was fourteen at the time and had fetched and carried materials for the men doing the work. Still, he didn't leave for the day until everyone else left. Three *makiwaras* adorned one wall while mirrors covered the entire opposite wall. There were two heavy bags in the back — one hanging and one free-standing. On the wall with the *makiwara* was a rack with several *Bo* staffs, *Jo* staffs, and *Bokken* as well as a *kamiza*.

Alex unlocked *Sensei's* office and went in, closing the door behind him and throwing the keys and mail on the desk. He changed into his *gi* and sat in sensei's chair. As he went through the mail to make sure there wasn't anything urgent, he could hear students coming through the front door. He walked out onto the dojo floor, bowing as he crossed the line from the office to the dojo, and pulled on the ends of his belt, cinching it tighter. Alex looked at the large clock on the wall. It was time.

"Line up!" he shouted, walking to a point on the floor at the center of the wall holding the makiwara. The students ran to form a line in front of him. The highest rank was on Alex's left down to the lowest on his right. He waited until everyone had sorted themselves out and pivoted in place until he was facing the same way as the students. He called out *"Seiza!"* and he and all the students knelt down and sat back on their heels, their backs straight. There was a *kamiza* on the wall in front of Alex, about six feet off the floor. It contained an eight by ten photograph of Chojun Miyagi, the founder of Goju Ryu, calligraphy of the Dojo *Kun,* and a small flower arrangement in a delicate vase.

The most senior student shouted, "*Kamiza... ni!*" All the students and Alex shifted until they were facing the *Kamiza.* The student called "*Kamiza... Rei!*" and everyone bowed. They placed their right hands first to the ground, palm down, then their left hands. They touched their foreheads to the ground, and then, sitting back, their right hands and then left hands came back to the tops of their thighs. Alex pivoted on his knees, facing the class. The senior student yelled "*Sensei...ni!*" and the class turned to face Alex. The student again called out "*Sensei...Rei!*" and the class bowed to Alex. He bowed in return.

Alex said "*Mokuso,*" and the students closed their eyes and cleared their minds *Moku-So* translates to "still thoughts." This was the essential meditation before class. Each student sat perfectly still while Alex intoned, "Concentrate on your breathing. In...out. In...out. With each exhalation, feel the tension leave your body. With each exhalation, feel yourself sinking deeper into your center. With each exhalation, feel your mind calming." Alex continued the meditation for another couple of minutes, then called "*Rei!*" Everyone bowed and got to their feet.

"*Junbi undo,*" Alex called, beginning the series of warm-up exercises that started every class. Starting at the toes and working their way up, the students, Alex leading, did toe raises, ankle circles, knee circles, hip rotations, waist twists, shoulder rolls, arm circles, and wrist stretches. The students then did leg swings, dynamically stretching the hamstrings by swinging their legs to the front and then stretching the inside of their legs by swinging them to the sides. Alex began the static stretching while standing with their legs spread wide, reaching down to grab their ankles and pull their heads toward their knees. Then they did the same thing while seated. After those came partner stretches against the wall with one person stretching their partner's legs and then holding the stretch at their maximum limit.

"*Hojo undo,*" Alex called out and the students formed back into a single line. *Hojo undo* meant "supplementary exercises" and included everything from basic movements to specialized pieces of equipment. In the beginner's class, Alex confined the conditioning exercises to squats, push-ups, and sit-ups. He ended the conditioning with the class standing in a low, squatting stance called *Shiko dachi* for three minutes. Three minutes doesn't sound like much until you realize that, at two minutes, your legs are shaking like a wobbly fawn taking its first steps. It was a test of endurance and mental fortitude. Alex noted the students who stayed down for the entire time and those who popped up momentarily to relieve the pressure on their legs. It had been his experience those who stayed down did much better and stayed with karate longer than those who did not.

"*Kote kitai,*" was Alex's next command. Students paired up for forearm conditioning. At this stage, their exercise consisted of one student punching and the other student striking their forearm with either a *shuto*, knife-hand, or *tetsui*, hammerfist. In more advanced classes, the exercise involved a middle-level block, cover, and strike for each punch. Adolescent boys and most men regarded this as a test of their manhood and tried to take the punishment without flinching, staring straight ahead, expressionless.

By now, everyone in the class was sweating and warmed up. Alex led the basic exercises which comprised blocking, punching, and kicking accompanied by stance work. A series of movements done from *Sanchin* stance involved basic blocks like *Age uke,* rising block, *Chudan uchi uke,* middle inside forearm block, *Chudan soto uke,* middle outside forearm block, and *Gedan barai,* low block followed by *Seiken Tsuki,* or punch. Blocking in Goju Ryu tended to be softer, even in these "hard" blocks, than other karate styles like Shotokan. The middle blocks, instead of smashing into the incoming fist, met the force and blended with it, as did the lower block with a sweeping, circular motion. The upper block, however, was a jarring, in-to-out block that could be used as a very effective close-in strike under the right circumstances.

The exercises progressed to using other stances like Goju's trademark *Neko Ashi Dachi,* Cat Stance, *Shiko dachi, and Zenkutsu dachi,* or forward stance. Each stance was useful for the techniques performed, maximizing the amount of energy transferred into the target. The weaving together of stances and techniques looks bewildering to a beginner but eventually becomes as automatic as breathing. Kicking techniques were interspersed throughout the basics and involved low *Mae Geri,* front kicks, *Kansetsu geri,* a low side kick to the knee, and *Hiza geri,* a knee strike. There were no flashy, high kicks like those prevalent in karate tournaments. Goju Ryu was at its heart a combative fighting art.

The students had been working hard now for nearly an hour. Alex called for the class to line up and gave them a ten-minute break. They bowed out, a line immediately forming at the water fountain in the back. Alex noticed a woman and her son were at the front of the school where some folding chairs had been set up for visitors. The woman looked to be Hispanic and was wearing a work uniform, pale green with white accents at the sleeves and collar. The name tag on it read "Esmerelda." He walked to the front of the school, smiling at them. As he got closer, the boy seemed to grow nervous and shy, moving subtly closer to his mother. He was also sporting a fresh shiner.

"Can I help you?" Alex asked.

The woman looked at her son, then spoke up, "We were wondering about taking classes."

"The both of you?"

"Oh. Oh, no. Just my son, Raymond," she smiled and looked at her son.

"Ok, well, I'm not the owner of the school, but I'm sure I can answer any questions you might have. Why don't we go back to the office and talk," Alex said. As he walked them back to the office, he called to the most senior green belt, a tall, angular kid named Danny.

"Danny! Give them a couple of more minutes to get water and then get them working on their kata."

"Hai sensei!" Danny said, bowing and trying hard to conceal the flush of pride on his face.

Alex ushered the boy and his mother through the door to the office, seating them in the two wooden chairs in front of the desk. He went around to the back of the desk and sat down. "How can I help you?" he asked.

"I am Mrs. Ramirez and this is my son Raymond. He got into a fight at school and I thought it would be a good idea if he learned to defend himself. He thinks so too," she said, turning to look at her son.

Alex shifted his attention to the boy. "Is this true, Raymond?"

He looked at his mother, then back at Alex, and nodded.

The mother broke in, "I pass by this school every day on my way to work and I thought maybe this would be a good place."

"I see," Alex said, shifting back to her son. "Raymond, could you tell me what started this fight?"

Raymond looked down and then spoke without making eye contact. "I was in the bathroom and this older kid started pushing my backpack from behind while I was trying to pee. He kept calling me a...a...wetback."

Alex could see his mother's face harden at the mention of the word.

"Then what happened?"

"I tried to get past him, but he had friends of his on either side of him. He shoved me. So I pushed him back and that's when he punched me."

"Anything else?"

"I fell down and then a teacher came into the bathroom and everyone scattered. I think someone must have run and told him there was going to be a fight."

"What did the teacher do?"

"He asked me if I was alright and I told him 'yeah'. Then the bell rang for class and he walked me to Algebra."

"Were you notified by the school, Mrs. Ramirez?"

"No. I have heard nothing from the school." Her reply was clipped, angry.

"What do *you* want, Raymond?"

Raymond looked up at him and for the first time, he made eye contact. "I want a black belt!" he blurted.

Alex sat back for a second. Then he reached under the desk and searched for a moment before coming up with a brand-new black *Obi*, still in the plastic wrapper and secured with rubber bands at both ends.

He slid the belt across the desk, shrugging. "Easy enough. That'll be eight dollars," Alex said.

Raymond looked confused, his mother even more so. Slowly, Alex saw comprehension dawn in the young man's eyes.

"No. I don't want to just buy a black belt. I want to get a black belt from the school," Raymond said.

Alex reached across the desk and took the belt back, "Ah, well, that's a different story. You want to *earn* a black belt. That will take you two to three years and more effort and sweat than you can imagine. Statistically, only about one to two percent of the people who take a karate class go on to become black belts. Are you sure that's what you want?"

Raymond was looking Alex dead in the eyes now and there was no hesitation in his voice when he said, "Yes. That's what I want."

Alex saw Raymond's mother smile.

"Ok," Alex said. "You'll need a *Gi*. That's what we call a uniform. Let's see; you're how old?"

"Fourteen," Raymond said.

Ah, he's small for his age. Probably another reason he's a target.

Alex swiveled in his chair. Behind him, along the wall, was a series of cubbyholes containing various items. He found a *Gi* he thought would fit and dug several pieces of paperwork out of the desk drawers.

"Here's your uniform, Raymond. Mrs. Ramirez, this is some paperwork you need to go over and sign," Alex said. Alex shifted his attention back to the boy.

"There's one thing we are very strict about here, Raymond, and that's your grades. You have to maintain at least a "C" average to be allowed to study here."

"That's not a problem. Raymond is always on the A-B Honor Roll," Mrs. Ramirez said.

"That's great, Raymond. You should be proud," Alex said. Raymond looked away, embarrassed by the attention.

"There is one thing…," Raymond's mother said, hesitating.

Alex looked at her and waited.

"I am a single mother and I work two jobs. How much money is it each month? And how much for the uniform?" She asked, her hands twisting together nervously.

"We are running a special this month and the first month, including the uniform, is free. As far as future tuition, well, there are always things around here that need doing. As long as Raymond studies and works hard, I'm sure we can find a way," Alex said.

She exhaled, relieved. Alex said, "I have some paperwork to do now so if you don't have any more questions...?".

Raymond, his mother, and Alex stood up at the same time. Alex shook her hand and then held out his hand to her son. He shook it solemnly. "I'll be seeing you in class, young man," Alex said to him.

"Yes, sir," Raymond said, smiling.

Alex ushered them out of the office, then turned back and retrieved his wallet from his pants. He took eighty dollars out, placing it in an envelope and sealing it, then writing Raymond's name on the outside. He placed it in *Sensei's* in-basket. It wasn't exactly true that they were running a special. Not exactly. Alex smiled.

Alex walked out onto the dojo floor to check on the student's progress. Some students were still working on *kihon*, basics, but most had progressed to working on the *Gekisai-dai-ichi or Gekisai-dai-ni kata*. Alex could see the students for the advanced class beginning to arrive. He moved through the class, making a small correction here or there, encouraging, always focusing on what the student was doing right. At the end of the class, the students lined up, bowing out as they had bowed in. Some people thought the rituals of the dojo were silly. Alex believed they were important, binding the class together as a unit, almost a family.

As the lower belts filtered out of the dojo, the higher belts came in. Alex greeted several of them as old friends which, after more than a dozen years in the dojo, they were. He glanced through the large window at the front of the school and saw a tall man in a hoodie, silhouetted by the dying light of sunset. He was looking toward the dojo.

Alaric? He thought, then chided himself for his paranoia. Still, the figure reminded him of the person on the Florida Power right-of-way.

"Hey, Alex! How's Eve doing?". Alex's concentration was broken by Eric Bellingham, his oldest dojo-mate and friend. Eric was a *Ni-Dan,* a second-degree black belt.

"Oh, she's fine. Complaining about how much she's going to look like a whale," Alex said, turning to Eric.

"Like that would be possible," Eric grinned.

"I know, but I humor her because, frankly, I think she can beat my ass."

"That's not even a question. You'd be toast," Eric said, nodding, looking serious.

Alex turned back to the school's front window, but the figure was gone. *Dammit!*

The class lined up and bowed in like the earlier class. Eric was *sempai,* the most senior student, and was at the end of the line to Alex's left.

"Eric *Sempai* will lead the class through *Junbi undo, Hojo undo,* and *Kihon,*" Alex announced to the class. Alex looked at Eric and motioned to his place. "*Dozo.*" Please.

Eric jogged up to the front of the class and Alex relinquished his position with a bow. Eric bowed as well and started the warm-ups. Alex went to the school office and closed the door. He took off his wet *Gi* jacket and put on the dry Gi top from his gym bag, He sat at the desk and picked up the phone, dialing Forriere *Sensei's* number from memory.

"Hello, Alex. How is class going?" came the gravelly voice over the handset.

"Fine, *Sensei*. How are you doing?"

"As well as can be expected. I can now be more than six feet away from a commode, so that's a relief."

Alex chuckled. "I signed up a new student. A fourteen-year-old boy."

"Really? What's he like?"

"Small for his age. Got into a scrape at school. Mom thought he should learn to defend himself. He seems enthusiastic."

"How old again?"

"Fourteen," Alex waited. There was a pause. *Sensei* did not want his school to turn into a glorified after-school facility, as so many *dojos* had. Although he knew full well the money in the martial arts business was in teaching children, he had resisted it. In his opinion, the idea of ten-year-old black belts was more than a little silly.

"Ok."

Alex let go of a breath he did not realize he was holding, "There's one more thing, *Sensei*..."

"Yes?"

"The boy's mother is a single mom, working two jobs, she didn't have the money...so I told her we were running a special on the first month with a free uniform."

There was a sigh on the phone, "Alex, is this another one of your 'karate orphans'?"

"Yes, *Sensei,* I'm afraid it is. Hey, the last one made it to brown belt. It wasn't his fault that his father got a job down south."

"All right. I know better than to argue with you about this. We'll work something out."

"Thank you, *Sensei.* I better get back to class. Good luck tomorrow."

"Thanks, Alex. I'm just praying the doctor has steady hands."

"*Like a rock.*"

Alex hung up the phone and grabbed his *obi.* He tied it on as he walked out onto the dojo floor. Eric was just finishing *Hojo undo.* Eric bowed to Alex, taking his place in the line. Alex started through an abbreviated set of basics, breaking a fresh sweat in his pristine *Gi* top. Finished with *Kihon,* Alex had them line up in two staggered lines and led the group through the *kata Sanchin.* After the entire group had gone through the *kata* once, he had them go through it again while he tested their techniques. He punched them in the stomach, testing how tight their abdominals were at the end of their *ibuki* breath, with all the air pushed from their lungs. He kicked them in their legs, sometimes sweeping them at the ankles to test the strength of their *sanchin* stance. He moved behind them and slammed his palms down onto their shoulders and up into their lats, testing their stability and the muscular contraction vital to a correct performance of the *kata.* Everyone was a little relieved when the *Sanchin* portion of the class was over.

After checking with the students and making sure everyone knew the kata *Seiyuchin.* Alex went through the kata once with the class and then had them go through it two more times while he checked individual form. Gi's popped with each strike, crisply, cleanly. The collective sound of their feet sliding along the floor started and stopped precisely together. The inhalations and forced exhalations of their controlled breathing reinforced their unity. He made a few corrections, then had the students pair up to work on *Bunkai*, the practical combative applications of the kata. *Sensei* always stuck with basic applications of the kata techniques, done with force and savage intent. One strike, one kill. Alex wholeheartedly agreed with him. He had seen *bunkai* performed by so-called grandmasters with willing, cooperative students that could only be described as, well, fanciful. Certainly, nothing that would work on the street against an aggressive assailant. Alex checked the clock and called a five-minute break for water. He motioned Eric aside to talk to him.

"You summoned me, Oh *Sensei*," he said with a lopsided grin.

"Yes, my loyal minion," Alex said as he arched one eyebrow like a cheesy Hollywood villain. Then, more seriously, "We're gonna do *Kumite* next. I want you to watch the brown belts. They're getting a little too enthusiastic".

"Oh, there's nothing more dangerous than a brown belt. They can almost taste that *shodan*."

"Were we like that?"

"Yeah. Yeah, we were definitely like that."

Turning, Alex raised his voice, addressing the class, "All right, we're going to be doing some sparring for the last twenty minutes of class. I want good, strong techniques in the spirit of *Ikken Hisatsu,* to kill with one blow. I also want to see *control.* We don't use pads in this school for a reason. Pair up. We will run two-minute rounds with a fifteen-second break to change partners."

Alex walked to the programmable boxing timer on the floor next to the dojo office door and turned it on. It was already set for sparring.

Alex turned to the class, "And Go!"

Immediately, the pairs of karateka began to circle each other like alley cats. Attacks came in either single, lunging strikes or combinations meant to confuse the opponent. Each decisive attack was accompanied by a *Kiai*, the yell punctuating the sound of feet shuffling back and forth. Although light contact to the body was allowed, there was no contact to the face, groin, or other vital points. Two brown belts clashed repeatedly. They were getting out of hand when Alex nodded to Eric. Alex peeled one brown belt off the pair and Eric got the other one.

Alex paired with a muscular teenager named Mitch. He was a good kid but tended to get emotionally involved when fighting. Right now, Mitch had a look of concern on his face as he looked at Alex. The buzzer sounded for the end of the previous round and they waited for fifteen seconds for the others in the class to find new partners. The buzzer started for the next round. Alex and Mitch bowed to each other and began to circle. Mitch tried a backfist-reverse punch combination that Alex blocked. Alex shot a punch toward Mitch's face to back him up a little. As they circled, Mitch stopped for a moment to adjust his stance and Alex moved forward with a foot sweep to Mitch's lead leg while he grabbed his lead arm for control. The bottom of Alex's foot hit Mitch above the ankle and moved his leg just enough to throw him off balance. Alex planted his sweeping foot and executed a roundhouse kick with his other leg to Mitch's face. Mitch, already off-balance from the sweep, managed to get his right arm up and Alex's instep smacked his forearm solidly. Alex dropped his kicking leg and used his forward momentum to land a reverse punch to Mitch's face, pulling his lead arm down, stopping barely a half-inch from contact.

Alex and Mitch separated and assumed fighting posture, or *kamae,* again. Mitch tried a backfist and side-kick combination that Alex swatted down and then a roundhouse-spinning back kick Alex just backed away from. As Mitch got back into a *kamae,* Alex lunged in suddenly with a *Kizami tsuki* jab with his left hand, following up with a reverse punch to the face, causing Mitch to lean back, taking the weight off his lead foot. Alex stepped in and slammed his shin against Mitch's calf, causing him to rotate to his right and, again, be off-balance. Alex grabbed his *Gi* with his right hand to control him and stepped down with his right foot, punching Mitch in the ribs with his left hand. Although the punch was controlled, it still took the wind out of Mitch's sails. Alex released him and Mitch put his hands on his knees, trying to catch his breath.

"You okay?" Alex asked him.

Mitch nodded and held up his hand but didn't say anything. Alex checked with Eric and he nodded, indicating he'd had similar results.

Alex clapped his hands twice after the next buzzer and said, "Line up!". He went over and turned the timer off before returning to the front of the class.

"Good class, everyone. You're all working hard and I appreciate your effort," he said, then nodded to Eric. The class bowed out and some, who were not involved in the *Kobudo* class, were leaving. Alex caught up to Mitch.

"You sure you're alright?"

"*Hai, Sensei*," he said. "Just got the wind knocked out of me."

"You're doing fine, Mitch. Remember: fight smarter, not harder."

Mitch smiled. "Thanks, *Sensei*," he said and bowed before leaving.

Alex went into the office, retrieving his *dojo* bag with the weapons in it. Since it was his class, he decided they would work on *Bo-Sai Kumite* today. Maybe throw in a little *Tonfa* at the end. He counted the class and it was an odd number. That brought a smile to his face. It meant he would get a chance to work with Eric. He called the class to order and they bowed in.

"Okay. Find partners. We're first going to work on some *Bo-Sai Kumite*. So half of you will have *Bo* staffs and the other half with be using a pair of *Sais*," Alex instructed. The students went to their bags along the wall; some, including Alex, got *Bo* staffs off the wall.

The class worked back and forth across the dojo floor, practicing strikes and blocks with the *Bo* against the *sais*. They had to be careful to rotate their forearms so the shaft of the

Sai lay along their ulnar bones. If they didn't, the *Bo* made contact with them, not the weapon. After basics, they began to work on a *Bo-Sai Kata*, with pre-arranged moves that involved attack and defense. After they had been on both sides of the form, Alex told the class to grab their *Tonfa*.

Alex got his own *Tonfa* out and lectured the class. "The origin of the *Tonfa* is said to be an agricultural tool. The handle to a rice mill grinder or some such nonsense. That just isn't true. You can find the same weapon, just a little longer, in China where they are called 'Iron Crutches,' or 'Bodhidharma's cane.' In any country, they are very versatile weapons. When you grab it by the handle and align the long, extended portion of the weapon with your forearm, you can block and strike with the short end."

Here Alex demonstrated a normal karate punch with the *Tonfa* in his hand. "You can strike with the forearm," Alex explained as he executed a chopping forearm strike with the shaft of the weapon. "Or you can use an elbow strike if your *Tonfa* is the correct length and protrudes past your elbow by an inch or so," Alex said as he demonstrated a side elbow strike.

"But the most singular use of the *Tonfa* is a centrifugal weapon, like the nunchakus. If you swing your hand forward in a short, tight arc, the end of the *Tonfa* follows that movement and makes the weapon swing out with increased velocity and power. In effect, it multiplies your strength and speed." Alex said as he demonstrated and the *Tonfa* cut the air in front of him with an audible *whoosh*.

"You can also do the same in reverse." Alex did so with the same speed. "You can vary the angle and do what is referred to in *Kenjutsu* circles as *Happo Giri,* cutting in eight directions. Only you'll have a *Tonfa* and not a sword." Alex used the *Tonfa* to inscribe a downward figure-eight in front of him. Then he reversed directions and executed an upward figure-eight. He then swept the *Tonfa* side to side, horizontally, before cutting the air both down and up in a vertical line directly in front of him.

"The *Tonfa* is not nearly as well known as the *Nunchakus* but, in my humble opinion, they are superior. So grab your *Tonfa* and I'll show you why I think so."

The class then went through basics with the *Tonfa* until they were sore and had blisters before Alex called it a night. The class bowed out, everyone collecting their weapons and meandering out the door in small groups. Eric was the last to leave.

"You staying?" he asked.

"Yeah. I'm going to work on a little *Hojo undo.*"

"You ought to go home and work on that wife of yours."

"I did. That's why she's in her current predicament."

Eric laughed. "Got it, man. See ya," he said as he walked out the door,

Alex locked the door behind him. This was when he liked the dojo best. When he was alone there with his art and his thoughts. He checked the office to make sure everything was in its place, then he went to the back of the dojo, to the training equipment. Alex looked at it, deciding where to start. He had worked on hand, wrist, and forearm strength for years, after reading a story in a book. *The Weaponless Warriors* by Richard Kim. The story concerned a man named Agena, who was from Gushikawa village in Okinawa. From this story,

Alex had been obsessed with becoming a man like Agena with "iron fists" and "steel fingers." Alex's hard work had paid off in multiple ways on the job. Once he grabbed a suspect, he stayed grabbed. No one ever got away. He had gotten pain compliance more than once just by just squeezing a suspect's triceps muscle or some other tender area.

When he had gone through his physical for the police academy, one of the tests had been grip strength. The corporal administering the test had been a bit distracted by a busty recruit when he gave Alex the dynamometer and told him to squeeze it as hard as he could. Alex had squeezed it and had handed the equipment back to him. With a bored look, the corporal had taken it and started to write down the number but then stopped.

"Did you squeeze this with one hand or two?" he had asked, suspicious.

"Just one," Alex had said.

"Right," the corporal had replied, resetting the machine, "Show me." He had handed Alex back the dynamometer and had stood staring with his arms crossed.

"Okay," Alex had said and squeezed again. Then he had handed the equipment to the corporal who looked at it and handed it back.

"Do it again," he had said. Alex had done it four times in all before the corporal had written down the number 210 pounds. A strong man has a grip strength of 140 pounds, an average man about 110. Since that time, Alex had closed the Captains of Crush Handgripper at a number three which is registered at 280 pounds.

Back at the dojo, Alex started with the *Makiage Kigu* or what would be called 'a wrist roller' in the west. It was comprised of a wooden dowel rod with a hole drilled through the middle and a rope threaded through it, The dowel was placed on a wooden support with the rope tied to a set of weights on a loading pin directly underneath it. As Alex rolled the weights up and down in either direction, he could feel the burning in his forearms. He did this exercise until his arms felt exhausted.

Next, he grabbed a pair of *Nigiri Game,* or grasping jars. These ceramic jars were filled with sand and had a lip on their slightly fluted end. Alex gripped the jars with his fingertips and began to walk up and down the dojo floor, first in *Sanchin* stance and then in *Shiko dachi.* Sometimes, he just held them to see how long he could do it. He had gotten to the point that he got bored before his grip gave out.

He put down the *Nigiri Game* and picked up a *Chi Ishi,* a short pole with the weight at one end. There were several traditional Okinawan models which had a stone on the end, but Alex preferred the more modern approach of a dumbbell with the plates loaded on one side. This allowed for variable and increasing resistance. He went through multiple traditional manipulations of the *Chi Ishi,* all of which involved his forearms. Then he isolated just the radial and ulnar deviation, concentrating on each repetition. At last, he sat down on a bench and placed his forearm on his thigh. He began to rotate the *Chi Ishi* back and forth, pronating and supinating his hand. When one arm gave out, he switched to the other.

He ended his solitary workout session by pinch-gripping iron weight plates. After he stopped, he looked at the veins in his forearms, standing out like river tributaries, writhing as he flexed his forearms and gripped his hand into a fist. He felt a certain sense of pride and accomplishment.

I wonder if Popeye started this way? he thought, grinning.

Alex began gathering his gear and then thought about the guy in the hoodie he saw earlier. He closed his dominant eye as he got his things together. It was an old trick his FTO had taught him years ago, after Alex's first bar fight where he went in from a well-lit parking lot to a dark, chaotic, drunk-filled environment. He'd almost gotten his clock cleaned because he couldn't see anyone for about thirty seconds. Later, on the way to the county jail, George had leaned back in his seat with one foot up on the dashboard, tilted his Stetson down over his eyes, lit a cigarette, and told him to close one eye a minute out from any bar fight or any place he thought might be dark. That eye would take over in the dark bar and you could see almost as well as someone who'd been in the bar for hours.

Alex turned out the lights and let his non-dominant eye adapt to the increased level of darkness. He stayed inside for a full minute, then scouted out the street in front of the dojo. Not seeing anything suspicious, he exited the school, locking the door behind him. He checked his rear-view mirror all the way home but didn't detect any tails. He even took a few detours.

Either Reed and Malloy have upped their game or they just aren't following me tonight, he thought.

He pulled into the driveway, hearing Khan's welcoming bark, which was distinctly different from his non-welcoming, 'I'm-gonna-bite-the-crap-outa-you' bark. The porch light was on as was the light in the bedroom window, which meant Eve was waiting up for him. He smiled and opened his car door, getting out. He stopped for a minute and then walked to the back of the house and looked up the power right-of-way. Nothing there but the looming iron giants holding the weight of civilization on their shoulders. He sighed, promising himself he would stop being so worried, and immediately knew, as soon as he made it, he would break that promise. Alex opened the unlocked carport door and Khan greeted him frantically. He took a moment to pet him, telling him what a good boy he was. He never understood people who didn't have pets. It seemed unnatural to him.

He walked down the hall to the open bedroom door to see his wife in one of his x-large t-shirts, propped up in bed, reading through papers that were piled up on the bed around her, her reading glasses down on the end of her nose. Ominously, she held a red marker in her hand.

"How were your karate doobies?" she asked, then looked up at him and grinned. Alex had made the mistake of telling her his mother always referred to his karate practice as "karate doobies", which drove him nuts as a super-serious fifteen-year-old. *Mo-om, they're called KATA!,* Alex could hear himself saying. *Whatever they are. Dinner's ready,* was always the reply. He'd give anything to hear her say that one more time.

"Oh, my 'karate doobies' were just fine young lady," Alex said as he dropped his gym bag and jumped into the middle of the bed, landing on his hands and knees, scattering her papers.

Eve squealed as she tried in vain to grab the paperwork. He leaned forward and kissed her on the cheek with an audible smack, then he sat down and helped her gather the papers. She glared at him in mock reproach.

"Maybe YOU would like to try grading these papers, Mr. Big-Shot Detective?" she said.

"Oh no, not me. 'A man's got to know his limitations'. Movie?" Alex asked, his eyebrows raised.

"I have no freaking clue," she responded.

"Magnum Force. Clint Eastwood. You know, I'm trying to complete your education here. Chaucer will only carry you so far in life."

"Yes, well, if you don't mind, I'll stick to the classics."

"Clint Eastwood IS the classics. Have you seen how old he is? He probably knew Chaucer on a first-name basis. What was his first name, anyway? Fred?"

"Geoffrey. Jeff to his friends."

"There you go. No doubt Clint and Jeff shared a beer or two at the local pub."

They finished gathering up the papers, including a few that had fallen to the floor while they were talking. Alex handed them to her and she kissed him on the lips. She took all the papers and set them on her nightstand.

"I'm glad you're home," she said.

"Me, too. It's been a long day."

"Anything interesting happen?"

Alex considered telling her what had happened that day, but he wasn't too clear on it himself at this point. Maybe tomorrow. Yeah, he'd know more tomorrow.

"No. Not really. Same shit, different day. You?"

"You saw the end of my day when you walked into the room. And that was pretty much the high point."

"Speaking of coming into the room," Alex said, "How come you're not locking the carport door?"

"I left it open because I knew you'd be home in an hour and I didn't want to get up and upset my careful bedspread filing system which, by the way, you ruined. Besides, would you come through the door if you didn't know Khan?"

"Hmmm. Good point. He is pretty formidable."

Khan had perked up upon hearing his name and now sat at the side of the bed, Shepherd grin prominently displayed He shifted his gaze from Alex to Eve, depending on who was talking. Occasionally, he would tilt his head as though thinking deeply. Alex reached over and scratched him behind his ears.

"I'm going to catch a shower. Believe me; I need one," he said as he headed for the adjoining bathroom.

"I believe you, babe," Eve said, rolling over on her side, pulling the covers up under her chin, and turning out the bedside lamp, "I'm going to sleep. Don't wake me up unless you mean business."

Alex laughed, "I won't. That's a promise."

Chapter 25

Alex stopped by a local donut shop on his way into work Wednesday morning, mindful of the "request" made by Joe the afternoon before. He got an assortment of a dozen donuts and was about to check out when the baker came out of the back with fresh apple fritters in a basket, still too warm to eat, the glaze not yet hardened. Normally, he could stop himself from eating things like baked goods, but these were his all-time favorite. He got another half dozen.

Alex made it into work at about a quarter to nine and, as he walked into Investigations, was the immediate object of attention. Pritchard noticed first. Alex swore he air-scented the donuts.

"Hey, Alex, whatcha got there?" Pritchard asked, sniffing. "Did I ever tell you that you're my favorite detective of all the detectives back here?"

Pritchard had been talking to another detective, Randy Crile, "Hey, what about me, you fickle sonofabitch?" Crile said, looking hurt.

"No one touches a donut until Esposito gets here. He has first dibs."

"The Walrus?" Randy groaned. "We're screwed. They're gonna all be gone."

At that moment, Alex's phone rang. It was Joe at the front desk. Carstairs said he'd bring him back and Alex took that time to hide the apple fritters.

Joe walked into Investigations a short time later, sniffing the air, "Ah, I see you didn't forget," he said, looking at Alex, beaming.

"I swear, if there's a prison break, we're gonna hook you and Pritchard up and use you to track down the escapees," Alex said.

"A - that would only work if your escapees were made out of baked goods of some sort and B — my knees would give out long before my nose would. Now, where are those donuts? I skipped breakfast on the off chance you wouldn't forget."

"Well, I have a dozen donuts here," Alex said, showing Joe the box on his desk with a wave reminiscent of Vanna White on Wheel of Fortune. "Or...or, you could have what's behind door number two."

Joe frowned, his eyebrow arching, "You're toying with me in a situation where donuts are on the line? Are you insane, man?"

"Your choice," Alex said. Pritchard and Crile were listening with rapt interest. Even Deni had prairie-dogged up out of her cubicle to see.

Joe's eyes narrowed, regarding Alex through those slits with both suspicion and hunger. "Fine. I'll take a chance. I'll take what's behind door number two."

Alex reached into the next cubicle over and retrieved the box containing the apple fritters. He popped open the box and presented them to Joe as though they were precious diamonds on a black velvet cloth.

"Oh. Those are...those are just beautiful. I think I might cry. I'd marry you right now except for that whole you've-got-a-wife-already thing."

"Don't get carried away, big fella. Two of those are mine. Take what you want and throw the rest to the wolves over there," he said, indicating the other detectives.

"Here, we only have the finest in culinary ware," Alex said as he brought out a roll of paper towels from the next cubicle. "Wrap your fritters in these and we'll eat in interrogation room one."

Alex looked over at Deni getting a coconut-covered chocolate donut out of the box, "Will you be joining us today?"

"Nah, you boys go on without me. I've got court today and the subpoena says *Duces Tecum* so I gotta go to evidence, get whatever I've got on the case out, and try to figure out why I put it in there in the first place."

"Well, that sounds like a pain in the ass. Good luck."

Deni gave him a half-smile and a one-finger salute before sinking slowly back into her cubicle until only the finger was visible.

Alex and Joe got some coffee and took their still slightly warm apple fritters into the interrogation room. In an effort to be a kinder and gentler police department, the administration had re-named an interview room, but Alex still used the old name. They sat down with their case files and spread out the information, taking care not to get any icing or coffee on the paperwork. They had covered a decent amount of the financial district and figured they could probably get the rest of it covered in the time allotted.

"I've got an appointment at 1100," Alex said.

"Oh, Hell, that means we have to take two cars. I was getting used to being chauffeured."

"Stop whining. It's unattractive in a man of your years."

"Hmm," Joe mumbled as he licked his finger and chased a piece of icing around on the tabletop until he cornered it. He got it on his finger and licked it off with his eyes closed in bliss, a smile on his face.

"You know we interview all kinds of people in here and have never cleaned the table, right?"

Joe's eyes popped open, "Not until just now. Thanks."

"I wouldn't worry about it," Alex said. "You've probably had your shots. Look, it's close to ten, why don't you head downtown and I'll go to my appointment and catch up with you later."

"OK," Joe said, getting to his feet, adjusting his belt with both hands. "Thanks for the fritters."

"No problem. You know, I was on midnights when I discovered they came out fresh every morning at 0300 hours. So, me and a bunch of other cops were always there at exactly

0300 hours. You could have taken out most of the night squad with one grenade. They came out so hot you could barely eat them and tasted so good your eyes rolled into the back of your head. Then, after two weeks, I found I was up five pounds, so that came to a screeching halt."

"See? That's my problem. No screeching halt. Hell, no halt at all, really," Joe sighed as they headed out the door.

"Hey, can you find your way out? I need to check email."

"Yeah, no worries. I know the way. Catch you later," Joe said, and walked out of Investigations.

Alex settled into his cubicle and brought up his desktop. He signed in using both password and biometric identification and then pulled up his email and began to read. He looked for more emails from Alaric but found none. Toward the end of his session, he found an email from Lt. Benton, IA, which would be Internal Affairs, a wholly-owned subsidiary of the Professional Standards Bureau. The email ordered him to report to IA for an "Administrative Inquiry" at 0900 on Thursday. It did not specify what said inquiry was about.

Alex racked his brain. *Fallout from the shooting?* That was closed. It could only be re-opened if they found new evidence. Alex assigned that a low probability. *Something arising from him screwing with Reed and Malloy the other night?* He didn't think either of them would admit to being caught like a couple of rookies. *Choking out the biker?* Maybe. Whatever Reed and Malloy were ordered to follow him about in the first place. He thought about looking them up and seeing if they knew any more than what they'd told him but that could go wrong in so many ways he rejected it out of hand. In the end, He decided to call his PBA Rep. And he sure as Hell wasn't going to do it from inside the department on a PD phone line. He'd call from his cell on the way to the library to meet "Alaric". On the way out the door, he checked out a portable bug sweeper from Investigations.

Alex got in his car, heading toward the library. About a half-mile from the PD, he pulled into the bay of a do-it-yourself car wash. He got out and scanned the area but saw nothing resembling a tail. He went over the inside compartment of the car slowly and methodically with the bug sweeper but didn't find anything suspicious. *So if they've bugged me, it's not something that's going to relay me talking. It could just be a GPS device that tracks my movements.* He swept the trunk, not finding anything there, either. Assuming it's an active tracking device and gives real-time updates concerning his location, it would probably be hooked up to the car's electrical system and would emit radio waves. If it was a passive tracker, it could be anywhere, downloading his travels to an internal memory, and would have to run on a small battery. That would be very hard to detect. Alex was betting on them wanting real-time information if they thought it was important enough to bug him in the first place.

He popped the hood, searching the engine compartment, where he found the active GPS tracker. It was hooked up to his fuse box. Alex examined it, deciding he could pull the wire powering it for the time he was at the library, and then re-attach it. He was betting on no battery backup, at least for the active tracking. *It might still download my trip to the library but, really, so what? At least this explains why Reed and*

Malloy aren't up my ass every day. A grim, tight-lipped smiled crossed Alex's face as he pulled the wire and got back in the car.

*   *   *

Alex, like most cops, paid dues to a union. In Florida, it was generally either the FOP, Fraternal Order of Police, or the PBA, Police Benevolent Association. The reasons for belonging to a union were many and included, of course, wages and working conditions. Beyond that, however, the PBA would be at your side ASAP in the case of a shooting. Rick Norton, Alex's PBA Rep, was on the scene of his shooting before the lieutenant could get there. There was also something in Florida called the Police Officer's Bill of Rights. It safeguarded officers against unscrupulous practices by police administrators and delineates the procedures involved in Internal Affairs investigations. It only took one bad boss to make you a believer in the union. Alex believed.

Alex dialed Rick on his cell phone. Rick picked up on the second ring.

"Alex! How ya doin'? Everything all right?" Rick asked.

"Yeah. At least, I think so. I got this email from Benton. He wants me to come in at 0900 hours tomorrow for an 'Administrative Inquiry', whatever that is."

"It's a fancy word for 'fishing expedition.' Do you know what it's about?"

"No. I caught Reed and Malloy tailing me a couple of nights ago and they didn't seem to know anything. No real surprise there. And, just now, I found a GPS tracker in my car. It's disabled now, but I don't have a clue why it was put there."

"Hmmm, well, it's their car, they can put a tracker on it if they want. Not a lot we can do about that. How about this... say I meet you at the station at 0845 tomorrow and go into the lieutenant's office with you."

"That'd be great, Rick. I don't know what I did to deserve this attention, but better safe than sorry."

"Okay, man. Whatever it is, we'll handle it. See you tomorrow morning."

"Thanks, buddy. See ya then," Alex said as he hung up.

Alex drove to the library, parking in the middle of the lot to give his nondescript car the best chance to be lost among the others. He set a waypoint after he got out of the car. *Better safe than sorry.* It was forty minutes after ten when he went up to the second floor and located the reference section. He walked slowly, cautiously, to the north side of the reference section and saw a small enclave with three small study carrels arranged in a triangle. The backs of two carrels were facing each other, and the third was at right angles to the other two. The sides of the carrels were about as high as a cubicle's walls. Only two of those carrels had seats and one of those was occupied.

Alex approached the carrels, worried and anxious about what he was going to find. As he got close, the person in the carrel leaned back, looking directly at him. Once again, there was the shock of recognizing his own face.

The man with his face said, "Hello, brother. I'm Alaric. We have a lot to talk about."

Chapter 26

Alex took a seat, looking his doppelganger over and scanning for weapons. He was dressed in a black shirt and jeans with a lightweight hoodie slung over the back of the chair. Doing a cursory visual search, he didn't see any weapons on him. Alaric looked relaxed. He had a half-smile on his face as though he found the whole situation amusing. Alex's frame of mind was entirely different.

"Yeah. Let's start with who the *actual* fuck are you?" Alex said, staring a hole through Alaric.

"I'm exactly who I said I am. Alaric. Your twin."

"Bullshit. Alaric's dead."

Alaric sighed, "He is. In *your* universe. In mine, you're the dead one. Hell, I imagine in the next universe over, we're both dead. Or alive. You know, whatever isn't forbidden..." he paused.

"Is compulsory," Alex finished. Alaric nodded.

"Do you have any idea how inconvenient it is to end up here, where I'm dead and have no history? No Social Security number? Nothing?" Alaric asked, leaning forward, lowering his voice. "It's been a huge pain in the ass. Fortunately, some of the people I knew in the last universe are still in existence in this one. And they have the same skills, thank God. So I'm now officially Michael Reston."

"How did you end up here, making my life complicated?" Alex asked.

"*Your* life? Huh. How about that little chase along the waterfront? You caught me the first two times. I imagine the Alex's and Alaric's in those universes had a tough time of it. On the third try, I hit on the idea of the bridge, having seen it raised my second time out."

"You mean you...?" Alex's brow furrowed.

"Yes. I bounced back to the point in time you found me. I automatically *twinged* and then ran."

"*Twinged?* Is that what you call it?"

"Yeah, named it after the feeling you get between your shoulder blades. Why? What do you call it?"

"Setting a waypoint."

"What...like on a GPS? That's kinda complicated. I like *twinged* better."

"I had no idea that I'd chased you before," Alex said.

"Now you know what the rest of the world feels like when you do it. Both times you chased me to a place I couldn't escape from. One was a blind alley, the other a seawall. By the way, any idea where this ability comes from?"

"Not a clue. How did you discover yours?"

Alaric took a deep breath. He frowned, then hunched forward, clasping his fingers together between his knees, his forearms resting on his thighs. "Dad died when I was between five and six. I can only vaguely remember him. Mom seemed lost without him and then hooked up with this abusive asshole. I got regular beatings from this putz during my youth. Especially when he was drinking. I guess I was twelve or so when I did something that really pissed him off. I don't even recall what it was now. I ran down the hallway with him right on my ass and had a choice between left and right at the end. I was scared shitless. I felt the *twinge* between my shoulder blades but it kind of blended in with the fear. I went left and immediately realized I was trapped. I can still remember how he seemed to fill the doorway, a sadistic smile on his face. I could smell the reek of beer on his breath. I was terrified. And then I suddenly found myself in the hallway, faced with the same decision, and I went right. That room had an open window I dove out of and escaped," He paused. "And you?"

"Much less dramatic. I just got embarrassed in high school," Alex answered. "I'm surprised at mom, though."

Alaric shrugged. "Mom had some personal frailties I assume were kept in check by dad. Your mom ever show any signs of being an alcoholic?"

Alex shook his head. Alaric regarded him with a look on his face that seemed equal parts fascination and envy. "You had dad almost all your life." He said it with a completely flat tone, like it was somehow Alex's fault.

"Up until the crash, yeah, I had both of them," Alex said, staring at Alaric, tense, wary.

Alaric shook himself, then relaxed, leaning back in his chair, "It's funny how something like that can be the pivot upon which your whole life turns. If dad had been around, I'd have probably turned out to be....well... like you," Alaric smiled, like they were sharing a joke.

"Which brings us to why you're not me and what you're currently doing for a living."

Alaric did not seem to want to let go of the idea. "I *could* have been you, though. And you *could* have been me. Then I'd have a wife and a job. Hell, I'd be a respected member of the community," Alaric appeared to be considering the idea. "You know, on second thought, it sounds a little boring," he grinned.

Alex could not get over how eerie it was to be, almost literally, talking to himself. *He seems to be very sure of himself. I'll try a different tack.* "So...why *this* universe, in particular."

"I have no idea why I ended up in this particular universe. Quantum fluctuations? I can tell you what I did to get here, if that's any help."

"Go ahead."

"I was pulling a job, as usual, when I got jammed up by something you can never account for. The random shit that just happens. In this case, the random shit took the form of a cop on patrol. She was in the right place at the right time. Well, for her. For me, it was the wrong place and the wrong time. She called in the cavalry and I got trapped. I'd gotten sloppy. Usually, I *twinged* well before engagement with the job. That way, if anything went wrong, I'd bounce back and walked away like I was never there, which, factually, I wasn't. But, this seemed like such a cake job..." He shook his head at his stupidity. "There I was, like a rat in a trap, so I did the only thing I could think of: I *twinged.*"

"What does that even mean?" Alex asked.

Alaric's snorted, his smile lopsided, rueful. "I assume you've run into the three *twinge* limit?"

Alex nodded.

"I started *twinging* like mad. Hitting the limit and going for the fourth. Every single time, I shifted into a different universe. I did this over and over until the cops simply weren't there anymore. And I was here. In this universe. And of course, they weren't there. I don't exist here so, naturally..."

"You couldn't have been there committing the crime," Alex finished.

"Exactly," Alaric said. "I found that out in short order when I went home and found someone else was living there. Then I found my credit cards didn't work. Also, I had none of the resources that were available to me before. In retrospect, it probably would have been easier just to let myself get caught."

"Certainly would have made *my* life easier," Alex muttered.

Alaric smiled, "I guess so. Fortunately, I always carry a large amount of cash as well as gold coins sewn into my belt. I suppose it's a consequence of my criminal lifestyle. Drives TSA nuts."

"One of the first things I did was research myself to find out what happened to me. As you can imagine, it is somewhat disconcerting to find you have been wiped from existence, which is what I discovered when I accessed the internet from my friendly local library. I looked through online records and found I had died at birth. As grisly and morbid as it sounds, I have visited my tiny little grave. A grave that, in my original universe, is occupied by you. During the research, I also found that my twin brother, dead to me all these years, is alive and, by some odd quirk of fate, a cop. So, I resurrected myself with a new identity and began to ply my old trade. Pretty successfully, I might add. I also did some recon on you."

"You were there under the power lines and outside the dojo," Alex stated flatly.

Alaric looked thoughtful, "Hmmm...apparently, my ninja skills need honing, but, yes, that was me. It's interesting. We are both involved in the martial arts, you in the Japanese arts and me in Chinese gung-fu, but then, we *are* identical twins."

"If we're so identical, why are we on opposite sides of the law?"

"The difference in our childhoods, I suspect. Also, I hear that the line between cop and criminal is very, very thin. Both exist, to some extent, outside society. One to protect it, one to prey on it. Tell me you haven't noticed the same thing."

"Oh, I've had this conversation before with other cops. The best cops are the ones that can mimic how criminals think. And you can't fully mimic something you aren't similar to or familiar with. So, yeah, I get the argument. The question is: what do we do now? Where do we go from here?"

"I'm afraid, dear brother, that your best option is to kill me and destroy the body utterly. Not a trace of DNA left. Acid, maybe. Or fire."

"I'm not going to kill you," Alex drew back, repulsed by the suggestion.

"No? Have you thought about how inconvenient I would be? How difficult would it be to explain my existence? You could claim that I somehow survived the birth and my death was faked for some reason. Of course, if they exhumed my tiny little casket, I'm fairly sure the body would yield DNA which would prove that to be untrue. Frankly, I don't think you could make up a lie that good. We'd probably both end up strapped to a lab table somewhere in a secret, underground governmental lair."

"That's a little over the top, but I've had some of the same thoughts," Alex said. "How about you just disappear? Go someplace else and, for God's sake, don't get caught. You've got to have enough money by now, if the FBI is right, to live for some time without, well, let's call it 'working'."

Alaric chuckled, "I do have a considerable amount of money but not as much as you might think. I have expenses, too. Overhead, as it were. Fences get their cut, the lawyers and shady accountants I use get theirs. It's a vicious circle. I'm already looking into various places to live as an expatriate. Belize and Costa Rica are on my list, as are several Eastern European countries. But I'm not there yet in terms of money."

"Why here, man? Why right in my backyard? Just want to rub my nose in it?"

"No. Not at all. I did want to meet you. You have to admit; it's kind of fascinating to look at someone who is, for all intents and purposes, you. If we had both survived childbirth and had grown up together, we'd be used to it. But we didn't. And we aren't."

"Besides," Alaric continued, crossing his ankle over his knee, "I have a specific target in mind. Murman Financial. They're as dirty as it gets. Up to their eyeballs in corruption."

"You'll never get past the alarm system," Alex said.

"The tomographic system? I'll grant you it's pretty slick but I have an idea. Let me bounce this off you. If I set up a sort of rhythmic *twinging* where I'm not really in either the extended position or the bounce-back position, could I be detected?"

"You're talking about existing in a state of superposition?" Alex looked at Alaric doubtfully.

"Ride the cosmic wave, baby! Schrodinger's kitty alive and dead at the same time."

"How is that even possible?".

"Actually, Alex, I don't know that it is. But I'm gonna find out," Alaric grinned.

"Great. You get caught and then I'll have to explain it," Alex said, a sour expression on his face as he got up. He glanced at his watch. "I have to go. I'm supposed to be protecting the city from you. Stay the hell away from Murman Financial. I mean it. This isn't over."

He turned to go when, over his shoulder, he heard Alaric say, "Now, see? This is why people don't like family reunions."

Despite himself, Alex laughed.

Chapter 27

On the way to the financial district, Alex pulled over in a parking lot and reattached the GPS device under his hood. He could only imagine the relief of whoever was monitoring the signal. He got back into the car and called Esposito.

"Thank God you called. Those apple fritters will only last a man so long, Dorn."

"How sharper than a serpent's tooth is the tongue of an ungrateful detective. What's your twenty?"

"In front of the Chinese buffet where you should be."

"The one at Bradbury and Lincoln? In the shopping center?"

"Of course. It's all you can eat crab legs day and I like to see the look of fear in their eyes when they see me coming through the door."

"I'll bet. Be there in a minute."

Alex pulled up in front of the restaurant and saw Joe standing impatiently in front of it, hands on hips, glaring at him. A light blue Ford Taurus had been pacing him for the last half-mile. To be fair, he was expecting a tail since he had gone dark for over an hour when he unplugged his GPS. Predictably, the Taurus turned into the parking lot but at least they went down to another entrance.

"Howdy-Ho, partner. You hungry?" Joe called, as he walked up.

"I could eat," Alex said as they both turned toward the restaurant. It was set into a strip mall shopping center that housed a chain grocery store and drug store as well as several independent businesses, the Forbidden City Buffet and Chinese Restaurant among them. There were two stylized Chinese dragons painted onto the windows, facing each other with claws raised and the door between them. The front of the building, above the windows, was built up to look like a pagoda, with green tiles, fluted ends, and a gate in the center.

As they approached the plate-glass windows on the front of the restaurant, Alex talked to Joe without turning his head toward him.

"So, Joe. I want you to take your time and look at the menu like you're reading it. While you're doing that, look at the reflection of the light blue Ford Taurus."

Joe pretended to be reading the menu and said, "Okay, I got it. What about it?"

"I think they're following me."

"Oh, for cripes sake! I got news for you; you're just not that important."

"I know that. And you know that. But whoever attached a GPS tracker to my car doesn't know it."

Joe looked at Alex askance and raised an eyebrow, "Should I not be seen associating with you?"

"Might be safer for you if you didn't. Anyone you recognize?"

"Too far away for me to make anyone in the car. A Taurus, though, that's pretty generic. Could be anyone."

"Yeah. I can't make out anyone either. Let's eat."

They went into the Chinese restaurant and were immediately assailed with delicious and exotic aromas. They stopped by the cash register area which, along with a low wall, separated the dining room from the take-out waiting area. Alex's stomach growled as the Asian hostess approached. She was walking from the back of the restaurant, past the buffet steam tables, clad in a red, ankle-length *cheongsam* decorated with gold dragons that accented her figure. Her coal-black hair was pulled back in a ponytail, her face smooth and unlined though Alex placed her at around fifty years of age. She moved gracefully, unhurried, as she approached the front of the restaurant, pausing only to pick up two menus by the cash register before she spoke.

"Two for the buffet?" she said, not seeming at all overawed by Esposito's size. Alex nodded and she turned, deposited the menus back into the slot by the cash register, and escorted them to their seats.

"I hope you gentlemen will enjoy your lunch," she said, the trace of an accent limning her voice. "Your waitress will be right with you," she said as she smiled and turned back to the front of the restaurant.

Waiting for the waitress to take their drink order, Alex turned to Esposito and said, "She did not seem all that impressed by you, Joe."

"Oh, she was. She probably has standing orders not to scream when she sees someone like me and...hello, what's this?" Joe cut his eyes toward the door.

Alex looked over to see Reed and Malloy standing at the entrance, waiting to be seated. He raised his hand, motioning for them to come over and sit with him and Joe. The hostess walked them over to the table and they sat down, looking a little sheepish.

"So, I assume that's you two in the Ford Taurus out there?" Alex's question was more of a statement.

"You assume correctly, Kimo Sabe," Reed said, idly unwrapping his chopsticks.

"Aren't you guys breaking protocol right now?" Alex inquired.

Reed and Malloy looked at each other. Malloy cleared his throat and spoke up, "Look, we figured you found the GPS tracker on your car and disabled it because you wanted to go someplace where you didn't want company."

"Drove the lieutenant apeshit, by the way," Reed chimed in, grinning.

"Right. Anyway, after you re-enabled your GPS and we picked you up, we expected that you would be looking for a tail and we've already been down this embarrassing road once. Plus, we were hungry and it's crab leg day," Malloy looked at Joe. "Can he be trusted?"

"No speakee English," Joe deadpanned.

"Yeah," Alex said. "He's good."

That seemed to satisfy both Reed and Malloy. The four detectives had lunch together, chit-chatting about departmental gossip, speculating on promotions and transfers, and generally putting the intelligence-gathering capabilities of the NSA to shame. Alex tried to gently pry more information out of either of the detectives but didn't get much.

Finally, Reed said, after a hearty belch which was only partially smothered by his napkin, "I'll tell you this much. Vice is involved somehow. I saw Chapman coming out of the Lieutenant's office the other day and he had a guilty look on his face."

"He always has a guilty look on his face because he's always guilty of something. Was he slithering on his belly like a reptile? That's his usual method of travel," Malloy said.

I guess there's no love lost there, Alex thought. Aloud he said, "I'll grant you that he bears more than a passing resemblance to Wormtongue, but I don't know that I've done anything to attract his attention."

The other three detectives looked at him puzzled. "Who?" asked Joe.

"Grima Wormtongue?"

Nothing.

"Lord of the Rings?"

Still nothing.

"I hate you guys," Alex said, sulking. The other three laughed.

Malloy cupped his hands into a makeshift bullhorn over his mouth and made an alarm noise "Nerd Alert! Nerd Alert!"

"Do you know how many ways I can kill a man with a pair of chopsticks?" Alex asked, picking up his unused pair and twirling them through his fingers.

"Well, looks like lunch is over," Malloy said as he and Reed got up.

"Great. You made him angry and now I'm stuck with him the rest of the day. Assholes," Joe lamented to no one in particular.

Malloy stopped, "Remember: this lunch never took place. We never met today," he said, dead serious.

"Got it. Thanks, guys, for at least being honest."

"No problem," he said, looking vaguely embarrassed.

Joe watched them walk away, "Not really bad guys," he said. "Ready to get back out there and do the FBI's work for 'em?"

"Sure," Alex said. He'd continue to go through the motions and collect names, addresses, and contact numbers for the security studies but it was useless. He knew exactly where Peter Perfect was going to strike. He just didn't know when. And, even if he did, he couldn't tell anyone.

Chapter 27

When Alex got home, he took Khan for a walk which delighted his furry son to no end. As he walked along their well-worn route, he was lost in thought. He couldn't figure a solution to the problem of Alaric. *Literally, my evil twin.* He grimaced. If he caught and arrested him, there was too much to explain. It would consume his life. If Alaric moved on, there was always a danger he would be caught, and exposed, and again it would ruin Alex's life. He began to seriously consider killing Alaric and disposing of the body.

Legally, he doesn't exist. So is it murder? Of course, it is, you idiot. It doesn't matter that he's from another reality; he's still a thinking, feeling human being. There's no way of getting around that. Plus, he's your brother. Did you forget THAT, genius? The arguments kept bouncing around inside his skull as he walked along behind the dog. In the end, Alex came to two conclusions. The first was that killing Alaric and hiding the evidence made the most logical sense. The second was that he simply couldn't do it.

He arrived back at the house after forty minutes of internal debate during which Khan had urinated on every vertical surface within reach. He took the leash off after he opened the door.

"Well, at least one of us accomplished something," he said.

Alex decided to make one of Eve's favorite dinners, spaghetti and meatballs. The first time they'd had it, she'd insisted on reenacting the famous "Lady and the Tramp" scene. He'd learned it was messier in real life. He mixed the meat with spices, Italian breadcrumbs, and a raw egg, formed the mixture into balls, and shoved them in the oven. He checked the clock, deciding to wait on the pasta. On a whim, he went to the back of the house and looked up along the power line right-of-way and, there, along the ridgeline, was a figure with binoculars.

"Son. Of. A. Bitch," Alex said. He went back to the bedroom, getting his spotter scope out of its case in the closet. It was a beauty. A Swarovski Optiks 20-60 scope with an eighty-millimeter objective lens and a tripod. It was his father's, who'd used it for rifle practice with an old army buddy and, oddly enough, birdwatching. He took it to a window in the back of the house and, after checking to make sure he wasn't backlit, looked up the slope again, focusing the scope until the figure resolved clearly enough to tell it was Alaric.

Alex brought the scope down, letting it dangle in his hand by his side. *He has some kind of obsession with me. He's not going to let this go.* That thought crystallized into action. Alex went back to the same closet he'd retrieved the spotting scope from and pulled out a large, rectangular, matte-black Pelican case. He laid it on the bed and opened it up, exposing his father's rifle, an old English Enfield L-42 sniper model. It was his dad's favorite and one of the few guns he'd kept after his parents passed. It wasn't the newest or the best long-range rifle by far, having been originally designed and built in 1895. But his dad loved its history and the beautiful, well-oiled walnut stock. Alex checked the action and saw that it was loaded. He went to his *dojo*. It was dark after he turned off the hall light and opened the door eighteen inches, sliding along the wall until he got to the edge of the glass doors. He unlocked them, slipping one side open about eight inches, praying that Alaric wouldn't notice the movement.

He went out onto the floor of the *dojo,* well back from the glass doors, going to one knee and then easing down onto the floor in a spot that lined up with the open glass door, the faint figure still visible on the hill. He bent his knees, aligning about forty-five degrees with the target, the fore-grip balanced in his left hand; the strap wrapped around his forearm. His left elbow pressed against the top of his left thigh just above the knee. He ran through the checklist in his mind, one that had been drilled into him by his father. The butt end of the stock was pulled back firmly against his right shoulder. His right hand was in position to shoot, his index finger laying along the stock, staying there until it was time to pull the trigger. He consciously, inch by inch, centimeter by centimeter, tightened the connections between himself and the rifle, taking the slack out of his body until he and the rifle were one unit.

Alex put his eye behind the scope mounted on the weapon. It was a Bushnell, dialed up to a 12x magnification. He snugged his face up against the leather cheek rest on the stock. He found the target and placed his finger on the trigger. The maximum range of the rifle was two thousand yards. Its effective range was closer to six hundred. Alex estimated the target range to be about seven hundred yards. At this distance, the shot was like a trigonometry problem. He adjusted for distance and bullet drop, settling again behind the scope.

He could see Alaric clearly. *Pull the trigger. Pull it!* His finger lay on the trigger but it wouldn't move. Alex's jaws knotted as war raged inside him. On the outside, he was as still as a stone, his breathing shallow and slow. *Pull the damn trigger!* Alaric turned to start back down the blind side of the hill. *Now! Now!* Still, his finger did not move as beads of sweat popped out on his forehead, Alaric slowly disappeared behind the rise.

"Shit," Alex said, pulling his head up and putting the rifle in a vertical position between his knees. He let out a long sigh, the tension draining out of his body. Khan started barking at the door and Alex realized Eve would soon be home. He got up, moving quickly to the bedroom, and replaced the rifle in its case. He closed the case and put it back in the closet along with the scope. He looked at everything to make sure it looked normal and then took a moment to roll his neck muscles and listen to his spine crack.

He made it to the living room in time to see Eve coming through the door, greeting Khan. He took a moment and settled himself. She looked up at him, a wide smile on her face as she sniffed the air appreciatively.

"Is that my favorite meal I smell cooking?" she asked, putting down her paperwork and bag.

"Why, yes. Yes, it is. And it was cooked by your favorite husband," Alex said, putting on a smile and gathering her into his arms for a hug. He could feel the "baby bump." He felt happiness and contentment sweep over him, something he'd never felt before. All the tension of a few minutes before seemed to slide away.

Maybe this is what Alaric envies. Maybe this is what he wants. But it's mine. Mine.

Eve broke free from the hug and, placing her hands on his hips, kissed him lightly on the lips. "I'm going to change. I love you. And thank you for fixing dinner," she said, pirouetting in place before gliding down the hall to the bedroom.

"I love you and you're welcome," Alex called.

I should have pulled the damn trigger.

Chapter 28

The next morning, Alex got to the PD at eight-thirty. He sat in the visitor's parking lot until eight fifty when Rick drove in and parked. He had a bright yellow Camaro, so it wasn't difficult to spot him. As Alex approached the car, Rick looked up, waved, and put out his cigarette — one of the last of the unrepentant smokers.

Rick got out of the car and shook hands with Alex, "What's shakin', bacon?" he said with a grin. Rick was wearing tan slacks and his ever-present PBA polo shirt, white this time. He smoothed back his thinning blond hair, parted in the middle and a little mussed from driving with the window down.

"I guess we'll both find out in few minutes. I have no idea what these assholes want."

"What they want is to have a little, informal IA without being encumbered by the Police Bill of Rights. It's my job to make sure they don't get what they want. And I love my job," Rick grinned.

Alex knew it to be true. He'd seen Rick reduce administrators to impotent, apoplectic fury. He'd once seen him piss off the Chief so much he'd closed his eyes, waving his hand in front of Rick saying, "I don't see you. I don't see you", like an eight-year-old trying out a new Harry Potter spell. Alex's jaw had dropped when it happened. He truly regretted not having his phone out at the time to capture that moment forever. If he had, it would still be on Youtube, in all its glory.

As Alex and Rick went into the PD together, Alex saw Carstairs still stuck on the front desk and waved at him. Hank knew Rick from the shooting investigation and waved them both through. They went up to the second floor and Alex knocked on Lt. Benton's door. Benton was on the phone and could see Alex through the open blinds on the windows bordering the door. He waved at him to come in.

The lieutenant smiled at Alex but then looked past him to Rick, and his expression instantly hardened. "Let me call you back," he said over the phone and hung up.

"Reporting as ordered, lieutenant," Alex said, affably.

"What is *he* doing here?" Benton said, jerking his head in Rick's direction.

"Nice to see you, too, Lt. Benton," Rick said, in his most agreeable voice.

"I thought I made it clear, Detective Dorn, that this was simply an administrative inquiry and did not require union representation."

"I don't recall you mentioning anything about the union, Lieutenant, but I'm still a little jumpy after the shooting and all, so I thought I'd have my rep here, you know, just to make me feel better," Alex explained.

"I don't think he should be allowed in here, personally…," Benton started.

"Is there any way that this line of inquiry could result in discipline for Detective Dorn in any way, shape, manner, or form?" Rick interrupted.

Benton stared malevolently at Rick who gazed placidly back, his face as bland and innocent as an angel. Benton fumed silently for half a minute before trusting himself to speak, "Fine. I'll take into account Detective Dorn's recent trauma and allow you to stay, Norton."

"Thank you, lieutenant, I appreciate that," Rick said.

Benton grunted, straightening out some papers on his desk, "Well, I'll get right to the point then. Vice has had an establishment under surveillance for about three weeks. It's a pawn store that is suspected of several things, like receiving and dealing in stolen goods."

Alex frowned, "How'd Vice get involved? Wouldn't that be property crimes?" he asked.

"I'm getting to that," Benton said sharply. He paused, taking another deep breath, "Normally, yes, it would be property crimes. And they have worked the business before but haven't been able to make a case. Vice was working a different angle, drugs and porn. Possibly child porn."

"Which pawn shop is this?" Alex asked.

"You tell me, Detective. You went into it."

"What?" Alex said, surprised. "I haven't been in a pawn store for…let's see…seven or eight months when I was looking for jewelry for my wife."

"That's not what the vice officers say and they know what you look like. It's not like you're a stranger."

"So you don't have a violation to charge Detective Dorn with; you're just on a fishing expedition here?" Rick interjected.

Benton stood bolt upright, leaned over his desk, pointed his finger at Norton, and yelled, "YOU need to shut the fuck up!"

Rick started to jump right back at Benton when Alex said, quietly, "Where and when was this supposed to have occurred?"

Both Benton and Norton stopped like two dogs going after each other, brought up short by their leashes. They both looked at him. The lieutenant sat back down, collected himself, and looked at his notes, "Three Coins Pawn on Monday afternoon around 1400."

"Hmmm," Alex said. "Can I borrow your phone?"

Both Rick and the lieutenant were looking at him a little strangely now. Benton pushed the phone across the desk to Alex.

Alex dialed three digits, waited until someone picked up at the other end, and said, "Hank? Is Detective Esposito There? Yeah? Good. Would you escort him up to Lt. Benton's office, please? Thanks." He then hung up the phone.

"We'll sort this all out momentarily," Alex said. The next three minutes were very uncomfortable for everyone in the office. There was no small talk. The lieutenant busied himself looking at, or pretending to look at, something on his computer. Rick fidgeted the way smokers do when deprived of their cancer sticks. He spent at least a minute smoothing his mustache with his finger. Alex kept turning the thought over in his head. *That was Alaric they saw. He's already screwing up my life. Sounds like he's lining up a fence to convert whatever he gets into something more negotiable.* A knock on the door caused everyone in the room to jump slightly. Alex got up and opened it to see Carstairs and Joe standing there, worried looks on both their faces.

"Thanks, Hank. Good morning, Joe. Come on in," Alex said cheerfully. Joe looked at him through narrowed eyes but said nothing.

When Joe got into the office, his bulk made it suddenly seem very cramped, his ill-at-ease demeanor doing nothing to alleviate the claustrophobia. The lieutenant nodded at Joe curtly.

"Joe, where were you at two o'clock Monday afternoon?" Alex asked.

"Whaddya mean? I was with you," Joe said, frowning, a little perplexed.

"And we were where?"

"The Anderson building. Downtown. Getting shafted by the FBI."

"Detective Esposito, other than your word for it, is there any other documentation of Detective Dorn being there?" Lt. Benton asked, staring at Joe, hostility underlining his every word.

Joe scratched his head, "I imagine so. Security was pretty tight. Almost had to give DNA to get in."

"So, Lieutenant, unless you're saying that Detective Dorn here can be in two places at one time, I think you're going to have to admit that you're barking up the wrong tree," Rick jumped in, not able to resist sticking it to Benton.

Benton brooded for a moment before looking up and smiling, though the smile didn't reach his eyes, "I guess that maybe a mistake was made. I'll double-check with Vice and see if there is any way they could be wrong, but for right now, it looks like you're in the clear, Detective Dorn."

"Yes sir, thank you. We'll get out of your hair, now. I'm sure you've got more important things to do."

Benton nodded and the three of them left his office.

"Did you honestly say "get out of his hair"? That was the worst toupee I've ever seen," Joe said out of the corner of his mouth, only feet away from the lieutenant's door.

Alex smiled, "He thinks it looks natural. That thing couldn't look any more *un*-natural if it had a chin strap."

"Could you guys at least wait to high-five until we get out of admin?" Rick said under his breath.

They maintained tactical silence until they got outside of the building. As soon as they cleared the door, Alex turned to Rick, "I know that didn't amount to much, Rick, but thanks for coming," he said, extending his hand.

Rick grabbed it, "No problem, amigo. That was fun watching Benton eat his words. I live for shit like this. You can call anytime you have a problem."

Joe looked at them both, "That's fine, but next time, could you not drag *me* into your tawdry affairs?"

"No promises man. You keep hanging around me and you're bound to catch a certain amount of crap."

Rick sketched a salute as he walked toward his car, "It's been fun, gentlemen but I have a Sheriff's Department contract to negotiate."

"Have a great time with that, Rick. Thanks again."

As Rick waved and got into his car, Joe turned to Alex, "This at least explains why Reed and Malloy are all over you."

"Yeah, maybe that'll stop now. Who knows," he shrugged, "I might actually miss 'em."

"Yeah, like you'd miss a case of bleeding hemorrhoids. What's on the agenda for today? More of the same ol', same ol'?"

"Unless you've got something better to do. Looks like we're going to finish in time, anyway."

The rest of the day went by quickly as they compiled more security stats. Several times, as he went by the Murman Financial Building, he wondered when the strike would be and whether Alaric could pull it off. *Being in a state of superposition, being neither here nor there?* It sounded crazy. At 4 o'clock, Alex called it quits for the day and both detectives headed home.

Chapter 29

Alex got home before Eve, letting Khan out into the side yard despite his obvious attempts to herd him to the garage door for a walk. He gathered up his *gi,* debated taking his weapons but decided against going to *kodudo* class. He was still thinking about the tomographic alarm system at Murman Financial and whether it could lock on to Alaric if he was able to achieve a state of superposition. He let Khan in, still preoccupied when he got in the car and left the house. He was halfway to the *Dojo* before he remembered he hadn't left a note for Eve.

Ah, well, it's Thursday. She'll know I'm at the dojo.

Alex pulled into the *dojo* parking lot early and opened the place up, turning on the air conditioners, checking the building for anything that needed to be done. He thought the floors needed an extra good cleaning. He made a mental note to have everyone line up at the end of the class with wet rags and race down the length of the *dojo* floor, pushing the rags in front of them, then do the same with dry rags, a cleaning method hadn't changed in hundreds of years. *Really, who am I to challenge tradition?*

Alex checked the class log sheets to see if anyone had been missing more than a few classes. He was especially watchful where teenagers were concerned. He'd seen the martial arts straighten kids out who were headed in the wrong direction and he had a vested interest, as both *sempai* and police officer, to see kids got the best shot they could in life. There weren't any red flags that jumped out at him, and he wondered if Raymond Ramirez would show tonight for his first class. The first class was always the most intimidating when you didn't know anyone and had no idea what to do. The only answer was perseverance. *A Black Belt is just a white belt that never gave up. They should put that in a fortune cookie.*

Alex dressed in his *gi* and cinched his belt tight just below his belly button. The ends hung down to the middle of his thighs. *Anything lower than that looks silly. Well, in my august opinion.* He grabbed a *suburito* from the wall. It looked like someone didn't quite finish making a wooden sword. It had the handle of a wooden sword but, above where the hand guard would be, the graceful arc of the sword was replaced with a somewhat ungainly looking block of wood that was thicker than a wooden sword and a little longer. The effect was to make it much heavier. He began to practice *suburi*, overhead strikes that started with the handle at maximum extension above his head, the tip of the *suburito* tapping his lower back, and ended with a controlled, focused stop at waist level in front of him. He worked his way up and down the *dojo* floor, going one way with his right foot and hand forward, using a slide-step, coming back with the left hand and foot forward. Each strike was accompanied by an exhalation of breath and complete mind-body focus. After ten minutes, he was sweating and warmed up, his shoulders, arms, and forearms burning.

He had just finished when the first students for the beginner class started filtering in. Alex saw Raymond among them and he smiled, waving at him. Raymond already had his *gi* on and had attempted to tie the belt. The knot was wrong; one end hung lower than the other. Alex went to where he was standing nervously near the wall.

"Here," he said, "let me help you with that belt. Go ahead and untie it." As he said it, Alex untied his belt.

Alex lined himself up with Raymond, standing to his left and facing the same way, toward the back of the dojo. "Grab the belt by the middle so you have equal lengths on each side. Got it?" Raymond nodded. "Okay, take the middle part of the belt and place it against your lower abdomen just under your belly button and right at your hips. Okay, now cross it in the back and bring the ends out in front of you. Still even?" Raymond nodded again. "Good. Now cross the left over the right and tuck it under both pieces of the belt. Bring it out. Now cross right over left and pull tight. See? It's a square knot and the ends are, well," he smiled, looking at Raymond's belt, "pretty even." Raymond turned to face Alex and look at both of their belts to compare them.

"You'll get better. Don't be sloppy. Sloppy makes *Sensei* frown." Alex affected a cartoonish frown but Raymond was looking past him and not laughing.

"Oh, makes me frown, does it, *sempai?*"

Alex stopped, tilted his head back, and closed his eyes, grimacing. Then he opened one of them, squinted at Raymond, and stage-whispered, "He's right behind me, isn't he?"

Raymond nodded, but he was smiling this time.

Alex turned. *Sensei* Forriere was standing two feet behind him dressed in his *gi*, his arms crossed and a stern look on his face. Sensei Forriere was two inches shorter than Alex, thin and tan with his gray hair cropped close to his skull. There wasn't an ounce of fat on his body. Alex stood at attention, suppressed a smile, and said, "Oops."

"Oops, indeed," *Sensei* said. He looked past Alex to Raymond, "Pay attention to what *Sempai* Alex tells you. He's right. Sloppy makes me frown." Then he smiled, "But not too much. Alex, could I see you in my office?" And with that he strode toward the back of the *dojo*, his back ramrod straight, his feet gliding across the floor.

"*Hai, Sensei,*" Alex answered. He walked behind *Sensei,* turned, and mugged a look of fright for Raymond, who barely stifled a giggle.

They entered the office with *Sensei* going behind the desk and taking a seat. Alex sat in one of the seats in front and waited for him to speak. *Sensei* looked at some papers on his desk for a few minutes, then looked up.

"So I take it that young man is your new project?" he asked, one eyebrow raised.

"*Hai, Sensei*. Raymond Ramirez. I get a feeling this might be the one that makes it all the way to black belt," Alex answered, his expression serious.

"I hope you're right. Lord knows I love to see kids work their way up the ranks and accomplish things. I suppose I'll have to find things around the *dojo* for him to do," he sighed. "Why do you do this, Alex? You know you're just making work for me."

"I guess I see kids that need a little help and I know how much karate helped me. Besides, you know the old proverb about 'as the twig is bent, so grows the tree'?"

Sensei nodded.

"Ever try to straighten out a full-grown oak?" Alex asked.

"I take your point," *Sensei* said. "Now get out of here and go teach the beginner's class. I have some paperwork to catch up on now that I'm no longer indisposed."

"Oh, right. How did things turn out, *Sensei?*" Alex asked.

Sensei stared at Alex, stood up, and gravely reached down to the seat to retrieve an inflatable donut. He held it up for Alex's inspection, "Does this answer your question?" he asked.

"*Hai Sensei,*" Alex said, not breaking a smile. "I guess I'll just get out there and teach that class now."

Sensei grunted, replaced the donut, and sat back down. Carefully.

Chapter 30

The classes that night went smoothly with Alex teaching the beginner's class and *Sensei* teaching the advanced class. Alex looked for any sign he was in pain or not able to teach but his techniques were, to Alex's eyes, flawless. *Sensei* had originally studied while serving in the Marines Corps, having been stationed on Okinawa in the 1970s. He had studied at the *Jundokan* under men like Eichi Miyazato. Miyazato had studied directly under the founder of Goju Ryu, Chojun Miyagi. *Sensei* was in his sixties but was still as fluid as a tendril of smoke and as hard as a cypress knot. For Alex, he perfectly encapsulated the Goju philosophy of uniting both hard and soft, as reflected by the name of the style: *Go-* Hard, *Ju-* Soft.

Alex finished the classes and helped close up the *dojo*. He climbed into his car for the ride home, taking a moment to relax and consider how he was feeling. He realized that, for the first time that day, he felt relaxed. Karate did this for him. Centered him. Brought him peace. He felt as long as he had *this*, he would never need a psychiatrist. He took a deep breath and started the car. He assumed the GPS tracker was still on the car but didn't let it bother him. At least it gave Reed and Malloy time off to go home and be with their families. As a matter of course, he checked for tails but found nothing. Everything seemed to be as it should.

When he pulled into the driveway, he could hear Khan whining. Eve opened the door and let him out to maul Alex. Khan seemed wildly happy to see him, even more so than usual. He would not stop whining or jumping up to lick his face. Finally, Alex grabbed him by the neck ruff and held him in place, talking to him calmly, rubbing the side of his face against the dog's. Khan calmed down to a reasonable level, which was usually just this side of Tasmanian Devil.

Eve stood in the doorway and said, "I'm glad to see *he's* back to normal. And look, you got your regular car back. That was fast." She smiled and turned to go back into the house, leaving the screen door open.

Alex followed her inside; Khan glued to his side. "What do you mean 'got my regular car back?'" Alex asked.

"Honestly, are you going senile? I'm the one with pregnant brain. If you lose it too, no one in the house will be a competent adult."

"To be honest, that was always debatable for me anyway but, seriously, what about the car?"

Eve had been drying dishes and stopped, regarding him with a dishtowel in one hand and the other planted firmly on her hip.

"Okay. I'm going to go through this s-l-o-w-l-y so that you can get it all. When you were home earlier and Khan was acting all weird around you, you had a different car. You said that they took yours in for some work and this was a loaner. We talked for about twenty minutes and then you went to karate. I guess there wasn't too much wrong with the car because now you have it back. That's not as important as Khan. I'm really glad he is being his normal self now. He was acting like he wanted to be near you but then shied away when you tried to pet him. I've never seen him do that. Maybe you got some funky bad-guy smell on you.

"There! Happy now? All caught up?" Eve asked sarcastically, then turned away, returning to the dishes.

Alex stood inside the doorway, frozen. His face was a mask, as he processed what Eve had told him. *Alaric! He was here! In my house! With my wife! Fuck!* Trembling slightly, he turned to Khan, who was more than glad for the extra attention. He knelt down and began petting him, masking the rage that gripped him. *Not my wife, you son-of-a-bitch! Not ever!* He used every speck of control he'd garnered through the martial arts and slowed his breathing. After a few moments, he got control of his breath as he consciously relaxed his shoulders and sunk his body into his core. The rage was replaced with a cold fury; something as cold and hard and unforgiving as the edge of a knife. He compartmentalized all the rage, the anger, the fear. The whole process took about thirty seconds.

"Well, Khan seems fine now, babe," Alex said as he arose. "Maybe you're right. I just got something on me only a dog could smell and he just didn't like it." *Couldn't fool Khan, could you? Could you, brother?*

Alex went up behind Eve, encircling her waist with his arms, pulling her back into him. He stuck his nose into the hair at the nape of her neck, inhaling deeply. *God, she even smells beautiful.* He slowly rocked from side to side, "Do you know how much I love you? Always. Always and forever."

She relaxed into him, putting her arms over his, smiling, "You'd better, mister, 'cause I'm not going anywhere." She spun in his arms and they were facing one another. They kissed, tenderly, then passionately. In the middle of this, the thought came to Alex that without her, his life would be meaningless. Literally. He had never felt this way about anyone else, nor was he likely to again. This was a one-shot deal he would guard this with everything he had. He reached down and, still kissing her, picked her up and carried her toward the bedroom.

As they entered the bedroom, she murmured, "Better enjoy doing this while you can, Buck-o."

Alex looked down at her, "I'll be doing this when you're nine months pregnant."

Anything she had to say after that was muffled by Alex's mouth and soon, she didn't want to say anything at all.

After they'd made love, Eve rolled onto her side, falling asleep whispering, "I love you." She was snoring gently. Alex waited until he was sure she was fast asleep, then got up and checked every point of entry in the house, padding naked from room to room with his compact Glock .40 in his right hand. Khan accompanied him, seeming to sense his urgency.

He was all business, shadowing Alex on his rounds. Satisfied, Alex returned to the bedroom and eased into bed. Eve stirred slightly, then settled back to sleep. Alex stayed awake for some time after that. Khan came over to his side of the bed to check on him. Alex lay there in the dark, scratching Khan behind the ears and planning. Eventually, he fell into a light and fitful sleep.

Chapter 31

The next morning, Alex got up and was fixing an omelet when Eve came up behind him and put her arms around him, wrapping them across his belly, laying her head against his back.

"Good morning, lover," she said, her voice husky. "Thanks for last night. You were mah-velous."

"That may well be the worst impression of Billy Crystal doing an impression of Fernando Lamas EV-AR! Fortunately, you're still cuter than a basketful of puppies holding kittens and I love you," he said. "If you would like to take your seat madam, I have your special-order ham and cheese omelet with whole-wheat toast coming right up. Gotta keep momma and baby well-fed."

Eve released him and poured herself a cup of coffee. "Given up on calling our little bundle of joy Alaric?" she asked, looking at him over her coffee cup as she took a sip.

A dark look passed over Alex's face, disappearing nearly as soon as it appeared. He turned to face her, smiling,

"Yeeaahh....I've been re-thinking that. It is a little ghoulish and kind of an unusual name to hang on a kid."

"Glad you're finally seeing things reasonably which of course means how I see them," she said, sitting down at the table.

Alex brought her plate over to her and set it in front of her, laying the silverware on the side. She looked up at him and asked, "Aren't you forgetting...?".

"Oh, no, I've got it," he said. "Right here." And produced a squeeze bottle of ketchup from behind him, placing it in front of her, "I assumed you'd want to desecrate your eggs in the usual manner."

Wearing a wicked grin, Eve grabbed the ketchup bottle and popped the top open. Then, holding it above her plate with both hands and laughing, "Bwuhahahaha," she sprayed her omelet from one end of her plate to the other.

"I think you got a little on your toast, there," Alex offered, helpfully, as he sat down with a whole wheat English muffin slathered in peanut butter. He picked up his cup of hot tea and held it to his lips, inhaling the scent of Bergamot oranges that gave Earl Grey tea its distinctive taste and aroma. He took a sip and sighed. *Ah, Jean-Luc, I share your vice,* he thought. And then, *Good Lord, I really am a nerd.*

"No eggs for you?" Eve asked between forkfuls.

"Nah. Didn't feel like it this morning," Alex said, taking a deep breath. *Here goes.* "I want to discuss something with you concerning our household." *Damn it! That came out more seriously than I intended.*

Eve's fork full of ketchup-smeared omelet paused on its way to her mouth, "Sounds ominous."

"Well, not really," Alex smiled, trying to take some of the edge off. "It's just that there's been some burglary and home invasion robbery stuff going on lately and I wanted us to keep the house locked up. Even when we're home."

"You think anyone in their right minds would break in after hearing Khan, behind the door, baying for their blood?"

"Probably not. I just want to be careful. Do it for me? Please?"

Seeing he was serious, Eve just said, "Sure. I can do that."

"One more thing before I go to work. I think we should have a safe word."

"Really? I'm pregnant and *now* you want to get kinky? Something about fat women turns you on, big boy?"

Alex chuckled, "No, not *that* kind of safe word. I mean a word only we know that would verify our identity in an email or text."

"Ok, Captain Paranoia. How about 'Ladyhawke'. That's unusual enough."

"Unless we're at a Rutger Hauer retrospective. Why don't we use the word Vice uses on all of its takedowns: *Winnebago.*"

Eve almost spit out her toast, "Winnebago? Seriously?"

"Oh, yeah. I'm surprised drug dealers can go by an RV Park without hitting the ground and going spread eagle."

"Hmmm," Eve demurred, pushing some spilled strawberry jam onto the last bite of toast. "I'm not feeling the whole 'Winnebago' thing." She thought for a moment and then a light came into her eyes, "I've got it. 'Gravity's Rainbow.' That's our safe word."

Alex laughed, "Perfect," he said. He kissed her as he got up and grabbed her plate, letting Khan lick the egg remains off before putting it in the sink.

"Ewwwww," Eve said, making a face. "Do you know where his tongue has been?"

"I am 86% certain that common dish washing soap will kill all the germs. Even his butt germs," Alex said, walking back to the bedroom to dress for the day.

Alex decided to go casual for the day, wearing black BDUs and a red polo shirt emblazoned with the PD insignia over the left pectoral and his name over the right. He carried his compact Glock Model 27 in a positive retention Serpa holster on his right hip and a lightweight Ruger LCR .38 on his left ankle. *Two is one and one is none.* The Ruger was a relatively new acquisition, constructed mostly of plastic polymer, except for the inner workings, hammer, cylinder, and barrel. It was so light Alex sometimes forgot he was wearing it. As a bonus, it had a Crimson Trace laser sight on it. Point and shoot, no aiming required.

He looked over the array of knives in his top dresser drawer. After a moment, he selected a Cold Steel Recon 1 knife. Cold Steel made knives that would stand up to anything. They frequently posted videos of themselves torturing their innocent cutlery with a fervor that would shame the Spanish Inquisition. His last addition was a Gerber Impromptu Tactical Pen, which was more of a weapon you could write with than the other way around. Constructed of machined steel, it could be used as a *Kubotan* or *Yawara* stick and had an integrated glass breaker. He slid it into the sleeve pocket on his left arm.

Alex kissed his wife goodbye on the way out and Khan followed him to the door to be sure a tragic mistake had not been made and he was going to take him for a walk. Khan got to the door and sat, looking up expectantly. Alex scratched his ears, sadly leaving without him. The door had not even finished closing before Khan had wheeled around and started trotting for the bedroom and his last chance for a walk. Alex watched him through the window by the door and shook his head. The dog was a serious addict – a walkaholic.

He looked around the front and then walked to the side yard to look up into the right of way. It was empty. He stopped for a moment, establishing a waypoint. He planned to do this throughout the day as fallback options. As he could feel one easing, he'd dissolve it and establish another and he would do this until he came home tonight. It would be a little taxing and definitely uncomfortable, but he felt it was a necessary evil until the Alaric crisis was resolved. He returned to his car, inspecting it and the surrounding ground before unlocking it and opening the door. He inserted the key, thinking about how nice it would be to have an automatic ignition mechanism. He steeled himself, preparing to reset to the waypoint, then turned the key. *Nothing happened. Well, the car started but other than that, nothing.* Alex backed his car out of the driveway. *This is not gonna be a fun day.*

Chapter 32

Alex's drive to the station was uneventful, so he used the time to plan his day with Esposito. With any luck, they could finish this FBI thing by lunch and use the afternoon to format their report. It wouldn't do at all to hand in second-class work to the Feds. He was still thinking about it when he parked his car and walked through the parking lot to the station. He opened the door to find Hank Carstairs waiting for him in the stairwell. Before Alex could say anything, Carstairs started talking a mile-a-minute.

"I've been watching for your car all morning, detective. Lt. Benton came in early today, like at eight o'clock, and that NEVER happens. Your lieutenant, Lt. Blakely, is also in early. A couple of guys from Vice are in, including Chapman, which also never happens. I started putting two and two together and I figured it had something to do with you. I even heard Chapman mention your name when I went to the break room to get coffee," Carstairs paused to take a breath.

"One of the advantages of being a rookie is that no one notices you," he finished and grinned. If he was a puppy, he would have wagged his tail. Alex almost patted him on his head.

Alex looked at Carstairs and marveled at the informal information system that existed in every police department. You can't stick a bunch of suspicious, nosy people who don't trust you into a building and expect to keep secrets. It just couldn't be done. *I think I've done some of my finest detective work inside these walls.*

"Thanks, Hank. I appreciate the heads-up. Sure you don't want to be a detective? That was some pretty good investigating," Alex said, clapping Carstairs on the shoulder.

Carstairs blushed slightly. *My God, he's that young.* "No," he said, "Not yet anyway. I just figured I owed you and besides, those guys are dicks." Carstairs stopped and listened to some movement on the other side of the door leading to the stairwell. Whoever it was moved past and went down the hall. "I'd better get back. I took my break as soon as I saw you coming in."

As Carstairs started to turn around, Alex asked, "Mind if I make a suggestion?"

Carstairs stopped in mid-turn and turned back around to face Alex. "Sure," he said, looking puzzled.

"Go out this door to the parking lot and walk around for a minute within sight of the cameras before going back to the front desk. Better yet, walk around and go back to the front desk through the front door. Create a plausible and trackable reason for your absence. Don't make it look like you went right to someplace and then came right back from it. It looks like you had a place to go and a reason to be there. The other way, you're just wandering around and getting some fresh air. The best way to get away with something is not to be questioned in the first place."

Carstairs smiled, "I guess that's why you're a detective," he said.

"Yeah. That and my dashing good looks. Thanks again, Hank," Alex said as he extended his hand. Carstairs shook it.

Carstairs nodded then and left through the door Alex had entered. Alex took a moment and let his last waypoint slip. He stretched for a minute, enjoying the lack of tension between his shoulders, then created another waypoint. *I might just need this one,* he thought, opening the interior door and starting toward Investigations.

Alex had just cleared the doorway demarcating Investigations when the trap was sprung. The sergeant from Professional Standards, Charles Morris, was in Investigations when Alex walked through the door, seeming to be engaging in idle gossip with one of the detectives. He immediately stopped talking when Alex cleared the doorway, orienting on him. *Jeez, could you make it any more* obvious? *If you were a Shepherd, your ears would have popped up.* Nearly simultaneously, Reed and Malloy had appeared at the doorway behind him, bracketing him perfectly.

Alex stopped about halfway into the room and glanced over his shoulder. Reed and Malloy had also stopped. Everyone but slick-sleeved rookies knew about Alex's martial arts expertise and most were more than willing to give him a wide berth. Morris had abandoned all effort at pretense and approached Alex, albeit somewhat cautiously. With unerring cop radar, every detective in the room was now focused on the scene before them.

"Any particular reason for bracing me like this, sergeant?" Alex asked.

" I'm sorry if you got that impression, Detective Dorn. I'm just here to escort you to Professional Standards to speak with Lt. Benton," Morris said, wearing a wounded look. The insincerity in the tone of his voice overlaid his expression, giving it a noxious and oily feel. "The detectives," he nodded toward Reed and Malloy, "are here to ensure that we don't have any difficulty."

Alex turned and looked at Reed, the closer of the two. He had the look on his face every cop gets when he's being ordered to do something he doesn't want to do. Both he and Malloy looked apologetic and Reed half-shrugged before looking down at the floor.

"Well, let's not keep the good lieutenant waiting," Alex said and began walking toward the door. Reed and Malloy stepped aside as Morris, caught unawares, nearly ran to get in front of him. Unfortunately, his gait was kind of mincing and not at all authoritative. One of the detectives watching laughed, cutting it short when Morris glared at him as he flounced by. Morris's need to appear to be in charge only amused Alex. *Insecure little bastard.*

Morris turned and caught Alex grinning, his jaws knotting as his teeth clenched. "This way, Detective. Now", Morris ordered gruffly, turning on his heel, furious. He walked quickly out of the office, attempting to put on an air of command presence. Alex stopped, the two detectives behind him almost running into each other, Keystone Cops-style, trying to come to a halt.

"Uh...Alex? What are you doing?" asked Malloy.

"Wait for it," Alex said.

Every detective in the section had completely disengaged from anything resembling work and was watching the growing drama with rapt attention. You could feel the anticipation in the room as the sergeant's fading footfalls could be heard in the silent room as they faltered and then stopped. Alex held up three fingers...two fingers...one. Morris' footsteps were coming back toward Investigations at a quickening pace, becoming louder as he approached.

Alex stood in the aisle between the cubicles with his right hand folded loosely in his left, both hands just below his belt and in line with the buckle. His shoulders were relaxed and his expression was calm as Morris rounded the corner with his face red and clenched like an angry fist.

"What the fuck!?" he screamed as he came around the corner, entering Investigations, his voice coming out in a near falsetto, "I gave you a direct order, Dorn! Are you disobeying a direct order? I can have you brought up on charges of insubordination for that, you sonofabitch! I could have you fired!"

In his rage, Morris had failed to take into account his headlong pace that carried him to within three feet of Alex. Alex took a step forward as Morris stopped, closing the gap between them. Morris' expression went from apoplectic to frightened in a half-second as he raised his hands, involuntarily jerking his upper body away from Alex. Unfortunately, the carpeting had needed replacing in Investigations for some time and the areas that were walked on most, like the area right at the doorway, were worn slick. Morris' dress shoes lost their traction as his center of gravity shifted backward and he fell, unceremoniously, on his ass. At this point, there was no holding back the laughter from the detectives in the room as Morris crab-walked backward to the door and then stood up.

"Tha...that's it, Dorn! I'm gonna have your fucking *job* for that little stunt," Morris stuttered, his face going crimson, a vein standing out on his forehead looked like it was going to burst. Morris glared around the room, marking people for future retribution. The laughter subsided.

Alex stood motionless and with a bland look on his face inquired, "Aren't I allowed to contact my PBA Rep?"

"NO! No, you goddamn well are NOT!" Morris yelled, taking a few moments to gather himself. "Now, get out the door," He said in what was, Alex thought, supposed to be a low and menacing tone.

Alex started out the door, Morris waiting for him to leave, not wanting a repeat of his previous misadventure. After they cleared the doorway, Morris once again pranced past Alex to get to be the head of the procession, turning sideways in the hallway and skipping to avoid any contact with him. People took notice of them as they passed and seemed subdued like Alex was going to his own execution. *I should be yelling "dead man walkin" for effect.* Their merry little troupe finally arrived at the door of Lt. Benton in Professional Standards. It was open, the Lieutenant and Chapman from Vice sitting inside. Sgt. Morris made a show of coming to an abrupt halt and, almost standing at attention, knocked on the side of the open door. *I'm surprised he didn't click his heels together.*

"Detective Dorn to see you, sir," Morris snapped, standing aside.

"What, not coming in, Sergeant?" Alex asked. "I'm sure we could make room."

"Just get inside, Dorn," Morris snarled, his lip curling into a sneer.

"I get the feeling we won't be exchanging Christmas cards this year, Charles," Alex said as he stepped through the door. Morris' scowl hardened even more as the lieutenant smiled. Reed and Malloy suddenly found other more interesting things to look at in the office area.

Alex came to a halt inside the door, glancing to his right at Chapman, who was already seated. Chapman refused to make eye contact and kept looking at the lieutenant, his beady little eyes, oily hair, pronounced overbite, and perpetual inability to grow a competent mustache lending him a rodent-like air. That and his penchant for running to admin with any minor transgressions committed by other cops earned him the nickname "Ratboy." Legend had it there was a trail worn into the carpet from Ratboy's mailbox to the chief's office; a trail that terminated in a pair of knee pads under the chief's desk. Alex kept staring at Chapman until it became too uncomfortable for Ratboy to keep ignoring him.

Chapman twisted his neck up and around to the left to look up at Alex, "Hello, Alex."

"Hello, Jim. If I'd known you were going to be here, I'd have brought cheese," Alex replied, pleasantly. Malloy stifled a laugh.

"That's enough, detective," Lt. Benton said. "Sit down. We have a serious problem to discuss."

Alex closed the door and sat in the chair to the left of Chapman, after moving it from its position directly in front of the door. He didn't enjoy having his back exposed, especially in this weasel pit.

"Do I get to talk to my PBA rep before we start this meeting, Lieutenant?" Alex asked. "Oh, and by the way, just so everyone knows, I'm recording this meeting on my phone." Florida was one of the few states to require that all parties in a room know they are being recorded.

Chapman glanced at the Lieutenant with a worried look on his face and Benton narrowed his eyes, squinting at Alex. "Do you really think recording this is necessary?"

"Yes, sir. I do," Alex replied, meeting his gaze.

Benton looked down, straightened some papers on his desk, then looked up at Alex. "Very well, then, let's get down to why we're here. Some information has been brought to my attention, Detective, that may or may not require I institute an internal affairs investigation against you for conduct unbecoming an officer as well as possible other charges. This is not an internal investigation at this point, but simply a fact-finding mission to ascertain if one is needed," Benton paused.

"Again: do I get union representation or not?" Alex asked, pressing the issue.

The Lieutenant leaned forward in an effort, Alex assumed, to be more assertive. "No. You don't. I thought I made it clear: this is not an investigation. I will not say that again."

Promise? Alex thought but kept it to himself. Aloud he said, "Then there's nothing in this that can lead to formal or informal discipline for me, right? Okay, I'm good with that. So, why am I here?"

The Lieutenant hesitated, flustered he'd lost control of the meeting but at a loss as to how to get it back. He took a deep breath and started, "Yesterday, detective, Vice Officer Chapman was again engaged in surveillance of the Three Coins Pawn Shop...and *this* time, he was using video to record the surveillance."

Benton grabbed the sides of his computer monitor and, with all the drama of a magician about to do the big reveal, spun the monitor around, intoning, "And THIS is what he recorded."

Benton punched his keyboard and the screen animated, showing the Three Coins Pawn Shop around dusk. It was a plain store front in an average strip mall with three other businesses in it. The facade was brick with large windows protected by iron bars and jammed with every kind of merchandise desperate people might sell to raise cash. Alex knew the store; every cop did. The proprietor was known as "Honest Abe" because, of course, he was anything but. Abe had skirted the law for years, staying just on the legal side. Just.

As Alex watched, several people walked across the viewing area. Then someone approached from the left that looked familiar. *Alaric.* As he got closer to the entrance, the camera focused in on the face. Alex's features leaped out at him. It was undeniable. Alex looked up to see that Benton had a smug look of self-satisfaction on his face and Chapman was smirking.

"And your point?" Alex asked, blandly.

Benton's face clouded, "What the fuck do you mean '*my point*'? That's you on the video, Dorn. Don't bother to deny it." Benton was breathing hard now.

"Oh, you've got *someone* on the video. Someone who looks like me. But it's not me. Period. End of story," Alex said.

"Don't hand me that horseshit, Dorn! What were you doing at that pawn store? We *know* it's involved in illegal activity. What are you trying to pull?" Benton was nearly screaming now, standing up behind his desk, spittle flying from his mouth.

Alex also stood and with exaggerated precision said "Lieutenant, I have twenty to thirty people who can verify my whereabouts teaching karate classes last night"

A vicious smile creased Benton's face, "Oh, I'm sure you could get any number of your little cronies to vouch for you."

Alex leveled his gaze, "Well, lieutenant, one of them is the mayor's daughter. So, unless you want to call him up and tell him his daughter is a lying sack of shit, I think we're done here."

"We're done when I SAY we're done, detective. SIT. DOWN," Benton screamed, punctuating his last two words by stabbing his index finger at the chair.

"I don't think so," Alex said, turning to leave. He grabbed the doorknob, opening it to find Sgt. Morris blocking his way.

"Move, Charles," Alex said, taking a step forward. Morris put his right hand on Alex's chest and said, "You heard the Lieutenant. You stay put."

Alex had put up with enough shit for one day. He grabbed Morris's hand with his right hand, twisting it until the thumb pointed down. With his left hand, he hooked Morris's right arm at the elbow and bent it until it was in an "S" shape. Alex dropped his weight and bent forward at the waist, executing *Nikyo* from *Aikido,* forcing Morris to crouch to avoid the pain. As Alex was still partially in the doorway, he pushed the sergeant's right elbow in toward his face, causing his body to rotate away from Alex and catapult toward the ground. Alex kept the pressure on, forcing Morris' face to slide across several feet of carpet, ending up right at Reed's feet.

Reed stood, dumbfounded by events, with his mouth agape; uncertain of what to do. Malloy, on the other hand, was clawing for his Taser. Alex realized this had gone too far. Fearing a Taser jolt might undo his waypoint, he concentrated for a moment and felt the *pull* between his shoulder blades and...

Alex was in the stairwell once again. Carstairs had just left. Alex gathered himself and shook off the feelings still coursing through him, the echo of adrenaline in his blood, feelings from a universe he was no longer a part of. *Well, on the bright side, I got to make Morris eat a yard or two of carpet.*

Alex considered what he knew of the administration's strategy and what they thought they knew of him. *It ain't what a man don't know that'll hurt him; it's what he knows fer a fact that ain't so. Was that Mark Twain or Will Rogers? No matter. I've gotta chop this thing off at the knees before it gets rolling. Time to bring in the big guns.* Alex got out his phone and dialed.

"Hey, Alex! What's up? More felonious douchebaggery in progress at the BCPD?" Rick Norton's welcome voice came over the phone.

"In so many words, yes, Rick. Yes, there is," Alex said. While being intentionally vague about how he knew, Alex briefly outlined for him his suspicions that the administration was planning to ambush him and what he thought the substance of their allegations might be.

After he finished, Alex said, "So, I don't want to go in there alone. Is there any chance you're nearby?".

"As it happens, my friend, I am only ten minutes from your location. Can you hold out that long?" Rick asked.

"I'll meet you at the donut shop at 4th and Magnolia," Alex said.

"Really, Alex? A donut shop?"

"Yes. It's convenient *and* delicious. See you there," Alex said, hanging up.

Alex thought about the layout of the PD and who might be able to see him leave. Like most police departments, the walls of BCPD held few windows as preparation for natural disasters such as hurricanes and for the more prosaic reason that people can't shoot you through a brick wall nearly as easily as they can through a window. The only real window in the place was the window in the chief's office and it was made of a clear, bullet-proof polymer. The only people who might catch him leaving were those watching the PD closed-circuit cameras, which were the front desk, currently being manned by Carstairs, and dispatch, who really couldn't care less. Alex figured he was clear.

Alex walked out into the lot, popped his hood, disabled the GPS tracker, and left the lot without incident. He wondered how long it would take them to notice he was no longer sending out a signal as he cruised to the nearby donut shop. He saw Rick parked there, backed into a parking spot. Alex pulled in, driver's side door to driver's side door in the familiar "56" position, named after the ten code 10-56 for "meet me at".

Rick was sipping his coffee and looked at Alex over the rim of the styrofoam cup suspiciously. "Why are you always in trouble?" he asked.

"I know, right? Lately, it's just been following me around like a lost puppy."

"It seems like it started with the shooting. I don't think you ever had a problem before that. And if that's the case, I'm gonna have to get in someone's ass," Rick was preparing for battle. He had an extraordinarily low tolerance for bullshit, which is why officers loved him.

"I don't know it had anything to do with that," Alex said, "but I would appreciate it if you could be there when they jump me."

"No problemo, man. I've got your six."

Alex left the lot with Rick in tow, gazing wistfully at the glass case full of donuts visible and inviting through the front plate-glass windows. He parked in visitor parking with Rick, walking through the front doors with him. Carstairs was at the front desk and they nodded to each other in passing. This time, as he was approaching the Investigations section, Alex noticed Reed and Malloy loitering by a water cooler down a hall as they passed it.

As they entered Investigations, Alex was in front of Rick intentionally, shielding him from the view of Sgt. Morris, who, predictably, brightened as Alex entered the room. Alex glanced behind him, finding Reed and Malloy had entered the room, as if on cue. Morris approached Alex from the front with a smile on his face. He was completely fixated on Alex, excluding everyone else in the room. Alex let him make the first move.

"Good morning, Detective Dorn. Lieutenant Benton would like to see you in his office," Morris said, a smug expression on his face.

"Great!" Alex said, smiling enthusiastically while stepping to one side, exposing Rick. "Can I bring a friend?"

Chapter 33

That meeting did not go like the previous one, Alex thought, as he was leaving the PD with Rick. *Oh, there was a great wailing; gnashing of teeth and rending of garments...but at least I didn't use Morris' lower incisors as a carpet cleaning tool.* He smiled, warmed by the memory.

Alex and Rick picked up Joe Esposito as they were leaving. Joe was agog with wonder.

"Dude! Seriously? Again? What is it about you, anyway?" Joe asked, incredulous. "I don't think I've seen I.A. twice in fifteen years and you top that in three days? Are you just an over-achiever or what?"

"Well, when I set my mind to something...," Alex started, but Rick interrupted.

"OK, kids, I got an I.A. to handle at the Sheriff's office. Look, Alex, it's pretty apparent they want to nail you for something. At this point, almost anything," Rick said, his brow furrowed. "That guy on the video looked a hell of a lot like you. You're sure your alibi will hold up?"

"Absolutely. There were between twenty and thirty people in the classes I taught that will all vouch for my whereabouts. One of them is Judge Whelan's wife. Another is the mayor's daughter."

"All right," Rick shrugged. "I guess everyone has a double somewhere. Unfortunately, yours is here. That complicates things."

You don't know the half of it.

"Look, I fully expect them to institute an internal affairs investigation at this point. I may have contributed to that by the way I handled the Lieutenant. If so, I'm sorry."

"Nah, you kidding, Rick? I loved watching that vein pop up on his forehead. I was placing mental bets on the odds of it bursting and him stroking out in the office."

"I do tend to have that effect on him," Rick said, grinning. "If they do start an I.A., give me a shout. What they tried to pull today is called a Weingarten violation. You absolutely have a right to representation. Remember that. I gotta go, guys. Have fun."

Rick climbed into his car and drove out of the lot while Alex and Joe watched him go. Joe turned to Alex and said, "Well, at least you kept me out of your bullshit this time. I gotta give you credit for that."

"Maybe next time," Alex said. "We still have to correlate all our data and make it all pretty for the Feebs. Where do you want to do this? I sure as Hell don't want to hang around here right now."

"Let's go to my place for a change. It's not as fancy as yours but, at least. for the moment, it appears to have fewer assholes in it. Also, Deni emailed me her data last night."

"Sounds good. I'll follow you," Alex said. "Wait a minute." Alex popped his hood and re-connected the GPS tracker.

Joe shook his head as he watched Alex work under the hood. "Do me a favor: if I ever talk about joining your department, shoot me in the leg."

"I may do that anyway," Alex said as he closed the hood.

Alex drove to Hampstead PD behind Joe on auto-pilot, letting his mind roam over the last several days. He had no control over whatever Alaric was doing but one thing was certain: his brother was precipitating a shit storm in his life. *I have a twin brother from another universe and he's cramping my style, Doc,* Alex thought, imagining himself on a psychiatrist's couch. *I doubt I could even say that out loud and, if I did, they'd Baker Act me. Yep. That would be a one-way ticket to looney town.* Alex's thoughts turned darker. When he thought about Alaric's contact with Eve, he again felt a cold, burning rage. He was certain he could now kill Alaric, with no remorse. *So what was that visit all about? Curiosity? Or something more. And if it is just curiosity, why watch my house from the power lines? Why take the chance with face-to-face contact with Eve? The thrill of it? Khan knew, though. He knew there was something wrong. Good boy.*

Alex was pulled from his reverie by their arrival at Joe's department. Much smaller than BCPD, HPD served a small feeder community on the outskirts of Bay City. The police department had, at one time, been housed with public works but when a federal grant had come through, a new city facility had been built, the PD got the whole building to itself. But even though it was now larger, the building was not designed to be a police department. There was no sally port, for example, to isolate prisoners when bringing them into the detention area. Suspects got walked into the department past an evidence processing area to get to the holding cells. The interior organization of the building was less than ideal, but they made it work.

They parked in the rear of the department by a patrol officer doing paperwork in his car. He was parked oriented toward the back of the PD while two young men slouched on a wrought-iron bench in front of him. They were out of the sun, under an overhang covering the rear entrance to the department, looking as comfortable as they could, under the circumstances. The circumstances being they were both handcuffed to the bench. They looked rather surly.

Both Alex and Joe got out of their cars at the same time. While Joe was still halfway inside the car, he called over to Alex, "Smaller than you're used to?"

Alex nodded, "I'll bet you have to say that a lot."

Joe was between the door and the car with his forearms on the top of the door and the roof of the car. He let his head slump downwards for a second, gazing down his expansive belly, and then picked it back up, regarding Alex, a grimace on his face.

"Only on the days I can find it," he said.

Alex laughed, shutting his door. As he walked toward the back door, he paused at the two prisoners and asked, "What's with the bench?"

"Ah, that's the felony bench."

"Felony bench?"

"Yeah. The chief instituted a new policy for using the holding cells that made it such a pain in the ass; we came up with this work-around. The officer can keep an eye on them and complete his booking paperwork at the same time. Genius, really," Joe said, waving at the officer as he passed. The officer waved back.

"I like it. Anyone ever try to run away carrying the bench?"

Joe shrugged, "A couple, but, Hell, even I can catch someone that stupid."

Joe let himself into the department by pressing his thumb into a biometric scanner. There was an audible click as the locking bolt on the door disengaged.

"Nice tech, Joe," Alex said, admiringly.

"Hey, we're not animals," Joe said, opening the door, allowing Alex to go first.

They went past communications where Joe stopped to exchange pleasantries with the dispatcher as Alex stood there, trying not to hear the gossip. Eventually, they exhausted their stores of new information and Joe led Alex to a room that functioned as a planning and training room. There was a large table inside with several chairs, as well as a projector. Alex threw his briefcase and assorted materials onto the table.

"Want coffee?" Joe asked as he headed toward the door.

"Any chance there's tea?" Alex inquired hopefully.

"You know, I think there just might be some. I'll grab it on my way back from getting my crap out of my office."

"My estimation of your level of civilization continues to rise, my friend."

Joe paused at the door, "Look, I *told* you we weren't animals, didn't I?"

Alex chuckled. "That you did," he said as he began to unpack his paperwork.

Throughout the day, the two detectives worked on their presentation. They coordinated their information into tables and checklists. They spent several hours on the creation of graphics to make the survey seem less boring than it was. They organized it so the information on any given target could be accessed in several ways. Throughout the entire process, Alex was working with only half his mind on the project. *There's only one survey in here that means anything at all and that's Murman Financial.*

They finally wrapped it up around six o'clock in the evening. Alex was rubbing his eyes from the strain of staring at print and computer screens for hours on end. Joe leaned back, belching, a satisfied look on his face. Alex stopped rubbing his eyes but left his hands covering his face, "Is that some sort of signal we're done?" he asked.

"No, it's a sign the onions I had on my burger at lunch are talkin' back to me," Joe said, idly rubbing the expanse of his stomach, "I wonder what Becky's fixing for dinner?"

Alex opened his mouth to say something as the dispatcher stepped into the room with a puzzled look on her face, "Detective Dorn?" she asked. Alex nodded.

"I've got a message from your department that you're to report to Lt. Blakely ASAP?" The statement came out as more of a question.

"How'd they know you were here?" Joe asked, turning to Alex and frowning.

"Ah, I left my radio in the car since I was out of the city and I'm guessing they still have the GPS locator working on my car, so it probably didn't take a genius to figure it out."

"I should have thought of that. My brain is fried. Do you think the Feds will do anything with this crap? I mean, besides wipe their ass?"

"I have no idea. I know I didn't want to end the week looking at the Lieutenant's smiling face. You going to store the presentation in your office since we're already here?"

"Yeah. One less thing for you to worry about. You, my friend, are a real shit magnet," Joe said, grinning.

Alex sighed, "Story of my life."

Chapter 34

Alex parked his car in the lot, taking a moment to let the last waypoint ease and instantly establish a new one. He wasn't sure what the lieutenant had for him but, going by recent history, it probably wasn't good. Alex also took five minutes to meditate, breathe, and center himself. It was the end of a long day and he wanted it to expire as painlessly as possible. He rolled his neck to loosen up, listening to the pops and cracks, and got out of his car.

There weren't many people around the department at six forty on a Friday night. Administration leaves promptly at five and Investigations had probably been empty by three in the afternoon. It was amazing how many crimes get solved on Fridays. A few patrol officers roamed the halls but most were out on the street. Alex greeted a few of them, nodded to others, and then found himself in front of Blakely's closed office door. He knocked.

"Come," the lieutenant said. *Really? Like a dog? Do I get a treat or a belly rub?* Alex opened the door to find not one, but two lieutenants waiting for him. He stepped into the office. Benton was in a chair to Alex's right, a position formerly occupied by Chapman. *That must be the asshole position. Two lieutenants. I must be in for a double screwing.*

"You requested to see me, sir?"

"Yes, detective. Please sit down."

Alex sat, ignoring Benton, his face impassive, waiting while Blakely organized some papers on his desk. Presently, he looked up.

"I've been conferring with Lt. Benton and we have decided, after much deliberation, that we must institute an internal affairs investigation into recent allegations against you. As you know, you have a right to representation," Blakely glanced at Benton, who looked away, "but, at this time, I am simply informing you of the allegations against you and your rights under Garrity. There is some paperwork to sign off on but there will be no questions asked of you today. Is that clear?"

"Yes, sir. May I ask who brought these allegations forward?"

"Lt. Benton made them, based on surveillance video and other intel. This will all be in your paperwork, detective."

There followed several minutes of Alex signing off on having received a copy of the Police Officer's Bill of Rights, his Garrity warning, a copy of the SOP governing I.A.'s, and a summary of the charges against him, the most serious of which appeared to be Conduct Unbecoming. *Conduct unbecoming? The disorderly conduct of I.A. charges? Benton must be really pissed off to come at me with something this weak. He's probably going to use this as a pretext to dig around and see if he can find something else on me.* Alex frowned. *He thinks I'm dirty.*

Lt. Blakely cleared his throat as Alex finished signing the papers, "One other thing, detective, you are suspended with pay from all duties and I will need your badge and gun. Please place them on the desk."

"What? For conduct unbecoming? This is bullshit, lieutenant!" as Alex said this last, he leaned forward in his chair and stabbed the desk with his finger. Blakely recoiled slightly, looked at Benton for support, then collected himself. Benton steadfastly refused to make eye contact.

"The department feels that, with the recent shooting, this is the best course of action. Now, your badge and gun. That is a direct order."

"I was cleared of any wrongdoing in that shooting, lieutenant," Alex said as he stood, frustrated, knowing it was futile as he said it.

He took his service weapon out of its holster and holding it up in front of him, pressed the magazine release. The magazine slid smoothly out of the well and into his left hand. He placed the magazine on the desk. He racked the slide back with his left hand, allowing the round to fly free into the air, catching it with his left hand, and put it on the desk next to the magazine. He locked the slide back and then placed the gun on the desk by the single, upright bullet, framing it between the weapon and the magazine. He then took the badge, with its badge holder off his belt and threw it on the desk, badge side down. It skipped across the blotter on the lieutenant's desk and nearly end up in his lap.

"Anything else?" Alex asked, his voice low and controlled, nearly a snarl, gritting his teeth, his expression set in stone.

"Ah, yes. We aren't going to take your car, at least as of yet. You'll be restricted to your house during your normal duty hours and will inform this agency should you need to leave the city for any reason. Is that clear?" Blakely asked.

"Crystal, sir. If we're done here, I believe I need to call Rick Norton," Alex said.

Alex had the satisfaction of watching the expressions on both of the lieutenants' faces darken at the mention of Rick's name. *It's like he's kryptonite to these assholes.*

"You can call whoever the fuck you want to, Dorn," Benton spat the words out, finally making eye contact, "You're not getting out of this." Blakely looked over at Benton with a look that said, "Shut up. Right now."

Blakely returned his gaze to Alex, "Yes, detective. We're done for now. Thank you for coming in. This isn't easy on any of us."

A hell of a lot less easy for me than you, pal. Alex nodded at Blakely and turned to leave the office. He stopped in mid-turn to stare at Benton. They locked eyes for several seconds before Benton looked away. *Thought so.*

Alex left the Lieutenant's office and headed for his desk. He scarcely noticed the few people he passed; his facial expression caused people to avoid eye contact. He made it to investigations which was, true to form, devoid of life at this time on a Friday evening. He sat heavily in his chair and slumped forward, placing his forehead on the desk, feeling the cool surface, letting the anger seep out of him. He stayed there, motionless, for ten minutes before raising his head. He looked around the room, blinking.

"Feeling sorry for yourself is useless. It's worse than useless, Alex. Stop being an asshole," Alex said aloud, talking to himself in the empty room.

"Easy for you to say," he grumbled, but immediately felt better, smiling at the idea of giving himself a good talking-to. *Clearly, someone needed to.*

Alex sighed and pulled up his email. He noticed the Lieutenant lost no time in informing everyone of his suspension. *He must have had that in the can, ready to go. Typical.* He responded to a few emails concerning some cases and then, impatient to be done with the day, scrolled down to see if there was anything more urgent and found an email from Alaric. Alex stared at it for half a minute, considering just how much more bullshit he could take today. Reluctantly, he opened it.

The message was simple: "Tonight's the night!" Alex checked the date and time on the email. It was today just after noon. He looked at his watch. 1915 hours. Alex began making plans for dealing with this new problem when the alert tone went out over the radio parked on Pritchard's desk in his charger.

"34-Baker, copy the call, 34-Adam, 32-Adam, K-2 monitor, Alarm at Murman Financial, 1724 NW 2nd Avenue. Motion detected inside. No perimeter breach indicated."

Alex was already moving toward the door when he heard Deni chime in, "Delta Five Nine, I'm near. I'll be en route."

Today is never going to end. Reflexively, he dissolved his previous waypoint and set another.

Chapter 35

Alex ran out of the PD, getting in his cruiser before remembering the GPS locator. He popped the hood and didn't bother with any of the niceties of disabling the device. He ripped it out by the wires and threw it into the front seat. *Fuck 'em. They can send me a bill.* He turned left out of the lot and punched it while bringing his in-car computer system online. Two blocks and three near-collisions later, he had the call on the screen.

Alex read as he weaved in and out of traffic. Officially, he could not respond to this call. That would be insubordination and, with his recent history, immediate dismissal. Everything he did would have to be clandestine and off the air. He chafed at this. Being unable to communicate with other units hampered him. The call-taker indicated the subscriber, Mr. Petrelli, would be responding and had an ETA of thirty minutes. Alex figured he was fifteen minutes out. Twelve if he drove recklessly. *Okay, MORE recklessly.*

34-Baker checked out on the scene and reported the front was secure and that he was going to check the north side of the building. 32-Adam called over the radio that he would be at the rear of the building in five minutes. K-2 advised he was still 10 minutes out and to secure the scene for a building search. Alex began to relax. *The cavalry was on the scene.* Then Deni called over the net.

"Delta Five Nine, I'll be checking out a service alley on the south side."

Alex remembered there was a long, thin alleyway connected to a secondary alley on one side of the building. Petrelli had said it was useful for bringing in clients that did not want their presence to be known. Celebrities and the like, he'd said. Alex included it in the briefing even though he thought it a less likely route of approach due to the narrowness and length of the alley. Now, with the back and front covered and K-9 on its way, that alley was Alaric's only viable escape route. Deni had worked the financial district when she was on patrol and was familiar with that alley. The third shift cops were all new officers, with less than two years on the job. In any department that bids for shifts by seniority, the junior officers almost all end up on afternoons. That's just the way it works.

Alex was thinking he was going to be there in a few minutes when he caught a traffic jam caused by a minor crash. He was stuck behind a group of college kids who were pissed they were being held up. They were in a Mercedes convertible and the two idiots in the back seat were standing up, yelling and cursing at the stalled traffic in front of them. Alex looked at his options, deciding he could make it past them by mounting the curb. Mostly. He might lose a little paint but considering the day he'd had, he was all right with that.

Alex got his right wheels up on the curb and moved ahead, squeezing between the Mercedes and a light pole. There was a rending, screeching sound as he moved past the convertible, scraping down the entire side of the car and removing a large patch of paint. The chrome on the side of the car peeled up and away as the college boys stopped what they were doing and watched the slow-motion destruction of the side of their luxury vehicle with mute horror. It was only as Alex made it past them that they re-animated and began cursing and screaming at him. Alex put his left arm out the window and gave them the universally understood single-digit salute.

He was moving again at speed as he approached the mouth of the alley. He got out of his car, rounded the corner, and saw Deni's car partially blocking the narrow alley. Down the alley was a solitary figure that was running but had stopped, back lit by the reflection of the fading sun, looking at him. *Alaric. But where is Deni?* Alex sprinted toward the junction of the access alley and the city alleyway. He found her slumped against her cruiser, in front of the access alley, her torso soaked with blood. She'd been stabbed multiple times in the chest. Alex knelt and pulled her into his arms, holding her up. *No, no, no.* Her eyes flickered open; recognition flashed in her eyes.

"A-Alex. Bu-but you were just...you were just... there. Why...Why...?" she said before collapsing into his body, limp. She managed one last wet cough through the blood in her lungs, one last attempt to breathe before giving up. Alex felt her die. He looked back toward the mouth of the alley at the other end but the figure was gone. Alex felt the tears coursing down his cheeks, over his lips, hot, salty. They fell in slow motion onto Deni's face, mixing with the blood she'd coughed up.

Alex looked up the alley again. Anger and resolve transformed his face, "Not today, you son of a bitch. Not today," he whispered. He reached back with his mind to the area between his shoulder blades and felt the knot of the waypoint there. He grabbed it and puuullled...

And he was back in Investigations, starting to move toward the door. All of his feelings about Deni's death still raw in his chest, the hot, coppery smell of her blood still in his nose. He wiped his face and ran.

He popped the hood and ripped out the wires before jumping in the car and heading toward Murman Financial. Alex no longer needed to use his computer to find out about the call. He drove like a maniac with his full attention on the road. As he hung a tight left, cutting off another car, he took the Ruger out of his ankle holster, placing it under his left thigh. He took a route that bypassed the fender bender that had stalled him before, sliding to a stop behind Deni's car parked just outside the alleyway. Alex swung the door open as he bailed out of his car, grabbing his gun from under his thigh. He cleared the mouth of the alley as Alaric was approaching Deni. He pelted down the alley toward her, the Ruger LCR at arm's length, the laser-activated. She had her back to him, concentrating on Alaric, who was smiling as he approached her. He looked up as the laser flickered over his face and saw Alex coming at him at a dead run. His eyes went wide. He turned and ran down the alley, away from Deni.

Deni turned, seeing Alex running toward her with a gun out. She instinctively drew hers.

Alex yelled, "GET DOWN!"

Deni hesitated a moment before she went to one knee. Alex had ceased to care what explanation he might have to offer for a corpse that looked exactly like him. He had ceased to care about anything but killing his twin. The red dot of the laser bounced all around the alley, the odds of hitting Alaric with a two-inch barrel at a run were nil. Alex didn't care. He just wanted him dead. He had no shot at this point but kept the gun leveled at Alaric. He came to a stop before getting to Deni, who was still holding her weapon, looking unsure about whether or not to shoot Alex.

Alaric turned the corner and disappeared. Alex pulled up by Deni, breathing hard. "You're...alive," he said, grinning between gasps of air.

"No shit. And I just saw you twice. Once over there," she indicated over her shoulder, "And once here. And then I saw you running toward me with a gun out looking like you wanted to kill yourself. Or your double. This is some seriously weird shit. Do you have any kind of explanation? Any at all?"

"Nothing that would make sense right now. Or ever. Look, I can't be here. I'm suspended. Can you just go with me on this? Leave this out of any report? I know I'm asking a lot," Alex looked at her anxiously.

Deni seemed to be gauging him. Applying a metric only she could read. In the end, it boiled down to how much she felt she could trust him. After a long moment, Deni nodded her head.

"Okay, but you owe me an explanation for this. Soon. What if there's a break in the door down this alley? What am I supposed to say? Or write?" she asked.

"There won't be. This will go down as a false alarm. You won't even have paper."

"Oh, so now you're the amazing Kreskin?"

Alex looked around, knowing it wouldn't be too long before 32-Adam or some other bored patrol unit came to check on Deni. "Actually, the Great Karnak. Look," he said, "go check the door. If there's a break, write it up. If not, we're good. Okay? I gotta scoot." Alex hesitated. "Tell you what... After you check the door and clear this call, meet me back at the PD and I'll explain as much of this as I can."

Deni's eyes narrowed and again she appeared to be engaged in some sort of mental calculus before she finally nodded.

Alex smiled and started jogging back to his car. Behind him he could hear Deni yell, "You owe me soooo much for this."

He got to his car and opened the door, looking back to where Deni was about to go down the service alley.

"But you're alive," he whispered. He could not stop grinning.

Chapter 36

As Alex drove back to the police department at a more sedate pace, he glanced over at the GPS locator on the passenger's seat, nestled in a tangle of wires. *Yeah. They're definitely gonna make me pay for that. Maybe days off. I wonder if they'd believe a squirrel got up under my hood and did the damage? A really big squirrel. On acid. Nah.* He thought about what he could tell Deni. Technically, no one is supposed to talk about an I.A. He'd already been warned in person and a warning was in the sheaf of papers he'd been given. It was like they believed they could invoke the Cone of Silence. *Not the Cone of Silence, Max! Yes, Chief, the Cone of Silence.* The reality was that officers talked about all I.A.'s all the time. Oh, maybe with a good friend while 56-ing in a dark parking lot, but still; they talked.

He couldn't tell her the truth. No one would believe that. He decided to go with the doppelganger theory. It would account for her experience in the alley and would already be documented by video in the I.A. He couldn't show her the video, but he could reference it when he talked to her and, eventually, it would become public record when the I.A. closed. Alex settled into his seat. *That seems reasonable.* He could account for his arrival on the scene of Murman Financial with his security survey, saying he knew about the service alley and thought it might be an escape route. It was a little weak but still plausible. Barely. *Don't dwell on it, move on.* He could say that, when he saw her in the alley with Alex 2.0, he knew his double would not be closing the gap with anything other than evil intent. Hence, the brandishing of his firearm. Alex smiled. *I give this a 70% chance of holding up. Deni's pretty sharp. She will either start poking holes in it or just accept it, warts and all. More likely, she'll poke holes in it privately and never let me know.*

Alex's thoughts turned to Alaric. There was no longer any question in his mind: Alaric had to die. Alex thought about what it would have taken to make him into his brother. He simply could not wrap his mind around it. The thought crossed his mind that perhaps they were identical in every way except in some executive brain function but, as much as he liked the idea, he rejected it. Genetics didn't work that way. Like it or not, Alaric represented some real portion of himself. Some dark side had laid quiescent in him but flowered in his brother.

Alex's thoughts drifted to the wolf/sheep/sheepdog metaphor originated by Lt. Col. Dave Grossman. It explained a good deal of police/citizen interactions. The idea was that most of the people of the world are sheep. Good, hardworking people who just want to live their lives without being hurt or hurting anyone else. The salt of the earth, these folks, with little to no capacity for personal violence. The wolves were exactly what they are in every fable mankind has ever written. Brutal, rapacious beasts who prey on the sheep. Sociopathic monsters with no need more powerful than self-gratification. Sheepdogs were, superficially at least, much like the wolves. They have the same teeth, the same capacity for violence, the same predatory instincts. What they possess that wolves lack is a deep personal commitment to their fellow human beings. They stand as a bulwark between the good, decent people of the world and those who would harm them. *Makes sense. Alaric is a wolf. I'm a sheepdog. We look exactly alike but our moral centers are different.*

But this similarity between the wolves and the sheepdogs makes the sheep uneasy. They also depend on the sheepdogs and this reliance breeds resentment. In some cases, this is justified. Cops go bad. Some become corrupt. Others take shortcuts that hurt people. This is when the sheepdog becomes the wolf and there is no greater betrayal. Alex could never understand the mentality that closed ranks to protect a bad cop. It made no more sense to him than sheepdogs accepting a wolf in their midst. It was the antithesis of everything the sheepdog is and stands for.

The uncomfortable truth is that every sheepdog has the potential to become a wolf. Every really good cop Alex had known in his career had a "touch o' larceny" in his soul. Every one of them could think like a criminal and used this talent to solve crimes and arrest perpetrators. Every one of them had a dark side. Alex was forced to admit to himself that he did, also. In Alaric, for whatever reason, that dark side had borne fruit. This made his twin's actions understandable, but not excusable. He had to die. Soon.

As Alex pulled into the drive, activating the gate for the secure parking lot at the PD, Deni pulled in right behind him. Alex had been meandering back as he thought through his explanation to Deni. *She must have hauled ass. She really, REALLY wants an explanation.* He pulled through the gate and parked the car, Deni parking right beside him. As he got out of the car, a piece of a song passed through his mind, *"Just as every cop is a criminal, and all the sinners saints..."* Yep. *Jagger was onto something there. Let's see how much of this I can get Deni to buy.*

Alex and Deni remained silent as they walked up to the door. Word was the cameras monitoring the parking lot had microphone pick-ups. That was unconfirmed but why take chances? As soon as they got in the stairwell, Alex turned to Deni.

"Do you want to talk here or......?"

"We can talk in Investigations. I swept it this morning. Not that I'm paranoid or anything."

"If you're not paranoid, you're not paying attention. After you."

As they got into Investigations, Deni selected a desk and leaned her butt back against it, crossing her arms across her chest and crossing her legs at the ankles. She regarded him coolly.

"Well?" she inquired.

Ah, jeez...crossed arms AND legs...this is gonna be a tough sell.

"So, you know I'm under an I.A. now, right?"

"I got the memo."

"Sooooo, the main accusation appears to be Conduct Unbecoming for associating with a known criminal element."

"Who?" she asked.

"Abe out at Three Coins Pawn."

"Really. And their reason for suspecting this is?"

"Vice has Abe staked out and Chapman swears that I was at Three Coins last Monday. Fortunately, I was at an FBI office when Chapman saw this."

"I'm assuming there's more".

"There is. Then I'm allegedly spotting hobnobbing with Honest Abe and this time, Chapman has video. I, however, was teaching karate at the Dojo at the time. Unfortunately, whoever *was* at Three Coins is a dead-ringer for me."

Deni pulled at her lower lip, "And that would be the guy I met tonight".

"Apparently so. Benton, and probably Blakely as well, sincerely want my hide tacked and drying on a wall. So they instituted this I.A. to go on a little spelunking expedition into my life, probably in the hope of locating something they can fire me for. I believe they think I'm dirty."

At this, Deni laughed out loud, "You suffer from an advanced case of smart-ass, Alex, but dirty you're not."

"Thank you for your support," Alex bowed.

"No problem. But here's the answer to your dilemma: I go on record as having seen the both of you in the same place at the same time. Like Clark Kent and Superman."

"Hmmm. Nope, I'm afraid that would put me responding to a call when I've been ordered specifically not to engage in police work. That's insubordination. A shitty case, to be sure, but that's all the daylight Benton would need."

"I could say I saw you at the scene when you weren't checked out there."

"Or anywhere, for that matter. That's not going to be very exculpatory. Also, I'm afraid that my GPS locator met with an untimely end."

"Meaning?"

"It's laying in the front seat of my car, along with a bunch of wires that go God knows where."

Deni reached down and placed her hands on the desk, lowered her head, and shook it in disbelief.

Uncrossed her arms. I think I'm getting somewhere. That was the trouble with cops talking to each other. Everyone was always reading body language.

"Besides, how do you know they're looking for my double? Not that they believe one exists, but I can't talk to you about the I.A. and if they think I have, that's another firing offense."

Deni looked thoughtful. "Wow. You are screwed."

"Yes. Yes, I am."

"I am puzzled by one thing, though. They have pretty good perimeter alarms at Murman Financial and apparently, some kind of super system inside. How did he set off the inside alarm without showing signs of a breach at the perimeter?"

Inside, Alex thought, *Well, my guess would be either quantum tunneling or superposition. Take your pick.*

Outside, Alex said, "I don't know. I guess he's just that good. Handsome fella, too, from what I hear."

Deni threw up her hands, "Okay. I've officially had enough for one night. Enjoy your vacation. I'm going home to a chihuahua that loves me."

"You know, he's just pretending to love you to get in your bed ."

She fixed him with a long-suffering look, "And you should, too. Wait." She held up her hand, knowing what would be coming next, "You should go home, that is," she said, clarifying.

She turned and walked away, "Good night, Alex," she called over her shoulder.

"Good night, Deni."

Chapter 37

Alex felt surprisingly relaxed on his way home from the department. Coincidentally, his suspension would give him time to hunt and kill Alaric. *Sooo, there's always a silver lining around that ol' cloud, a way to turn that frown upside down.* Alex paused for a moment. *Jeez, I even think in sarcasm. Maybe I have a problem. Maybe there's a Twelve-Step Program for sarcasm. Nah. No one at the meeting would take it seriously.* He smiled. *At least I crack myself up, so there's that.*

Alex turned onto his street and saw his house at the end of the block, sitting alone in the cul-de-sac. An island of comfort and light in the surrounding night. He wanted to get home, hug his wife, pet his dog, and go to bed. The very idea filled him with a sense of contentment, washing away the problems of the day. He rolled his neck and felt the vertebrae pop. He pulled into the driveway, shoving the gearshift into park. *Sometimes, I need to take a minute and realize just how lucky I am.*

He got out of the car, immediately feeling there was something was wrong, out of place. Not something that was there, but something that was not.

No whining.

No barking

No scratching.

No Khan.

Alex knelt down, slipping his Ruger out of its ankle holster. Rising, he turned and faded away from the welcoming pool of light by the carport door and into the concealing darkness. He started to work his way around the house, looking in windows for signs of movement, signs of life. There was nothing. He was torn between caution and anxiety. *Where is Eve? Where is Khan?* And then the thought, the dread, taking up residence in the darkest reaches of his soul and forcing him to the brink of despair. *My brother. He brought the fight to me. He has my wife.*

The thought very nearly unmanned him. It took every ounce of self-control he possessed not to become desperate. Unbidden, a line from *The Outlaw Josey Wales* ran through his mind, *"If you lose your head...you'll neither win nor live"*. Alex shook his head, centered himself, slowing his breathing and establishing a waypoint, feeling the knot draw up between his shoulder blades. It shouldn't be too long before Alaric realizes his initial hope for an ambush attack and a quick finish was not going to work out. Alex stealthily continued his recon of the house. There was no sign there was anything wrong, just an absence of what was right.

Alex's cell phone started vibrating in his pants pocket. He took it out and looked at the caller I.D. It was Eve. Alex pressed the screen to accept the call and waited.

"Well, by now you've guessed I'm in the house, so I don't think I'm going to get to finish this quick," Alaric said.

"Where's my wife?" Alex asked.

"Oh, she's here. In the house. Just indisposed at the moment."

"Have you hurt her?"

"Not a hair on her pregnant little head. She's sitting in a chair, duct-taped and blindfolded with noise-canceling headphones on. Listening to Bach, I believe. I'm surprised you haven't asked about the dog. I assume that's what tipped you off. The lack of barking?"

"I assumed you killed him."

"No...well, I might have. I had to dart him and I used a *lot* of ketamine. Do you have any idea how hard it is to get "Special K" these days?"

"Evidently not hard enough. How do you picture this going down?" Alex's gruff voice was in contrast to Alaric's light-hearted commentary. It grated on Alex's nerves.

"Well, first of all, thank you for not trying to shoot me in the alley. That was thoughtful. I assume you still have your gun? The one with the laser sight?"

"Yes, I still have it. I didn't want to draw every cop in the area down on me with a dead *you* to explain. If I'd known how things were going to turn out tonight, I'd have taken that shot and dealt with it."

"No doubt, hindsight being twenty-twenty and all. Can't bounce back to that point? Aw, too bad. You did get there in time to save that female cop, though."

"I didn't the first time."

"Really? Outstanding. I had no idea. This ability of ours can make for some strange outcomes."

"The only outcome I'm interested in now is getting my wife out safely."

"Is that all? I'm pretty sure you want to kill me as well."

"That's secondary, brother. Icing on the cake. Eve and her safety are the most important things."

"Hmmm, yes, getting to that. The problem I have is that I don't have a gun. And you do."

"So what is preventing me from assaulting the house right now and taking you out?"

"Two things. One: I can, without a doubt, get to Eve and kill her before you can affect a rescue. And two: I have rigged the house with thermite explosives hooked to a radio-controlled trigger. As you have obligingly built your house of wood, it should burn quite nicely. Did the cautionary tale of the Three Little Pigs teach you nothing?"

Alex knew he was being baited. He was past being angry. Alaric's taunts just forced the cold, hard edge of his mind into sharper focus. Eve's life depended on his actions. There was no greater incentive.

"What do you expect to get out of this, Alaric? You still haven't told me," Alex asked. *If I can keep him talking, maybe I can get into the house.* A plan formed in his mind. Alex worked his way to a point near the carport where he'd put in an old concrete birdbath that had been his parents. Its paint was chipped and faded and the stone swan residing in the dry center was missing a portion of its tail, but his mother had loved it. He checked the windows and could see no one looking out. He cradled the phone between his jaw and his raised right shoulder. Then he took the revolver in his left hand and pushed the cylinder release with his right thumb. Holding the gun muzzle up with his left hand and pushing the cylinder out with his fingers, he emptied the five shells into his right hand. He pocketed these and placed the gun in the birdbath, leaning up against the swan.

'Initially, I had hoped we might, perhaps, have become friends or, if not that, then at least come to some sort of working arrangement. I concluded, after I tried to kill – or, I guess, actually did kill – that cop, my hope was not going to be realized. I'm pretty sure you were going to try to hunt me down and kill me for that. Was I wrong?"

"You were not wrong," Alex said as he crept to the sliding glass doors of his home *dojo*. He took his tactical pen out, clutching it in his right hand.

"So what do you intend to do with me? Or with Eve?" Alex asked.

"Obviously, dear brother, you have to die. I was toying with the idea of killing you, setting the house on fire, and rescuing Eve. I could assume your place in this universe. Your corpse plays the part of the dead intruder. I'm not sure I have the chops to pull that off, though. I don't have your knowledge of police work and couples always have secrets only they know."

"What's your Plan B?"

"And what makes you think I have a Plan B?".

"There's always a Plan B."

Alaric laughed, "True. Plan B is that both you and Eve die in a tragic fire. I assume your identity and your corpse, once again, plays the part of the dead intruder. An intruder I kill, but, unfortunately, too late to save Eve. I, of course, am a shattered man. PTSD forces me to quit the police department and go on disability. Any oddities in my behavior are easily explainable by the trauma. It's definitely the easier way to go."

"Sounds like a no-brainer. Plan B is your best shot."

"Ah, but there's a Plan C."

"You *have* thought this through."

"I've had some time. In Plan C, both you and Eve die in a tragic fire and I fade back into non-existence. Essentially, what I have now. That's probably the easiest of the three."

"So. Either B or C then?"

"Logically, yes, but then, unfortunately, I'd have to give up Eve. Over the last several weeks, watching your comings and goings, I've grown quite attached to her."

I'll bet, Alex thought. Aloud he said, "Why not just shoot me?"

"That works for Plan A and Plan B, but not for C. Forensic people are notoriously thorough these days, and finding a bullet in you would put the lie to the story. They'd start looking for a suspect and I'd rather not leave a loose end."

"Understandable. So, exactly how *do* you plan to kill me... what with me having a gun and all?"

"Sword. Chinese *Gim*, actually. And that would be after you give up the gun."

"I gather if I don't, you'll kill Eve? That's your leverage?"

"Exactly."

"Okay. Gimme a minute. I need to think."

"Take all the time in the world. I'll give you two minutes."

Alex thought furiously, trying to map out every contingency. If he called Alaric's attention to the gun in the birdbath, that would put him at the carport end of the house. He could see Eve was not in the dojo room, so that would place Alaric past the spare bedroom, the master bedroom, and the study. Eve had to be in one of those rooms. If Alex could move him to that position at the end of the house, he could place himself between Alaric and Eve. Alex checked and saw his sword box was undisturbed. Inside was his *katana*. He thought about making it to the back bedroom to his gun safe but Alaric would be on him in moments and he couldn't guarantee Eve wasn't in one of the other rooms. Alex looked down at the tactical pen in his hand and, more specifically, at the integrated glass breaker. *This thing better work as advertised.*

"Alaric," Alex said on the phone.

"Yes?"

"Go to the carport door. Look through the window. There's a concrete birdbath on the other side. You'll see the gun there, sans bullets, of course."

"Of course. Standby," Alaric said.

Alex counted in his head. *One one-thousand, two one-thousand, three one-thousand...*Alaric's voice started to come over the phone.

"We..."

Alex dropped the phone and took two quick steps to the sliding glass doors. All glass has stress points that are formed during manufacture. Points that make the glass more breakable. Sliding glass doors are designed so the stress points lie along the outside of the glass sheet, where contact is unlikely. Alex chose the top right corner and struck the glass there, moving at speed and backhanding the glass, his white-knuckled grip on the pen welding it to his hand. The glass shattered and Alex was through the aperture, his eyes closed as the glass was falling, showering his head and shoulders. Another two strides and he flipped open the sword box, grabbing the *saya* with his left hand and the hilt with his right. He unsheathed the blade in one fluid motion, dropping the *saya* on his way to the door.

Alex ripped the door open and stepped through, *katana* in his right hand. He immediately oriented to his right and saw Alaric standing in the kitchen by the carport door, *gim* in hand. He looked surprised, if not astonished. Then he smiled, laid the sword on a countertop, and started a slow clap.

"Brav-o, brother. I did not see that coming," Alaric finished his clapping and picked up his sword. He looked down the length of his sword appreciatively. "In Mandarin, this is called a *jian*. It is the gentleman's weapon. Sleek, agile, and deadly. Before the Japanese had the *katana,* their swords looked much like this."

"We evolved."

"Or devolved. This particular *gim* is made by Cold Steel. It's made out of high-quality steel and is wickedly, wickedly sharp. It's probably the best sword of its kind produced today, at least in my humble opinion."

Alex let Alaric talk as he thought about his options now. Eve was in one of three rooms, all of them behind him. He couldn't determine which one without giving Alaric a shot at his back. He also couldn't risk having a sword fight in the same room as Eve. One wrong move and she'd be done. That left just the one option.

"As interested as I assume you are in my sword, Alex, I'm afraid we've reached the point where, as my late and unlamented step-father used to say, 'we're down to the nut-cuttin'."

"I suggest the dojo," Alex offered. He needed room to cut with the two-handed sword that Alaric did not.

Alaric seemed to weigh his options looking around the kitchen and living room area, an area Alex could navigate blindfolded and he could not. He nodded his head.

"After you?" he asked.

"'Fraid not," Alex said and backed up down the hallway, leaving room for Alaric to enter the *dojo*.

Alaric half-smiled and went through the door, watching Alex out of his peripheral vision. As he entered, he turned to face Alex at the door. They maintained eye contact as Alaric backed in slowly and Alex advanced at the same pace. The room had seemed more spacious to Alex before he realized he'd be facing another person with a sword in it. Now it seemed cramped, claustrophobic.

Alaric stood with his right foot and hand forward, sword in his right hand. Poised for maximum extension of the weapon as well as maximum protection of his body. Instead of the two-finger "sword hand" used in Chinese martial arts, however, his non-weapon hand lay close to his chest, out of danger. *That would be the influence of the Filipino martial arts. Probably wise considering how close we're going to be.*

Alex stood in the standard *Chudan No-Kamae*, with the sword in both hands, right foot and right shoulder forward and the left hand holding the hilt at the butt end, his left little finger at the pommel for maximum leverage on a cut. His right hand was behind the guard, almost touching it. The *kissaki,* the point of the sword, was pointed at Alaric's eyes. Alex willed himself to be relaxed, feeling himself fall into combat space. He eased his last waypoint and established a new one as he assumed Alaric was also doing.

"I've reached a decision. I think I'm going to kill you both. It's just the least trouble and, quite frankly, I'm tired. I think I knew we'd end up here eventually, anyway. The other options were just wishful thinking," Alaric said. He sounded almost wistful.

Alex launched his attack, stepping back slightly with his right foot, he lunged forward with his left in a maneuver that, in western fencing, would be called a *fleche.* The point of his sword blurred toward Alaric's throat, Alex's right hand pronating at the last moment. As terrifying as this thrust was, it was a feint, Alex hoping to draw a parry from Alaric, which he did. His brother swept his blade to the outside, moving his body in the opposite direction and Alex used that energy to draw his sword back in a circle for a *kesa-giri,* a cut that would take Alaric in his left shoulder and cut him to his right hip. The cut's name came from the robes Buddhist monks wore. It followed the line the robe made across the chest. Alex's right foot came forward as he made the cut.

Alaric saw his danger and angled to his left, bringing his sword up inverted in a modified shield block that allowed most of the force of the *katana* to slide off the *gim*. Even though the force was minimized by Alaric's angling and blocking, he could still feel the heaviness of the blow. It shifted him further to the left than he wanted to be so that, when he tried to counter, his blade barely caught Alex's back, behind his right shoulder. The point of Alaric's sword cut through Alex's shirt, tracing a long, thin line of blood along his back as he shifted to his left to avoid it.

Alex spun through the lunge, ending facing his brother in the same *Chudan No-Kamae*. Alaric looked shaken by Alex's attack but looked at his brother and said, simply, "First blood."

Alex nodded. *Alaric has the lighter blade. He'd prefer to counter-cut when possible. He plans to stay out of range. Cut me as I enter, defanging the snake. Even if I don't drop the sword, he'll bleed me until I'm diminished to the point that he can finish me off.*

To test his theory, Alex raised his sword as though to strike Alaric, sliding into range in the blink of an eye. Alaric angled to his left again, lifting his right foot in a classic stance, slicing his blade forward at an angle that would intercept Alex's forearm and cut it to the bone. Alex settled back into his *kamae* and wished for his short sword, his *wakizashi*. He'd worked with a visiting *sensei* once that had some experience with Miyamoto Musashi's *Nito Ryu* style. Using the two swords in concert would give him an advantage. *Yep, and people in Hell want ice water.*

Alaric suddenly closed the gap, stabbing toward Alex's face with a lunge, right foot forward. Alex started to retreat but sensed that this was a feint and stepped to the side. Alaric's attack unfolded as he stepped forward, his left leg crossing behind the right as he crouched and cut backward. If Alex had stepped back, he would have lost a foot. As it was, he was in position for a counterstroke and his backhand slash caught Alaric across the back and where his cut had been shallow Alex's cut was deep. Alex could feel ribs grating across his blade and a piece of organ tissue left Alaric's body as Alex's blade exited in a spray of blood.

Alex raised his *katana* over his head to administer the killing stroke when he suddenly found himself in the exact position he'd been in when the duel began. Alaric stumbled slightly as he still felt the ghost of the pain he suffered from Alex's sword cut. Alex was in *Chudan No-Kamae,* puzzled as Hell. If Alaric had bounced back to his waypoint, Alex should have no knowledge of what transpired in the universe they'd just quit. *In that universe, I would have won. In this one, we're still at the beginning of the duel. I shouldn't know any of this.* Alex slowly circled as he tried to work this out. *Quantum entanglement. We've become entangled. But he has no way of knowing.*

Alex formed a plan that relied on him making a fourth waypoint, something he'd never been able to do. He'd come close on several occasions but had never been able to hold it. This was either going to work or he was going to find himself in a different universe. It was an all-or-nothing gamble with the highest stakes imaginable. He let his last waypoint go.

Alex forced Alaric to retreat to the corner of the room near the dojo shrine and established his first waypoint. They fought back and forth across the floor until Alex relaxed his guard and Alaric started to get the upper hand. Alex was banking on his brother establishing a waypoint here in case he needed it. A waypoint where the fight was going his way. Alex created his own waypoint and felt it settle between his shoulder blades. Still, they fought, feint and counter-feint, attack and counter. Alex feigned fatigue, his twin seizing on the opportunity to finish the duel. Alex fought back and created another waypoint. He was one ahead of Alaric and at the end of his known abilities. The pressure between his shoulder blades was telling. As they contested in the middle of the dojo floor, Alex slipped and went to one knee. Alaric attacked savagely and Alex fought back to his feet, establishing the fourth waypoint. The pressure on his back was enormous. His concentration was absolute.

Alex was bleeding from a dozen cuts, but none of them were serious enough to end the fight. He barely felt them. He rushed his brother and went *corps-a-corps*, their sword guards pressed together. Alex was close enough to Alaric to see every drop of sweat on his face. *His* face. Then he forced Alaric's blade to one side and drew his blade across his brother's bicep, disabling his arm. Alex felt the waypoint established by Alaric spring into existence as he bounced back to when Alex was on one knee. Alaric attempted to leap over Alex's sword and side-kick him in the face, a maneuver that would have snapped Alex's neck. And it would have worked had Alex not been entangled with his brother, retaining his knowledge of the universe line. Alex's counter stroke took Alaric's leg off at the knee. Femoral blood spurted in an arc that went across the ceiling and then...

Alex found himself at the next waypoint, one at which Alaric was about to ram his sword through Alex's right eye. This time he nearly succeeded, as Alex dodged the fatal stroke by inches. He lashed out with *kansetsu-geri*, a low side kick to the knee, shattering Alaric's kneecap. Alex could hear the tendons and ligaments give way, felt the tearing as his twin's knee was forced to the ground at an unnatural angle. And then they were at the base universe. Alaric had no more waypoints.

Alex activated his last waypoint, dragging Alaric along with him. Alaric found himself at the *Kamiza* with a bewildered look on his face as Alex, without thought, blindly cut about, lopping off his brother's right arm just above the hand.

Alaric howled in pain, dropping his sword, involuntarily clutching the stump of his ruined right arm to his chest with his left hand. Alex stopped after the cut, motionless, stunned by the sight of his twin hunched over, trying to staunch the flow of blood from the stump of his arm. The hand and a portion of the forearm lay on the mat in front of him, the hand still clutching the sword.

Alaric looked up at Alex with dead, cold, hatred in his eyes. Alex stepped forward with his left foot and raised his sword to a vertical position with his right hand near his right ear, *Hasso No-Kamae*. He coolly regarded his dying sibling.

"It's over," Alex said, panting.

"I don't think so," Alaric said, reaching behind him and sweeping the *kamiza* clear, the objects flying at Alex's face as he reached into his pocket, retrieving a small object. Alex instinctively flinched away, then began to step forward to cut him down when the world exploded in a blinding flash of light.

Chapter 38

Alex awakened to a scene from Dante's Inferno. Portions of the wall were blown out into the center of the room, most of it burning. Alaric lay face down, unconscious, with a piece of the ceiling on top of him, in flames. Smoke was filling the room, choking Alex. He started to stand, finding he had to go back to one knee. His head was swimming. *Probable concussion.* He looked at his brother, feeling anger, resentment, loss, and relief. *He's dead. Good.* He managed to stand and his next clear thought slammed into his consciousness like a bucket of ice water. *Eve! I have to move! Now!*

Alex staggered to the *dojo* door, opening it. A wall of heat smashed him in the face. His house was burning in multiple locations, the refrigerator was lying out in the middle of the dining area, smoldering, while the side of the wall where it had been was engulfed in flames. Alex turned left and moved toward the master bedroom. *It's where I would have put her.* He opened the door and found he was right. Eve was sitting in a chair facing the door. She was blindfolded with earphones on. The bedroom had not been rigged with thermite but it wouldn't be long before the fire caught up to them.

He moved to Eve, took off the earphones, and pulled off the blindfold. She looked at him and started sobbing. *She's been holding in all her emotions. Trying to stay strong.*

"Alex! I was so afraid...I thought...I thought...," She stammered, tears welling in her eyes.

Alex cut her off, "We have to get out of here. The house is on fire," he said, moving to the back of her chair, pulling his knife out of his pocket, and opening it one-handed. He cut through the duct tape around her wrists, then stopped as a wave of nausea took him. He swayed slightly, holding on to the chair for support. It passed as he swallowed hard, moving to the front of the chair to cut the duct tape around her ankles. He stood up, Eve standing up with him, throwing her arms around him and burying her face in the side of his neck. He put his arms around her back, hugging her fiercely.

"I love you. I love you," she sobbed. "I knew you'd come for me."

Alex felt her tears on the side of his neck, another wave of nausea, "We have to move, babe. Now."

Reluctantly, she let go of his neck as he pulled her arms apart as gently as haste would allow. He kept his arm around her shoulders partly to reassure her, partly to balance himself. He opened the door, looking down the hallway to where the kitchen and dining area were now fully engulfed. *No getting out that way.* He closed the door, released Eve, and picked up the chair that she'd been tied to. He wished that he'd kept his tactical pen now to pop the window as he tested the weight of the chair. It seemed solid enough and its frame was made of metal.

"Stand here. Close your eyes," he told Eve. He took a running start, smashing through the window with the chair, holding onto it during the process, and adding his mass to the equation. The window shattered, partially coming out of the frame. Alex used the chair to clear away the remaining glass and placed it on the floor near the window. He grabbed the comforter off the bed, laying it on the windowsill.

"Come on, babe," Alex said, holding out his hand. Eve grabbed his hand and moved through the window with ease. Alex followed close behind her. They both went around the house to the front. In the distance, Alex could hear sirens approaching. They turned and looked at the house burning. It was mesmerizing, the carport end of the house was completely consumed by fire and it was spreading rapidly toward the master bedroom.

Eve's arm was around Alex's waist as he held her around her shoulders. *We're safe. Our family is safe and Alaric is dead.* He breathed a sigh of relief and then his breath caught in his throat.

He turned toward Eve, who looked up at him. He looked into her eyes, the eyes of the woman who meant the world to him. She smiled. He did not smile back. Her smile turned to a look of concern.

"What's wrong?"

Alex said one word, "Khan."

Eve inhaled sharply, turned her head to look at the conflagration that had been their house. Alex took his arm from around her shoulders, turning her to face him.

"I have to go back in."

Eve clutched his arms, "Into that? No. That's insane. That's..."

He cut her off, "I have to. He'd go back for me."

She refused to let go of his arms, "But...he might not be alive...he...", and then she stopped, seeing the look in his eyes, knowing that there wasn't a chance in Hell that she could stop him. She spared another look at the burning house.

"Come back. Go get our boy. But come back to me."

"Always."

Alex grabbed her face with both hands, kissed her, and was gone, running for the side of the house and the window they'd crawled out of. He rounded the side of the house and paused at the window to set a waypoint. He could feel it there but couldn't reach it, It slipped away from him. He paused, gathered himself, and pushed hard for the waypoint. A blinding, searing pain lashed across his forehead and he sagged against the side of the building, holding himself up with one hand against the wall. He took a couple of deep breaths as his vision cleared. *Concussion. Gotta be.* He looked at the window.

"Well, that's it," he muttered. "One shot. Do or die,"

Alex crawled back through the window, finding there had been a marked increase in the temperature from when they'd left. He grabbed the comforter off the windowsill and another one from the hope chest at the end of the bed, stepping into the attached bathroom. *Please let the plumbing be intact.* He got into the bathtub, turning the shower on. A jet of water shot from the showerhead and, within seconds, he had thoroughly soaked himself. A few more and both comforters were sodden and heavy. As he stepped out of the shower, nausea overtook him again and he almost lost his balance.

Most household accidents occur in the shower, he thought and giggled. As the wave passed, Alex blinked. *Dude, seriously. Focus.*

Alex had talked to a lot of firemen at scenes and was always stopping by the firehouse to use the bathroom when he was on patrol. He always showed up around dinnertime when Sam Lee was cooking: it was the best Lo Mein he'd ever had. Over the years, he'd learned a few things about fires. Everything he'd learned flashed through his mind. *Let's hope I learned enough.*

He took one comforter and wedged it between the wall and the curtain rod, pulling it over the rod and pushing it against the wall on both sides. He grabbed his dresser and shoved it against the bottom of the window, effectively sealing it. *A fire needs two things: fuel and oxygen. Can't let any more air get into the room when I open the door.* He got down on his hands and knees, pulling the remaining comforter over his head. He used the wet material to turn the doorknob. He could feel the heat through the cloth and thought he might have heard it sizzle. He opened the door to a scene from a horror movie. There were flames along the sides of the walls near the top. The heat was like a physical thing, beating him down. He looked at the ceiling and froze for a second.

The ceiling was a solid mass of flames rolling back and forth. Beautiful. *Rollover. Angel fingers. We might not be too far from flashover. That would suck. All it needs is a little more oxygen, then the air ignites and I get cooked. Great. Just great.* Alex started crawling forward.

The first door he came to was on his right. The study. Alex was coughing steadily now and the combination of the concussion, the heat, and the lack of oxygen was making him woozy. He couldn't see through the smoke and his tears. He reached up and opened the door, praying it wouldn't cause a flashover.

He pushed the door open and tensed, waiting for a second to be set on fire. When that didn't happen, he looked up to find out why. *Rollover in here, too.* Alex looked around the room and didn't see Khan. He started to turn around to try the spare bedroom when he caught sight of a bushy tail sticking out from behind the desk.

Khan!

Alex closed the door behind him. *For all the good THAT'S gonna do.* He crawled to his dog. Khan lay on his side. Alex wasn't sure if he was breathing. He lay his head on Khan's chest and thought he heard a faint heartbeat. It was hard to be sure. *Doesn't matter, boy, you're coming out with me.*

Alex started to crawl back toward the door, dragging Khan with him. Crawling and carrying a hundred pounds of limp Shepherd presented some unusual challenges. He began to open the door when a piece of the opposite wall peeled away and landed on the door as he opened it. Alex only just managed to shut it before the flames hit his face. He looked around the room, realizing there was only one way out. The window.

He considered his escape route. The minute he broke the window, fresh air would flood the room, igniting everything in it including him and Khan. He calculated his chances of breaking the window and surviving. They weren't good. He had one shot and, if that didn't work, Eve was a widow and his child fatherless.

Well, that's not gonna happen.

Alex took the comforter off his shoulders and hung it up on the curtain rods which, miraculously, were still there, the lacy curtains Eve bought to decorate his study having burned away. As he hung it, he felt the hair burn away on his forearms and smelled himself cooking. He was racked with a coughing fit, doubled over, and fell to the ground. He crawled to Khan and cradled him in his arms. Alex turned to face the window, gathering every bit of his waning strength. *One encounter, one chance.* The top of the comforter had dried out and was beginning to burn. *Now or never.*

Alex exploded from his crouched position with a scream, Khan in his arms, lunging toward the window covered by the smoldering, steaming comforter. As he launched, he twisted his body so that he made contact with the window on his upper back, hunching his neck in. The window didn't break. The frame, weakened by the heat, popped out of the wall altogether. Alex flew out into the cool night air, clutching Khan to his chest. He braced himself for impact with the ground.

At the same time, the air rushed into the room and ignited a flashover. A living, writhing tongue of flame leaped out of the window, chasing the puny mortal that had cheated it. Alex and Khan were falling away and down as the flame curved up, hungry, searching for them and barely missing. Flashover occurred simultaneously throughout the house, blowing every intact window out, flames shooting from every empty casement.

Alex fell, holding Khan tightly to his chest. His face screwed into a mask, waiting for the impact with the hard ground with a hundred-pound weight on his chest. The next thing he felt was water, all around him, up his nose and in his mouth. He thought for a moment, in his concussed and addled state, that it might be a miracle...and then he remembered the pond. He'd hit the Koi pond. He jack-knifed into a sitting position holding Khan's head above water. The pond was only two feet deep, but it was enough. He sat in the water for a moment, laughing between choking and sputtering, not entirely sane, and looked down at Khan. Khan looked back at him. And then he blinked. Alex cried, hugging Khan to him before looking up and remembering that he was still just feet away from an inferno.

Alex picked Khan up, staggering out of the pond and around the house. The dog couldn't move yet but was awake enough to lick the side of Alex's neck. Alex smiled as he navigated his way around the obstacles in the backyard and the carport area, giving the fiery death of his house a wide berth. He made it to the front of the house when he saw the fire engines pulling onto his street. He saw Eve sitting on the driveway; her legs curled beneath her, her arms stiffened, holding her upper body up as she cried, a keening wail, her head hanging suspended from her shoulders. *She thinks I'm dead.*

He got within thirty feet of her before calling out, "Honey."

She lifted her head, tears streaming down her face, looking at him in disbelief as he staggered towards her. With a strangled cry, she sprang to her feet and rushed him, colliding with him hard enough that it almost knocked him over. Her arms wrapped around him and Khan. They tottered back and forth for a moment as the firemen pulled up onto their front yard.

"Honey, let me put Khan down," Alex said. The shepherd was moving around now, squirming enough that Alex was in danger of falling and taking them all to the ground with him. Eve refused to let him go, but they somehow managed to get to the ground together, Khan lying between them, as the firemen began running hoses. Alex could see, over Eve's shoulder, a paramedic walking toward them, a concerned look on his face.

Alex's attention was wrested from the paramedic back to Eve as she grabbed him by his face and looked into his eyes, "Don't you *ever* do that to me again. I can take anything. Anything but losing you."

"I won't. Not ever. I love you," he said.

"And I love you. Forever", she replied, looking over Alex's shoulder at the house. "Our poor house."

"Ah, it's not that bad," he said. She looked at him, puzzled.

"Everything important is right here."

Epilogue

Cauterizing the stump of his right arm was, without a doubt, the most painful, most excruciating thing Alaric had ever done. He stumbled up the power line right-of-way toward the crest of the hill, loss of blood and shock making him weave drunkenly from side to side. He held the charred stump up in front of his face. *Well, Alex, we're no longer identical now, are we?* He giggled and then stumbled and fell, jamming his stump into the ground. He curled into a fetal position, cradling his injured arm, and screamed into the night. Slowly, he fought through the pain and got up.

Have to get to supplies, medicine, safe-house. He crested the hill and found his Jeep exactly where he'd left it.

Plan B. There's always a Plan B. Alaric giggled.

THE END

Author Bio

In 1968, I saw a group of men in funny-looking white pajamas punching and kicking in a public park. Fifty-three years later, I'm still practicing, with a 1st degree black belt in Japanese Shotokan and a 4th degree black belt in Okinawan Goju Ryu. Along the way, I picked up Chinese, Filipino, and Indonesian arts. In 1978, I started a career in law enforcement that would span the next 36 years, until I retired as chief of police of a small town. Along that journey, I was everything from a K-9 officer, to a traffic homicide investigator, to a hostage negotiator. After retirement, I decided to write a book, the kind of book I would like to read. *Decoherent* is the result.

Oh, and Khan is real. He's lying on the couch right now, looking at me and probably wanting me to take him for a walk.

The author can be reached via email at j.s.holley028@ gmail.com or Facebook under the name James Holley.

Made in the USA
Coppell, TX
09 February 2022

73178883R00198